I0579194

# THE ESFAH SAGAS:
# ARMY
# OF THE
# DEAD

BY

EDO VAN BELKOM

WITH

CHRISTOPHER D. SCHMITZ

A DRAGON DICE NOVEL

Edo Van Belkom &
Christopher D. Schmitz

© 2021 by Christopher D. Schmitz
All rights reserved. No part of this book may be reproduced, stored in a retrieval system, or transmitted in any form or by any means without the prior written permission of the publishers, except by a reviewer who may quote brief passages in a review to be printed in a newspaper, magazine, or journal.
The final approval for this literary material is granted by the author.
Dragon Dice and its terms including Esfah, Coral Elf (selumari), Dwarf (vagha), Lava Elf (morehl), Goblin (trogs), Amazon, Firewalker (empyrea), Undead (bloodless), Feral (ghwereste), Swamp Stalker (sarslayan), Frostwing (Areosa), Scalder (Faeli), Treefolk (efflorah), Dragonkin, Eldarim, Eldrymetallum, Magestorm! and Dragon Dice II: Gamer's Edition are trademarks owned by SFR, Inc.
Forgotten Realms and Dragonlance are trademarks owned by Wizards of the Coast.

PUBLISHED BY TREESHAKER BOOKS

# The Esfah Sagas

*Tales From the First Age*
Rise and Fall of the Obsidian Grotto
Cast of Fate
Army of the Dead

*The Relic Quests*
Ashes of Ailushurai
Rise of the Champions
Drakuwar

*The Cyrean Songs*
Chill Wind
Eye of the Storm
Secrets of the Shadowlands

## STAY UP TO DATE ON THE WORLD OF ESFAH!

Get a free copy of book 1 in the Esfah Sagas by visiting:

www.subscribepage.com/getfreedragondicenovels

Subscribers who sign up for this no-spam email list will get free books, exclusive content, and more! You'll get a *free book* immediately… If you would like more details or want to follow the authors, you can find their details at the end of this book.

# Background

Dragon Dice™ was originally created by Lester Smith and produced by TSR in 1995. It is an Origins Award winning strategy game where players create mythical armies using dice to represent each troop and is one of several collectible dice games that emerged in the 1990s. The game combines strategy and skill as well as a little luck.

After several years, TSR, now owned by Wizards of the Coast, had put Dragon Dice™ on hold to work on other projects. In October of 2000, SFR Inc. purchased the rights to Dragon Dice™.

Most of the races and monsters in original TSR Dragon Dice were created by Lester Smith and include some creatures unique to a fantasy setting and others that are familiar to the Dungeons & Dragons role-playing game. While the world of Esfah, where Dragon Dice™ takes place, has many similarities to that of Dungeons & Dragons, it is distinctly different in many respects. In some ways, there are greater unknowns and its history is both newer and older all at once.

Around the end of 1995, I was a teenager and avid board gamer who had a burger slinging job (which gave me a disposable income) and a car (that took most of my disposable income.) In addition to many other games I played as part of a regular quartet of gamers, Dragon Dice™ was one that we all enjoyed.

I fondly remember how the four of us would cut out of elective classes, study halls, and independent learning periods to meet up for gaming sessions. Dragon Dice™ came in a pocketable carrying bag which made it perfect for that.

We also had a mutual acquaintance. An older gentleman in town owned a new and used bookstore that also carried a limited supply of gaming products. Though he did not stock Dragon Dice™, he did have a copy of *Cast of Fate*, the first Dragon Dice™ novel which included a special promo die. I snatched it up right away, as the most avid reader of the foursome (which allowed me to become the dedicated DM for our role-playing game sessions and solidified my path as a story-teller). The included promotional die was our bright and shiny object for months.

*Cast of Fate* by Allen Varney was not the only book set in the world of Esfah, though it remains one of the few. As I write and publish more and more fiction (both Fantasy and Science Fiction), I tend to write the stories that I've always wanted to...and I've always wanted to have a voice in a shared universe. Creating a story within the Dragon Dice™ universe is something I've always wanted to do, so I give a special thanks to SFR, a company composed of true and like-minded fans who have kept alive a product that was one of the gems of the 1990s.

-- Chris

## FOREWORD

In eons past, when time was young and creation malleable, the four powers of Nature -- earth, air, fire, and water -- the children of Nature, gods in their own rights, brought forth two races of being to care for their fledgling world created by the all-father, Tarvanehl. One race, the selumari or coral elves, were created to husband the fluid forces of air and water. The other race, the dwarvish vagha, embodied the stability of earth and the tempering power of fire. Together, these two peoples worked to nurture their infant world into something glorious and beautiful.

But Nature had a nemesis in Death, the spirit of entropy. In imitation of Nature, Death brought into being its own races: The morehl, or lava elves, who worshiped fire and destruction, and the trogs, a race of goblins, who sprang from earth and corruption. From the moment of their creation, the morehl and trogs sowed conflict, defiling the very world that gave them life and corrupting the other races who tended it. War sparked over land and possessions. Soon, hordes of dispossessed selumari, vagha, morehl, and trogs swept across the lands of Esfah, locked in endless battle.

In their struggles for supremacy over the fledgling world, the First Races pressed other magical beings into their service. The morehl were the first to do so, bringing up fire-breathing Hellhounds and web-casting Driders from the deepest caverns below. The trogs followed suit, leading Trolls, Harpies, and other monsters into battle. In response, the selumari called forth Coral Giants from the ocean and swarms of Sprites from the skies. The vagha enlisted Gargoyles, Androsphinxes, and other creatures of the crags.

Conflict raged across the face of Esfah and Death delighted in the carnage.

Darkness battled against light. Each side pushed harder for victory and the battles grew ever more savage and desperate. New races arose, each pressed into the fray of bloody struggle with no end in sight.

Saddened by the bloodshed, Nature, the goddess-mother Ghaeial, dealt death to preserve life. Death, or Malgrimm the bastard child, son of Ghaeial and Selurehl and the god known as Void. Malgrimm reveled in the chaos, terror, and pain that war brought.

A tide of champions arose to safeguard the realm. Wars continued and an entire age passed. Pockets of tenuous peace grew from apathy--a new trick engineered by Death to soften the resolve of Nature's troops, almost seeming to abandon his playground for the comforts of the Abyss--but his attention had never truly waned.

Esfah has never known true peace. It is not in the planet's makeup: This is why the gods' children war on their behalf. Both old and new races struggle ever onward--creatures inspired to greater ends, forever in search of either an end to the bloodshed, or carnage renewed--as each is bent towards his or her own ends.

Esfah cannot know peace. Malgrimm--the god known as Death--will not allow it. Only a few know his true name. And to speak it aloud is to court Death himself.

For a short video overview of Esfah's origins, visit
https://youtu.be/JhF8RPFkF9I

For up to date information on the world of Esfah, and all things
related to the Dragon Dice universe, including products and specials,
check out:

http://www.sfr-inc.com

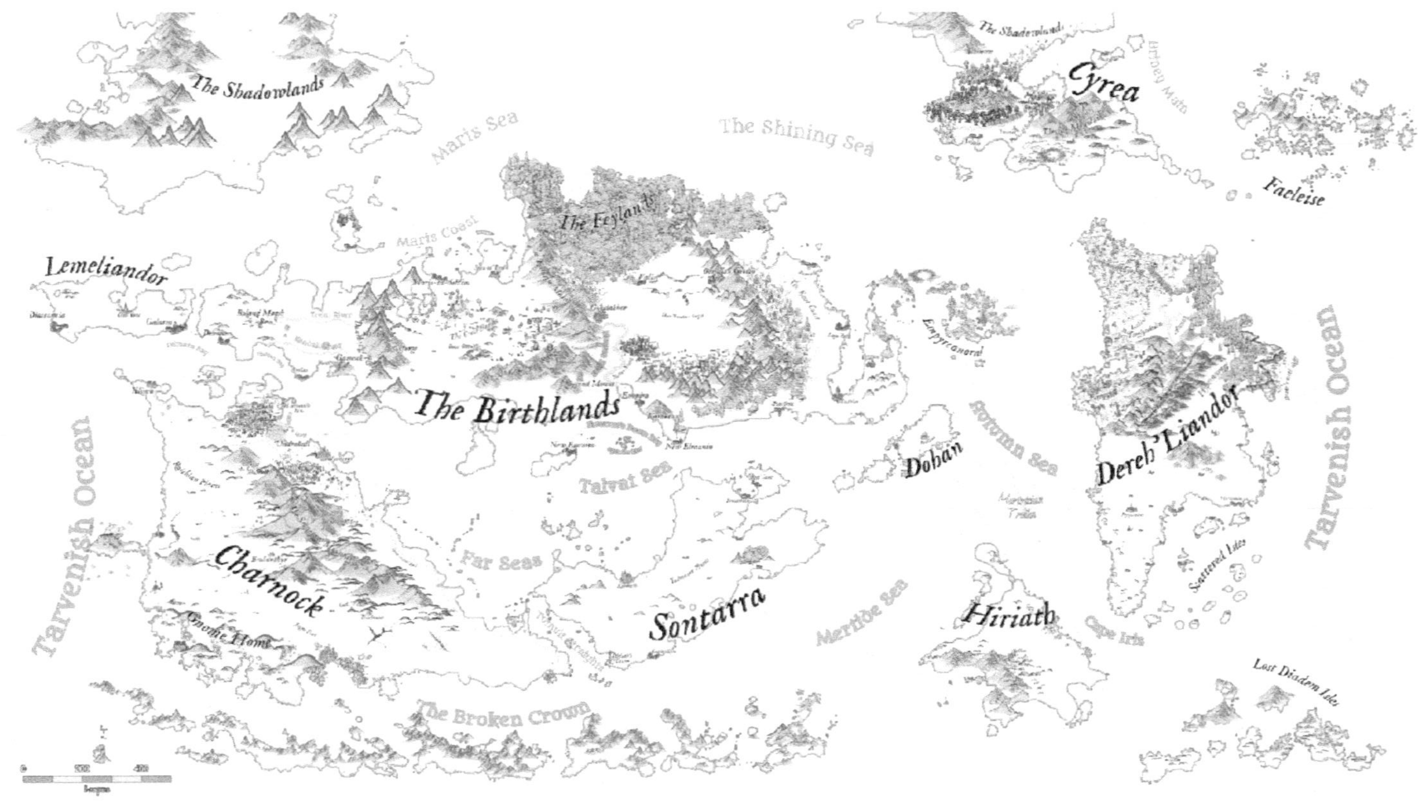
The Shadowlands
Gyrea
The Shining Sea
Maris Sea
Faeleise
The Feylands
Maris Coast
Lemeliandor
The Birthlands
Tarvenish Ocean
Doban
Autumn Sea
Dereh'Liandor
Tarvenish Ocean
Talvat Sea
Charnock
Far Seas
Sontarra
Meritoe Sea
Hiriath
Scattered Isles
The Broken Crown
Lost Diadem Isles

## PROLOGUE

536 First Age

Renata leaned forward upon her throne. For all the crimson-haired warrior queen's beauty, the words that fell from her mouth were ugly, and perfectly appropriate for an amazon in such a situation.

After exhausting the usage of every profane word she knew, she finally stood, and in a rage, hacked the wooden throne to pieces with her sword. Members of her royal entourage watched her and empathized with the woman's seething rage.

Last night, a gang of goblins had infiltrated and killed the queen's horses. To be an amazon meant being a leader of humans and being a member of the warrior elite. For her to suffer such a loss was a direct attack upon her pride and image among her people. Those two horses had been closer than sisters to Queen Renata as she rose through the warrior ranks to become ruler of her people. This amounted to the assassination of her family.

Renata whirled and stared at her generals and other advisers from within the skin hut where she'd made her home this last tumultuous year. The human Gwich'in, a kind of communal group that followed the mystic ways of the sages and the ancients, had built their village north of the Trent River after the lava elves of Mount Garnock began expanding into the human lands at the Wakefield Plain, the land between the Trent and Kendall Rivers.

They'd been emboldened by the events at Karakto in the east when the morehl there threw off their selumari oppressors and reignited the old war. Ever since that uprising, Garnock had consistently worked to expand its borders and grow its influence, by any means necessary. Negotiations had failed—even despite bringing in a morehl advocate for peace, the elf Orric had emerged from Karakto as a leader. Garnock had rejected him, too, and Renata had heard they tried to assassinate him, but it must have failed since Orric ventured east to find a free town on the coast far beyond New Elrannin.

Since assuming the throne, Renata had fought against the red-skinned morehl and their goblinoid trog allies in the Boland Marsh. Wakefield Plain was trapped between them. Without even engaging in open warfare, she felt the loss of her horses more deeply than any other.

"Do you have orders?" asked her primary general. He and three others stood near her. Beyond them, two other advisers waited patiently.

Renata nodded. "I had hoped the lull in this conflict had meant peace would arrive. Now, I want the lands scouted. There will be blood for this. I'll see the morehl killed quick and any trogs you find I want flayed slow."

"The cavalry will see it done," her chief rider said. The amazon leaders pounded the butts of their spears once in unison, and then turned on their heels and left the royal dome.

Flames flickered in the dwelling's central stone ring, and a curious old woman watched Renata drag a chunk of her throne and toss it upon the pyre. The middle-aged male, the other remaining adviser, waited near the door.

Leggara, the leader of the Gwich'in, put a hand on her daughter's shoulder and calmed her. "Peace does not come easy, and it commands a heavy price."

"I know. But this time it will be the trogs who pay it."

Leggara opened her mouth to speak, but Renata cut her off.

"I know all your sermons, mother. And this is a path I

must take. I cannot continue to shrink back and yield our lands. First, the morehl must die, and then the trogs. Our people are dying and we cannot remain hiding here at the Gwich'in. Enough is enough. We've lost good friends and family to those monsters."

Leggara waited for Renata to finish venting, and then she spoke slowly and intentionally, "Before you plow with intentions to plant, you must first count your cost. What would you pay to gain your satisfaction?"

Renata's face twisted wickedly. "Right now? *Anything.*"

She knew that beyond the dome, in the hospital tents of the human healers, many of her people lay bound up with wounds. Trogs, likely under orders from the morehl hordes, had begun setting traps to maim and wound Renata's amazons. They'd learned that a wounded amazon was nearly as ineffective as a dead one. Though there were plenty of corpses, too.

The queen was losing this war, and everyone knew it. That had made the respite at the nearby Gwich'in a logical choice—but it could not remain a permanent one, though it had begun to feel that way after a week.

"I may have a suggestion," the man stated, and walked forward.

Renata almost rolled her eyes. Peregrine was not a warrior, and his obvious flirtation with her could never amount to anything because of that difference in class. Despite her continued rebuffs, he kept trying to please her. Renata liked that, even if she couldn't ever admit to it, not truly.

Peregrine continued, "I am leaving in the morning, my queen. Word has reached me of a peculiar eldarim near the Trent River. They say he has a kind of medicine that none among the Gwich'in have ever studied before. It supposedly allows the healers to bring back even the deceased because of its powerful magics…"

This time Renata *did* roll her eyes. "That is nothing our healers cannot do already," she cut him short.

Peregrine shook his head. "No. Not *this*. This new medicine can supposedly restore someone *even after the spark of life is gone*."

Renata fixed him in her eyes, and they narrowed to slits. "That is not possible. Once the soul has left for the Eternal Lands..."

"Perhaps this calls it back?" Peregrine suggested. "I will not know until I've had a chance to study the stuff, provided the eldarim is willing to help."

Renata entertained the idea for several quiet moments. Finally, she nodded. "Make it happen. Whatever the cost. If we could restore our lost warriors, the remaining army would become so lionized that nothing could stop us from reclaiming the Wakefield Plain...*all* the Wakefield Plain."

Leggara raised a brow but said nothing. She knew as well as any that her daughter had long coveted the far side of the plains under the dwarves' jurisdiction.

Peregrine bowed low, bending at the waist. His motion brought him close enough to Renata that he nearly touched her. "I'm always leaving you," he said.

"And yet you always come back to me," Renata replied with an even voice that revealed none of her flattery.

"I just hope I can return with your miracle, before it is too late...before more trogs emerge from the Boland Marsh."

"You could leave tonight, then, to make every moment count," Renata stated, leaving no room in Peregrine's imagination that he might earn the right to steal a midnight kiss from Queen Renata.

Peregrine swallowed. "As you wish." He turned and departed.

Renata watched him go. After the tent flap finally stilled, Leggara stepped forward again. "That boy is madly in love with you."

"I am aware," Renata stated coldly. If anyone could read her, she knew her mother could—and Leggara would not need magic to do it.

Renata was not a foreigner to using magic; at one time, she considered following in her mother's footsteps and joining the Gwich'in, but she lacked the same potency her mother had and instead pursued a different path to power. She stared at the burning throne and felt as if it may have been a portent of things to come. Renata scowled.

She could have another throne made after the war. And who knew. If Peregrine's discovery turned out to be a boon, she might be able to finally entertain his advances and make *two* of them instead. She stared into the flames. "Until then…"

"Until what?" her mother asked.

Renata merely shook her head, letting the mystery of her words linger between the two.

"Soon," she vowed. "Soon the trogs will find their numbers depleted and the morehl will be defeated. And then… then it will be *my time*."

A scout hurried inside only moments after Peregrine had departed. "I bring word, my Queen. We have captured and interrogated a trog that was thrown from its mount when your raiders chased him back to the swamps."

Renata's brow rose. "He is still alive?"

"Yes. But his spine is broken…however that doesn't mean he can't feel pain. We got word out of him that they are mustering their army—all their army, in a slough at the edge of the Boland Marsh."

The queen grinned wickedly. "We could sweep in and knock them out of this conflict with one massive push." Renata stroked her chin thoughtfully. "My predecessor, Queen Starryi, had a pact with the vagha in Dehnlee. They will answer a call to aid."

"Do we need the dwarves' help?" Leggara asked. "Starryi would never engage an enemy she could not overcome with her own offensive force."

Renata glared at her mother. "She chose to engage *me*. Don't forget that was how I earned the throne almost two years ago." She shook her head. "But I am confident. They will never see us coming and are no match for our speed. The vagha are merely the anvil we might hammer the trogs against—but anvil or no, the hammer will smite those goblins."

She addressed the scout. "Send word to Warlord Adelric in Dehnlee. They have been harried by the trogs' lava elf allies in the south. We move quickly." She showed the messenger her hastily drawn battle plan on a map splayed nearby so he could relay details to their allies.

The scout nodded and then hurried away to fulfill his orders.

Peregrine dismounted the horse he'd taken from the Gwich'in and looked over the lagoon. It was a little more than a day's ride to reach the rumored location near the Trent River, but he was certain he'd arrived at the correct location. The river had created a still inlet where reed and rush formed a chest-high thicket; a winding, narrow footpath twisted through the tangled greenery and ended where a shingle building rose above the water and perched on gnarled legs ascending nearly ten cubits above the surface.

He felt eyes upon him as he approached and Peregrine waved to both greet the man and to demonstrate that he was unarmed.

The door of the strange shack opened and a very pale

person stood there, naked from the waist up. His robes hung about him and he pulled them over his shoulders and closed them, hanging the hood over his face.

Peregrine was not close enough to ascertain the carved and tattooed glyphs upon his host's flesh, but he was certain the man was shara: a pure member of the eldarim race undiluted by interbreeding with other Esfahn residents. Like others of his kind, the eldarim stood nearly a head taller than typical humans and had a broader, more flattened nose and thicker frame, but was otherwise almost identical.

An expectant tingle of excitement warmed Peregrine's belly. The eldarim people had formed the first settlements meant to train Esfah's younger races, the first of those being at Daur-Bor-Nin, and their ancient knowledges had produced the mystic sages who knew how to communicate with, and even bind, spirits. If any creature had devised a way to recall a soul from the afterlife and reunite it with its body as the rumor went, certainly he or she would be of the shara.

"Greetings! My name is Peregrine," he introduced himself. "I have heard that a great alchemist lives near here."

The eldarim nodded as he descended the rickety stair. "I am he. My name is Dhanriath, and I have dwelt here a little over a year; access to these waters have allowed me to study and tinker at my own pace."

Peregrine looked back and forth nervously. "May we speak openly? I am on a mission of some urgency and believe you may be a great help."

Dhanriath nodded and Peregrine continued. "I have come on behalf of Queen Renata whose people are under attack from both trog and morehl. I was told you had discovered a miracle cure: an elixir that prevented death and could recall even the departed spark of life and heal the long-since dead."

The eldarim nodded slowly. "I have found…something like that. And I assume you hope to employ this 'miracle cure' to revive the legions of dead lost to the goblins and lava elves as they pushed your queen back to the nearby Gwich'in?"

Peregrine nodded.

"Then we should be quick about it. The amazons already beat the drums for war," Dhanriath said. "Wait here." He turned and began to ascend the stairs of his hovel, which looked like it might tip over every time he advanced another step.

Peregrine muttered to himself, "I should have suspected her scouts would find the goblins so soon…Renata's outriders were skilled, and the trogs are not even attempting to hide. *Even I* saw evidence of them on my way here."

Dhanriath returned shortly with a bundle wrapped in coarse burlap. "Are you an amazon?"

"I am a human, but not a warrior. I never attempted to gain the title of amazon. My skills lie elsewhere."

"You are Gwich'in, then?" Dhanriath asked. "One skilled in magic and the ancient ways."

Again, Peregrine shook his head. "I am a healer, a physician, but I am not particularly skilled at magic. Not any more so than any foot soldier or archer."

Dhanriath said, "Then you have some skill with alchemy, at least if you focus on the medical sciences?"

"I do."

"Good," Dhanriath stated. "You will know how to use this, then." He turned over the bundle and Peregrine heard the clinking of glass vials within. "Now, be off. Your queen's need for you is great."

Peregrine found himself turning to leave without realizing it. His desire to please Renata moved his feet before his brain had engaged. He stopped. "But how do I make more of it? How does it work? I don't understand it at all…"

"*You will*," Dhanriath said.

"But how?"

"It is magic. Magic teaches its own. Trust your instincts,

my human friend. Right now, what do they say?"

Peregrine clenched his jaw. "That I must get back to Renata as soon as possible."

Dhanriath fixed him with a cold stare. "Then make haste and may Tarvanehl guide you."

Peregrine nodded, and then turned and made for his horse, holding the package close to avoid dropping it in the reeds. He climbed into his saddle and quickly left, feeling there was so much more to the mysterious elixir and to Dhanriath's presence near the river than he would ever know. But he was used to that feeling. All his life he'd felt like a side character in Renata's story, and his parents' story before that. Finally, he thought, this would be Peregrine's tale. Something larger and something *more* was happening than he was aware of—but at least Peregrine was at the center of it.

*Perhaps that will make her take notice of me. Perhaps* then *she will consider me worthy.* "Renata," he let her name slip past his lips.

Peregrine only looked back once and spotted Dhanriath standing at the top step of his stair and in the threshold of his hut. He distinctly felt multiple sets of eyes upon him, as if someone else also watched from Dhanriath's strange, elevated shack.

He turned back and rode, not able to hear the alchemist's words to those in the stilted building. "And now we strike, as our Lord Death commands us."

Three days had passed since Peregrine left her at the Gwich'in, and Renata's war took her further south and towards the Trent River. Here, the trogs had spilled out from their camps in the Boland Marsh and the river terminated in trellised, stagnant pools of muck and mire.

Goblins scampered easily across the peaty bogs, which stymied the horses that the humans rode and clogged up the wheels and axles of amazon chariots. The enemy stepped over the bodies of their fallen allies who bled yellow tinted blood from sword gashes and javelins that pinned their bodies to the grassy carpet. Even still, they kept coming.

Renata cursed as they fought their uphill battle. Despite so many goblin corpses laying strewn across the field of battle, the human casualties were mounting to nearly their equal, and she remembered how quickly the trogs bred and matured to fighting age.

She cut down goblins from her chariot where two new horses pulled. They were strong and young, but the wheels still turned sluggishly as they rolled over spongy ground and troggish cadavers. The wheels struck an amazon shield and bounced against the carriage.

A thought flitted through her mind. *Were my horses worth the lives of so many?* Her jaw set into a growl and she roared, "Yes," as she lopped off the head of a charging enemy. As a pure reaction to the next horde, she reached out to hurl a bolt of lightning at a troll that emerged from the fens and thought of her heritage in the Gwich'in.

The Gwich'in taught peace whenever possible. Renata's people had been displaced and hounded, but she felt certain her mother would disapprove. At least in *this fight. Is it truly worth these lives?* "Not Peregrine's," she mumbled, being honest with herself, which she only did in rare moments.

Renata hoped Peregrine was okay and would return at any moment, and not just because of the hope that he'd gone in search of, but because she needed him. He was not particularly useful; even as a healer, he was not overly skilled. But she never questioned his devotion to her and his support never wavered. She needed that in a time like this. Renata grinned, knowing she'd likely have the opposite feelings as soon as she was in his presence again. Her moods about him swung so widely and so fiercely ever since she could remember.

As the trogs fell to amazon spear and blade, a horn pealed within the swamp. The enemy whirled and made a hasty retreat. They fled back towards the swamp, even though Renata was certain they might have been victorious.

She locked eyes with one of her battle commanders, who shrugged. Renata wasn't going to let an opportunity to override a routing enemy get away from her. She raised her javelin in a clutched fist and howled, "Charge! Kill them all— first the trogs and then the red elves!"

Amazon horses and runners charged towards the goblins. Only moments before the humans could dispatch them with seeming impunity, acrid smoke and the barking of morehl flintlocks roared within the foliage, roaring with deadly aim.

The lava elf snipers let the trogs draw them in and then took down many horses and a huge swath of human soldiers. Trogs shored them up and began hurling bullet stones from slings with nearly the same force as the morehl ball shot.

Trogs riding war dogs and one on a muscular, mangy leopard surged from the undergrowth where they'd been hiding. They plunged into the fray and broke the morale of the charging humans and their cavalry. Amazons split in every direction as the trogs took their turn as pursuers.

One of Renata's horses fell, peppered with a barrage of high velocity wounds. It shrieked with a terrible noise that the stubborn amazon queen knew she'd never forget. Her other animal labored to pull the cart with its near-dead companion half dragged beneath the chariot's housing. Renata leaned forward and cut the dying beast free; her carriage bucked, nearly throwing her free.

She looked around and found her army fleeing. None

headed in her direction. They retreated, hoping to live, and many fell with morehl bullets or troggish stones, piercing their backs with exit wounds blowing bloody holes in their fronts.

"Where are they? Where are the vagha?" muttered Renata, scanning the horizon, hoping to spot a dwarven mammoth or pony force and laying the blame for her route at their feet. "Dehnlee has betrayed us—they've sent no aid. This is all their fault," she growled, fixating on failure and staring at the dead bodies of her warrior sisters where they lay motionless upon the grass.

Renata knew she could do nothing. The day was lost and she would need to marshal her forces at the Gwich'in. Finally, the proud queen whirled her horse back to the north east and snapped her reins.

A sharp crack echoed and slammed into her left shoulder blade, where a missile struck her. She spurred the animal away, curled an arm to her back, and wiped her side. Pulling it back, she found it slicked with bright blood that bubbled pink. *Lung shot… I need a healer while I can still breath—it's treatable but deadly—even Peregrine could fix this if addressed in time.*

Renata's animal howled. It pushed on, but with labored breaths and a wounded gait. Renata could see the gash across its belly. And by the time they'd cleared the edge of the battle and fled for the horizon, the wound had split further. The horse's innards had begun to peek out. A league later, its belly split entirely and the beast collapsed with a terrible neigh, spilling intestine across the grass.

"The river," Renata said with labored breaths, wondering if this was the River of No Return spoken of in the bard's poem, *The Soldier's Journey*. Her javelin dragged behind her as she staggered towards it. Finally, she dropped the weapon and continued forward, driven by sheer force of will.

A dark rage brewed within her, twisting around her guts like a black knot. Her thoughts came in ragged gasps provided by her only working lung, and a black haze crept in around her vision. *These trogs and their morehl masters tricked me… and the dwarves have abandoned me. But I will have my revenge. I swear it!* Renata knew that the gods sometimes honored mortal requests when one swore to become an acolyte—to forswear all other gods. Through ragged breaths she growled, "I would pledge fealty to whatever god helps me revisit my anger upon the bastards plaguing the Wakefield Plain."

A peal of thunder boomed across the sky as if a voice agreed to her oath. Renata became suddenly self-conscious. Gods and oaths were not a thing to trifle with, and she was uncertain exactly how committed she'd been when she'd invoked the divine.

Her footsteps echoed in her ears, and the pain suddenly disappeared. Everything turned shades of gray, as if the world was covered in ash and grown cold; sounds muffled like a morning after a fresh and heavy snow. Renata could see her breath and smell the crisp aroma of smoke in the air.

She stood straight and then turned to look behind her. Everything was wrong. Renata could feel the evil presence lurking somewhere nearby and she knew from the magical training she'd had in her early days with the Gwich'in that she'd entered a festration: a bubble of death magic. A festration always contained an evil spirit—a magic elemental.

Renata searched for it as she scanned in a circle. She was not a powerful spell caster, but had far more skill than many that she knew; she only hoped she had sufficient strength to bind a black elemental so that she could escape the festration—perhaps even enslaving the thing to her will. If she could do that, she might emerge from this failed battle more powerful than going in…even if she knew her mother would disapprove of using death magic.

Finally, Renata spotted the fiend. He looked like an ordinary man, dressed plainly and perhaps in his late teenage years. His age was difficult to determine, but he had every appearance of wholesomeness.

Fire and ice burned in each of the amazon queen's hands as she summoned magic to her aide. She found it far easier while within the boundary of the festration. The death elemental stood and locked eyes on her. He used a finger to write a burning symbol which hung in the air; it was a dweomernull sign that canceled Renata's magic, extinguishing all elements except for death.

Renata answered his anti-magic sign with her own. She likewise raked a finger through the air and made a sign of binding: a nearly forgotten art taught to the Gwich'in by the sages who specialized in spirits and elementals. She knew she was no sage, but had faith that her efforts would work, if this elemental death spirit was not too powerful, and the power of such fiends had dissipated since the binding of the four most powerful death spirits, the four Totems of Death.

"If you knew who stood before you, you would know better than to attempt such a trick," he said with a voice like an earthquake.

The woman's face blanched. Despite its benign appearance, she was certain the thing was powerful. It could have even been one of the seven Aspect spirits, the strongest elementals below Malfeus, Noxigant, Ghastamant, Surfeibese.

"W-who are you?" Renata's voice cracked.

"You know my name. *All* know my name … and none dare speak it without invoking me."

"Death?" Renata gulped. This was no mere spirit. He was the god of death.

His lips quirked into a smile. "Malgrimm is my true name." All on Esfah knew better than to speak it aloud; legend said that saying the forbidden name caused him to murder whoever spoke it.

Death paused and knelt over the equestrian corpse. He

dug his hands into the animal's innards and scooped them to his mouth, feasting on the gore. Finally, he stood and stared at Renata. "You have offered yourself to whatever god will grant your desires. I am here to collect an oath."

Renata's rage flickered anew, and a fire burned in her belly. "What will you offer me in exchange for service?"

Malgrimm's lip curled. "Satisfaction."

The amazon queen set her jaw. All her bitterness and malice rose to the top of her emotions. She wanted nothing more than to see spilled blood from goblin and lava elf… and anyone else she suspected might be an enemy. *The Wakefield Plain was* hers.

Continuing, the god said, "You must be loyal to me, my dear, if you choose this." Malgrimm turned his head unnaturally to look at something Renata could not see. "There are many who claim to follow me, but who secretly pursue their own aims. Their hearts are not pure, as yours will be." Lord Death turned back to look at her.

"All those on the Wakefield Plain will suffer!" Renata screeched, giving in and voicing her desires.

"Then I shall grant your wish. You shall have your vengeance." Malgrimm approached, and with a warm smile, lifted a hand. His forefinger had a wicked talon, and he poked his finger into the right side of her chest, puncturing her lung. He pointed to the Trent River with his other hand. "There is a boon upon the body at the river's edge. He carries something that you seek: the key to claiming your revenge…The thing that will let you spread your suffering across the Wakefield Plain."

With his free hand, he snapped his fingers. Renata could feel a shroud of silence fall over them. She did not understand what purpose it served, only that she and Malgrimm communed with words that only the two could hear.

She did not feel any pain, but was overcome with the sensation of the festration collapsing into a singular point. It crystallized into a purple, gleaming gem the size and shape of Malgrimm's finger.

"This is my gift to a loyal one, and this is what you have earned from our pact. A darkhold gem. There is festration inside of you now, and forever. Your magic is opened to you far more than ever, but you are my acolyte. No other gods will heed your call. The thirst will take you … drink of my ichor and create an army of my children."

"It's so … exquisite," Renata whispered as she looked at the gem. Then her mind caught up to the demon's words. "In-inside me?" She held out her hand expectantly, not understanding his prophetic meaning.

"My servant Melkior is gone and his underling is far away on a task of his own. I have need of a herald in this region. Spread my power and my will." Malgrimm withdrew his finger and plunged the darkhold gem into the hole in her chest as the festration closed around them. And with it gone, so was the god, Death.

Suddenly, thrust back into the real world, Renata gasped and choked on the blood welling up in her throat. She summoned healing magic enough to keep her lungs operating. Renata still felt as if she were drowning in blood.

Her eyes fixed on a body in the distance. The human corpse lay on the far side of the banks. It seemed to glow with a ruby corona. Renata could sense the nearby dead. A gift from the gem.

She staggered to the river and walked across its surface. It froze below her footsteps and created a bridge of ice as she struggled across it. Finally, with labored breathing and on the verge of collapse, Renata arrived at the body which she recognized.

*Peregrine!* The man lay dead with an arrow protruding from his chest. Someone had murdered him and he lay sprawled upon the banks, clutching a bundle. In his hand was a bottle of black, viscous fluid.

Sorrow welled up inside her. Peregrine was gone.

She paused, teetering on her feet. Renata did not see the trog riding upon the leopard as he rushed at her, club in hand, and cracked her across the back of the skull. The impact knocked a chunk of bone and gray matter free.

The rider and mount turned and growled victoriously. Renata's body lay over the other corpse and the trog spurred his mount. The large cat rushed into the distance in search of other fleeing amazons to eliminate; he and the other goblin cavalry headed in the direction of the human city which now had no defenders: the Gwich'in would burn.

## PART ONE

Face down, Renata reached back and touched the back of her head. She felt the jagged edge where her skull had been shattered and opened to the sky.

Renata lifted her head and brushed the shards of broken glass away from her facial wounds. Her face had smashed a vial of the black ichorous fluid and it seeped into her cuts and reanimated her. She did not remember how she got here. She barely remembered her name… *Renata*. And Renata knew that she felt rage and a fierce need for blood.

A hunger also rolled in her stomach. The black fluid called out to her with a powerful thirst. Renata unstoppered one of the black bottles below her and drank it like a dehydrated person chugging water. Finally slaked, she took the remaining bottles and began shambling north, unsure of what exactly she was supposed to do. Only impulse drove her, and the remnants of old emotion fueled her actions.

She walked towards the horizon. Her feet bore her ever onward until she disappeared out of sight. Only then did the magical sphere of invisibility dispel to reveal a trio of pale eldarim, Dhanriath and his two companions.

"What did Lord Death say to the woman?" Dhanriath asked. "He silenced their conversation to conceal it from us …Do you suppose he knew that we were here?"

"I think that much is certain," Burlaic stated. Both looked to their master, a tall eldarim with deep eyes.

"It does not matter," he stated. "We are not here for that;

we are here to study and learn the effects of the necralluvium to see if it is beneficial for us to use it."

Dhanriath and Burlaic nodded.

Burlaic laid his bow upon the dirt, squatted close to the cadaver, and examined Peregrine's body. The necralluvium moved like a tortured slug, sending tendrils to flail around and search for a host. The inky stuff found the wound where Burlaic had shot Peregrine a day prior. It pulled itself into the wound and disappeared within the deceased's body.

A bottle still lay in Peregrine's hand. Renata had left one behind.

The hand suddenly clutched the bottle as Peregrine's eyes snapped open. He sat up, grabbed Burlaic with his other hand, and sank his teeth into Burlaic's neck.

Burlaic screamed as the zombie's teeth tore a chunk of flesh free. His jugular artery flopped in the wound, pulsing great spurts of blood in slowing cadence.

Dhanriath and his superior watched Burlaic bleed out and die in a matter of moments. Peregrine finally released him and crawled to his feet, driven by the same urges that he'd had in the throes of death. Peregrine pulled the cork and drank the black fluid he'd placed so much false hope in before his death.

He dropped the jar. The necralluvium had no visible effect upon the reanimated Peregrine. The zombie turned and began walking into the distance, heading in the same general direction as Renata.

"Remarkable," Dhanriath said. "So this is what happens when a drone is created, but not under the thrall of any creator."

"We shall have to watch this situation unfold," Dhanriath's master said. "We could learn much about the strange substance as the war for the Wakefield Plain unfolds." He turned and looked at Dhanriath.

Dhanriath nodded. "The experiment goes well, but it will take time to learn all that we wish to know ... perhaps years, or even longer."

"That is not a problem. I have nothing but time and I am a patient man. I toiled under Sshkkryyahr the Drider. I watched the Karakto rebellion from the slopes of the Crooked Spine. This will be a mere heartbeat between movements and we must learn all we can before we spring our trap. We must not move too soon. We must be certain before we gather our mages, storm the gates of the abyss, and claim godhood for ourselves. By the end of this, all of Esfah will know the name of Nekarthis."

## CHAPTER ONE

541 First Age

The ax blade cut easily into the bright red flesh of the morehl bladesman, then crunched loudly as it smashed through the hard bone beneath.

He was a lowly soldier, probably pressed into service. The black-haired lava elf cried out as the vagha warlord raised his dwarven ax above his helmed head and prepared to deliver another blow. It might have been overkill, since the lava elf would likely die from the wounds already incurred, but none of these disgusting morehl had shown their enemies any mercy over the course of the war, and so the dwarf was hard pressed to show any in return.

And even if the morehl had been merciful and compassionate, the very fact that, as a race, they were attuned to the forces of death made them natural enemies of the vagha—a race of dwarves attuned to the element of earth. And although both races were attuned to the element of fire, for the morehl, it was a destructive force used for burning, searing, and destroying, while for the vagha, it was a beneficial force, used for warming, heating, and cooking... usually. They were violently opposed to each other by their very nature.

"No," the lava elf said, his voice a sibilant whisper with an underlying buzz to it. As he spoke, his eyes grew wide at the sight of the ax arcing over the warlord's head.

The morehl's plea went unheeded and Warlord Adelric, a dwarf of high military rank, brought the ax down once more, this time with all his might. He silenced the loathsome red elf once and for all before standing erect over his victim. He looked around to assess the ongoing battle.

Despite dispatching of the morehl fighter, the battle for his kindred vagha was not going well as a whole. There were too many morehl for the vagha forces to handle and if something did not turn the tide, the dwarven army would soon be overrun and their beloved city of Dehnlee would be left vulnerable, with only a token army left to protect it.

But what could be done now that hadn't already been tried?

Adelric's magicians had cast a variety of spells, but the lava elves were just as adept at fire magic as the vagha were and had been able to counter their attempts and gain an advantage through the use of magic. Furthermore, the ultimate result of their attempts at magic were geographic upheavals in the terrain of Wakefield Plain, and Tarvanehl only knew where else on the face of Esfah; creating tectonic shifts in the plains undoubtedly meant creating valleys and tsunamis elsewhere. The magic that had been used here would affect the terrain for leagues in any direction, and since what they'd already tried had not worked, more magic would only cause more devastation.

Adelric had even tried calling upon some of their monster allies, but the morehl had allies of their own. The resulting monster battle was a prolonged bout where each fought the other to its death and left a wake of destructive attrition in both sides' forces. Summoning monsters had no eventual outcome of the battle between such bitter rivals. The contest would only be won with ax and shield, blade and pistol—and relying solely on the desire of their troops to emerge as victors.

The warlord scanned the battlefield. Although his once fiery red hair had long ago been streaked with white, he was still an impressive and imposing figure. His squat legs and short arms bulged with taut muscles, and his ax was still as quick and powerful as any under his command. He had seen his share of wars during his lifetime—the scars on his gold-tinted skin attested to that fact—but his ability to fight had never diminished in all those years.

If anything had waned over time, it was his will to fight. In his youth, he served in the vagha army as a footman. He had relished every opportunity to do battle and the chance to swing his ax against a worthy opponent. But as he had grown older and had risen through the ranks, he became responsible for the lives of other soldiers in addition to his own; he realized that there was a high cost to doing battle, and most often, that cost was levied against dwarven blood and lives. And so, he began to cherish peace and tranquility. Adelric preferred it over war and chaos, almost to a fault.

However, in all his years, he had never ignored a single call to arms. A career soldier, he had answered such calls with all the skill and tenacity he possessed. The only difference now was that he looked more diligently for the quickest and easiest solution to a conflict and drew his ax only when peaceful negotiation and diplomacy had utterly failed.

Like now.

The morehl had been expanding their claims to the lands around their home of Garnock in the east. While some expansion over time was to be expected, the morehl had laid claim to huge chunks of Wakefield Plain, claiming that the rich mineral deposits in the rocky soil were necessary for the operations of their mills and forges. They'd pushed out the humans who lived there already; none knew where they'd emigrated to. While the plains possessed an abundance of natural resources, it was a poor excuse meant to justify a land grab since the Red Rock Mountains surrounding Garnock possessed all the raw materials the morehl would ever need—both for their own purposes and for that of export and commerce. Not that they could ever challenge the mining operations of the dwarves in the Daurhedge only a little further east.

Despite the dishonesty, Warlord Adelric had done his best to try to negotiate a peaceful settlement, but to no avail. The morehl marched across the plain and laid claim to it all. As Warlord of the vaghan city of Dehnlee, he had no choice but to settle the matter on the battlefield.

But now, with the morehl holding the advantage and threatening to overrun the vagha, they could lay claim not just on the Wakefield Plain, but the dwarven city of Dehnlee as well.

Incredible as it sounded, the fall of Dehnlee had become a possibility, and a very real one at that. But before the city fell, the warlord vowed that many, many morehl would die before any of them caught sight of the Dehnlee gates.

He finished his scan of the battlefield, noticed a vagha patroller fending off two lava elves, and decided he'd give the young soldier a hand. Adelric raised his ax and hurried toward the skirmish.

"Good day, Warlord," said the young fighter, a stout dwarf named Ackerly. "I could use your help about now."

"And you shall have it," said Adelric, cutting down the morehl with a sideways swipe of his ax. The tip of the blade caught the morehl just on the flesh of his flame-red skin, causing a darker line of red to bleed up to the surface; it leaked a slight wisp of steam when it contacted the air. It was only a scratch, but it proved enough to draw the enemy away from Ackerly, leaving the footman evenly matched against the second lava elf.

The wounded morehl scout returned Adelric's blow with the rapier he clutched, but the warlord easily deflected it with his shield. Undaunted, the morehl pressed his attack, managing to strike several more blows before Adelric returned them. When he did, the morehl's face twisted into one of shocked terror.

Adelric's ax lodged in the lava elf shield. He yanked it back, ripping the shield free of the morehl's hands. Then, he swung his ax once more, using the extended reach of the connected shield to smash the stunned morehl over the head, crushing his skull and laying him out prone on the battlefield.

Adelric wrenched his ax from the shield, and then turned to see if Ackerly needed help with his opponent. To Adelric's delight, the young footman had taken care of his enemy. A hard blow to the chest had easily cut through the lava elf's thin armor and stopped his heart.

"Well done, Ackerly," Adelric said.

"I've had good instruction, milord," Ackerly said in reply. Adelric had been the one to train all the recruits in close-combat tactics these past ten years.

Adelric beamed, but knew that such things were better celebrated after the battle was over. "Just don't start thinking you're invincible," he said. "All it takes is one moment of inattention and..." His voice trailed off.

"Yes, milord," said Ackerly.

"Head's up!" shouted a familiar voice. "There's more of them coming."

The call had come from the south. Adelric tried to place the voice and reckoned it belonged to Borvis, one of his best riders. A few moments later, Adelric's hunch proved right and Borvis rode up on his pony accompanied by his partner. A young dwarf named Darton straddled a second mount.

"What is it?" asked Adelric.

"It looks like additional reinforcements arriving from Garnock," he guessed.

Adelric nodded. "That sounds likely."

"What should we do?" asked the second rider, Darton.

"What *can* we do?" said Ackerly.

*Yes, indeed,* thought Adelric. *What can we do?* The battle's momentum was already in the morehl's favor, and now, their army swelled yet again.

For one of the few times in his military career, Adelric was at a loss for ideas. His scouts and soldiers all looked at him, awaiting an answer; a solution to their problem.

"We'll use our superior range weapons against them."

The voice was not Adelric's. It belonged to his younger brother, Evan, a battle-tested marksman who commanded the vaghan missile troops. *Good old Evan,* thought Adelric. Even though his brother was several years younger than himself. He could always be counted on in a pinch.

Evan acknowledged him with a wink of his right eye and a flick of his head.

Adelric looked around to see how the suggestion had gone over with the rest of the soldiers present.

"They have range weapons, too," said Darton.

"I've heard their flintlocks are quite accurate," said Ackerly.

"And has anyone ever heard the *zing* of one of our arrows fired by a skilled crossbowman?" asked Evan, his fists resting on his hips. "Would you ever wish to be on the receiving end of such missiles?"

No one said a word.

"Very well, then," said Adelric. "Get your troops prepared for fire whenever they come into range."

"Consider it done, brother," Evan said with a smile.
With a signal, a huge corps of crossbowmen followed him to intercept the reinforcements at a broken ridge, where return fire

would provide them with some elevation.

The vagha waited for the morehl to come into range. Then, the relative silence of the battlefield was broken by the whiz and whir of bolts as they arced over the heads of the vaghan soldiers still battling the lava elf hordes at the vanguard.

With deadly accuracy, the quarrels found their marks, striking morehl soldiers in the chest, legs, and arms. But almost to the second that the vaghan missiles began to soar, the air also filled with the crack and smoke of morehl pistols as they fired their shots in return.

The battle continued with troops fighting in close combat on the battlefield and others fighting a long-range war over the heads of the soldiers on the field. For some time, it felt like the two armies were locked in a stalemate. But slowly, the lava elf's shooters proved too skilled to overcome, even with the small cover Evan's ridge provided.

"We can't beat them like this," said Evan to his older brother.

Adelric had been watching the battle's progress and had not wanted to be the first to concede the point. But now that his brother had admitted it, he let his shoulders slump forward in a gesture that all but admitted defeat.

"What can we do in the face of so many?" said Adelric.

Evan did not have an answer at first. His usually bright face looked worn and troubled, and if Adelric hadn't known better, he might have thought he spotted a tinge of fear in the younger dwarf's eyes. "We could fashion pistols of our own," said Evan, a bright spark of life back into his eyes and a slight smile on his face.

"That's not going to help us right now, though, is it?"

"No, I suppose not," said Evan, looking to the ground as if thinking.

"Any other ideas, then?"

"Yes," Evan said, looking up at his brother with an ear-to-ear grin. "Why don't we charge them?"

"What? The missile troops?"

"Yes, they won't be expecting it."

"But your troops are trained with a crossbow, not the ax."

"Do you have any other suggestions as to how to stop them from picking us off one by one?"

Adelric had none. He said nothing.

"All right, then," said Evan. He raised his voice to address the dwarves under his command. "Put away your crossbows," he cried. "We're going on the march."

Adelric wanted to protest, to order his brother not to do it, but the young firebrand had already given the order and Evan would never forgive Adelric if he ordered him to stay where he was. Besides, Adelric had been the one to teach many of the crossbow toting fighters how to fight in the first place. Instead of holding his younger brother back, Adelric did the only thing he could under the circumstances.

"Good luck," said Adelric, slapping Evan on the back. "You're going to need it."

Evan looked across the battlefield at the morehl missile troops and said, "I know."

With his brother skirting the edge of the ridge so that he and his soldiers remained unseen by the incoming reinforcements, Adelric returned his attention to the battle nearby. Garnock's troops were advancing again, moving to fill in the gaps of their army.

Evan crested the ridge and led the charge across the battlefield toward the morehl. As the vagha soldiers ran, lava elf shooters fired as quickly as they could into the mass of charging bodies. Several vagha fell on their way to the fight. Many others took wounds, while a few lucky ones took grazing shots that their armor deflected.

Despite the injuries to the vagha forces, they continued across the battlefield, eager to take on the enemy. By the time they closed the distance between them by half, the morehl's resolve weakened. The dwarven charge was unorthodox to say the least, and the elven troops appeared to be younger and untested than those at the front. They were likely used to pulling triggers on flintlocks and had never crossed blades with a real enemy.

Some continued firing their pistols, but most of them looked too distracted by the charging vagha. They fumbled with their weapons, dropping shot and powder onto the ground, or jamming the pistols in their rush to take one last shot at them.

By the time the dwarves reached them, only a fraction had put away their pistols and drawn their weapons. The vagha, however, had been on the run with their axes raised high above their heads. They delivered blows the moment they arrived and scattered the morehl into disarray.

Lava elves fell, one after another, as the courage and tenacity of Dehnlee's missilers overwhelmed them. The roar of triumphant dwarves replaced the pistol cracks at Garnock's flanks.

All around his vantage, Evan could see his forces wielding their axes as skillfully as any heavy infantry. It was a proud moment for the dwarven warrior. As leader of the missile troops, he had spent a good deal of their training time instructing them on martial combat beyond what they'd learned as young recruits. Even though the warlord would never ask the ranged troops to fight such battles, Evan had always thought it best that his soldiers were ready for any eventuality on the battlefield.

And now he was being proved right.

He looked around for spots where he might be able to lend a hand, but his vagha had claimed the fight by this point. Many of the lava elves had already turned and run.

But then, out of the corner of his eye, he saw some movement. He turned and spotted a small morehl—perhaps only a boy—making his way toward him. The young lava elf struggled with the trigger of a flintlock, a pistol that looked extremely heavy in his small hands, judging by the way he carried it.

The boy looked too young, too innocent to be part of this fight. He had likely been conscripted as a sort of page or squire and now, with the final battle of this war in full swing, he was pressed into picking up a weapon to make his contribution to Garnock's victory.

Evan didn't want to harm the boy. He was so young, with so much of his youth to enjoy before the rigors of battle hardened him like blood-quenched steel.

"Put it down, boy," Evan said forcefully. "Drop it and run away!"

The boy kept approaching.

"Run, boy! If you do, I won't chase you and I won't kill you." Evan's voice was firm, as if he were giving an order to one of his troops.

The boy finally stopped and looked up at Evan. He'd cleared whatever jam had made the weapon malfunction.

Evan saw the boy's face for the first time. The boy was indeed little more than a child, not even old enough to be a page. Perhaps he'd accompanied his father into battle? Perhaps he'd even seen his father die at the hands of a vaghan soldier?

"Put it down and I'll let you live," said Evan.

The boy ignored the warning, choosing instead to slowly raise the pistol until it was pointed at Evan.

Evan opened his mouth to speak, but it was suddenly very dry and the words would not come. He saw the pistol flare.

Time seemed to slow for Evan. He watched the ball exit the barrel in a billow of acrid blue smoke.

The pitch of the battle had finally turned to favor Dehnlee.

As Adelric scanned the battlefield, he saw Evan's missile troops had overrun their opponents. The reinforcements had been killed off or had turned and run. He pumped his fist into the air. The fleeing enemies would no doubt stop when they'd reached the familiar lands surrounding the Red Rock Mountains.

"Well done, Evan," he muttered to the sky.

Best of all, his brother's victory had a direct effect on the larger, ongoing battle. It pitched the trajectory toward a new path: one that would lead to a dwarven victory, and none too soon. They'd been pushed to barely two leagues from Dehnlee's gates, and Adelric's troops received a desperately needed boost in morale. They suddenly fought with renewed vigor and determined not to be upstaged by the prowess of soldiers usually accustomed to fighting at a distance.

With their reinforcements suddenly gone, and advantage wiped out, Garnock's forces fought on their heels. They'd shifted to fighting defensively.

Minutes later, Evan's troops joined the main fray and harried the morehl flanks. Their numbers proved more than enough to firmly turn the tide.

Garnock's best floundered. Red-skinned soldiers fell dead all over the battlefield, leaking hot, red blood and steam into the soil of the Wakefield Plain.

Vaghan casualties dwindled to a fraction of their previous rate. An hour passed before the lava elves admitted the eventuality of the situation. The battle turned into a rout for the vagha, who chased away the vestiges of the morehl army before they could attempt to regroup. The cavalry pursued them for several hours until they could be sure that Garnock wouldn't be mounting a retaliatory charge any time soon.

*It was over,* thought Adelric. *At last, it was over.*

He wanted to thank his younger brother, Evan, whose actions had single-handedly reset the course of the battle and allowed Dehnlee to emerge the victors.

Adelric couldn't wait to congratulate him on a job well done.

"Evan!" called Adelric as he ran across the battlefield to the blood-soaked site, where his missile corps had recorded the magnificent victory. "Well done, Evan!"

But as he neared the sight of the battle, a bad feeling lodged in the pit of Adelric's stomach. Although the plain was littered with dead morehl, none of the surviving dwarf soldiers seemed to revel in their victory. In fact, their faces appeared drawn—long and full of sorrow.

"What is it?" asked Adelric. "What's happened?"

Rather than answer his questions, the soldiers simply averted their eyes. They looked at the ground or to the sky, busying themselves with the cleaning and care of weapons.

None wanted to be the one to deliver the dark message.

"Will someone tell me what in Tarvanehl's name is going on here? The battle is over and we've won! To look at your faces, you'd think we'd lost."

"Warlord," came a voice. Adelric looked over and saw his second-in-command, Sergeant Cadman, approaching.

"What is it?" Adelric groused.

"I think you should come with me," said Cadman.

The sergeant led him to a spot where a group of soldiers had gathered in a small circle.

"Make way," said the sergeant. "The warlord is here."

Slowly, the crowd parted and Adelric could see a soldier laid upon his back and on the ground. There was a large hole in his chest, no doubt made by a morehl pistol fired at very close range.

Suddenly, Adelric's heart slammed up and into his throat. He recognized him. The dead soldier was…

*Evan!*

The name screamed and echoed inside of Adelric's head, but the only word he could say was a weakly whispered, "No…"

"The magic-users tried reviving him, but he was too badly wounded," said Sergeant Cadman. "His spark had already left for the Eternal Lands…"

Adelric wasn't listening to Cadman. Instead, he knelt down beside his brother, cradled his head in his arms…

And he wept.

The victory celebrations were few and short-lived.

While everyone remained glad that the threat of the lava

elves had turned back, the residents of Dehnlee were each deeply saddened by the loss of their own Evan. No family or clan had escaped the viciousness of the morehl without suffering casualties.

Evan was the warlord's younger brother, but he had also been a favorite son of Dehnlee. Most in the city knew him as a symbol of their bright future; that loss, in addition to the funerals of clansmen, was deeply felt.

Although it had never been stated in so many words, it was understood that Evan would someday rise to the rank of warlord and take command of the vaghan forces from his older brother when Adelric retired. Now, that could never be.

And what of Adelric?

Much of the grief felt over Evan's death by the people of Dehnlee was felt for Adelric. Since he'd been a career soldier, he had practically been married to the military. He had no wife, few friends, and almost all of his non-military life had been interwoven with that of his younger brother. Evan was all the family he had. And now, that was gone.

But no matter how deeply he was affected by the loss, Adelric was too professional a soldier to allow himself to fall apart before his responsibilities were fully carried out. He'd dutifully presided over the burial of the morehl dead on the battlefield, as well as the transport of his kinsmen's bodies at the Wakefield Memorial, a league closer to the city, and had them interred there, before he allowed himself to feel any sorrow for his brother.

During the ceremony, Adelric did not single out his brother in any way, feeling it would be a slight against all the other vaghan soldiers—of which there were many—who had died just as bravely during the battle.

But while Adelric did not place any added outward significance on his brother's death, many others did in their speeches—even those who lost loved ones, children, and spouses during the battle. Many singled out Evan on Adelric's behalf and praised him for his courage and leadership.

The words of honor and kindness warmed Adelric's heart.

But only for a little while. After the words were spoken, the cold, hard reality of the situation returned to haunt his thoughts.

Evan was dead.

Adelric wondered if he'd ever be able to get over that fact.

Part of him didn't want to.

But another part of him knew that he must.

Eventually…

Someday…

But not just yet.

He left Wakefield Memorial as soon as the ceremony ended, heading back to his home in Dehnlee and looking forward to spending some time by himself.

Remembering Evan.

# CHAPTER TWO

One tenday later…

The view wasn't as pretty as he remembered.

Adelric stood on the gravel and sand covered ground behind his home on the western outskirts of the vagha city of Dehnlee. The semi-fertile soil stretched out before him, full of bumps, creases, and folds, looking much like the surface of a rumpled bed sheet after a particularly restless night. Luckily, the farmlands that were located further west seemed undisturbed by the tectonic disruption that had flowed over and into the borders of Dehnlee. Or at least, their crops had survived the war intact.

Closer to home, across the tract of land between the city and the farmlands, several plants and even trees had been uprooted and severely shifted during the battle. Many of them were now growing out of the ground at sharp and unnatural angles. To the right, an oak looked like an old dwarf trying to right himself with a scraggly wooden cane after being blown over by a particularly strong wind. To the left, the bark of a birch tree hung from its trunk with branches like the tattered clothes of a pauper.

Nearer the house, it wasn't much better.

The flowers and plants of Adelric's modest garden did their best to bloom and capture the warmth of the morning sun on their petals. But try as they might, nothing seemed to help them regain their delicate hold on the earth. The grass surrounding the flower beds had also been damaged by the war. The earth's upheaval had dried it out like desert fireweed, casting everything in shades of brown and yellow. Finally, the flat stones that lined the walkways through his garden were all askew, as if pranksters had swarmed through the garden and pulled up everything they could lay their hands on.

Such were the effects of war on the land.

Even though the last battle for the Wakefield Plain had taken place practically on the town's doorstep, the worst of the fighting happened a great many leagues further to the east. That was where the most magic had been used. Despite the fact that very few earth spells had been attempted against the morehl, the effects of the war had been felt all across the surface of Esfah. And like ripples moving across the surface of a pond, the waves of tectonic upheaval had made it as far as Adelric's backyard garden, and only Mother Ghaeial knew where else. That was the result of using magic to disrupt rather than heal; all the magic of the gods, except for the Death god, was intended to bring harmony and using it for war begged consequences.

Nature could sometimes be fragile for all her resilience. That was why Nature needed the first races of the vagha and the selumari to champion its cause on this fledgling world.

Adelric stared at his garden and let out a sigh. There was much work to do. It would likely keep him busy for a while, but perhaps a bit of hard work in his garden was just the thing he needed. If nothing else, it would help him clear his mind of war thoughts… and of his younger brother, Evan. Peace had returned to the Wakefield Plain, but not yet to Adelric's mind.

He turned and went back inside his house to gather a few tools and other items that might help him repair and reshape his land. Adelric had always been a keen gardener and kept a selection of simple tools and implements stowed just inside the back door of his low, stone-built house.

Although Adelric was a reputable vagha warlord and commanded a great many dwarves during times of war, during times of peace, he preferred to live a simple life and keep a modest home. He felt a large home with servants or soldiers to attend to his daily needs would feel too much like a reward for his countless days of battle. True, he had won more wars than he had lost, but how could he revel in the lap of luxury when many vagha, selumari, and amazons had died under his command over the years? How could he live well, when others had not even been allowed to live at all? And especially now, how could he indulge himself when his younger brother was dead and buried beneath the cold, hard ground of Wakefield Plain and he was left to tend the gardens?

Adelric did retain the services of a housekeeper named Hildegard; she cooked his meals and cleaned house for him once every tenday. Anything more and Adelric would have considered it an extravagance. But Hildegard was more than a warlord's housekeeper. After so many years of service, she had become a friend and confidante who looked after his most basic needs—such as seeing that he ate right, got enough rest, and kept his feet firmly planted on the ground. She often had to simultaneously remind him of his position. Even still, she kept him free from delusions of grandeur.

It was said that during wartime the warlord was king, but in times of peace, it was Hildegard who truly ran his house.

Adelric wouldn't have it any other way.

Besides, living simply and peacefully was the greatest reward a dwarven warlord could ask for on Esfah, where the various races—vagha, selumari, trogs, morehl, humans, and the fire-walking empyreans—were usually embroiled in one war or another. Somewhere on the planet, they swept back and forth across the land in a seemingly endless series of wars and battles. Adelric loved his home, but he didn't understand what drove the races to kill each other over tracts of dirt.

Adelric twisted his lips as he thought about it. He'd only seen a firewalker once, and that was years ago—the best warrior he'd ever laid eyes on. Empyreans were skilled in killing.

It had been years since he'd seen a human, though. Not since the early days of the war against the morehl. They'd come under attack first, as Garnock had expanded its power base. He'd always figured their proud warrior queen too stubborn to call for aid, and the last amazon Adelric had seen was a messenger gunned down by morehl flintlocks before he could reach the vaghan safety line. His message had died with him.

Adelric scowled. The lava elves understood the importance of severing communication and isolating their foes. Dehnlee kept many messenger birds. When the first skirmishes broke out with the red skinned invaders, they intercepted many of these birds. After exposing them to disease, they released them back to the dwarves so that they brought with them an avian plague that wiped out their entire population before the dwarves realized anything was amiss. They still hadn't been able to replenish their numbers. Were it not for that, Dehnlee might have been able to call upon Vhandria for aid and repel Garnock before they'd dug in their heels. But with the dwarven mountain forces dealing with trog raiders from the Brakishomme, Vhandria was too distracted with problems of its own to worry over policing any portion of the Wakefield Plain.

Despite how necessary the recent war with the hideous morehl had been, Adelric had come to realize in his elder years that it was a far better thing to lift a spade and work the land than to swing a sword in anger against an enemy. The former brought forth life. The latter only death.

With a heavy sigh, Adelric selected a long-handled spade with a sharply pointed iron blade off the rack next to the door, then he took a long-handled claw rake from where it rested against the wall. Finally, he picked up a small hand-held hoe and slipped its stubby handle inside his waistband.

He made one last check and, satisfied he had all he'd need, left the house and headed for the garden to begin his rehabilitation work.

Within minutes, he had the spade cutting into the ground with a satisfying *shiff,* again and again, as mounds of earth were quickly flattened and smoothed over. These mounds only moments before had been bulging out of the ground like diseased tumors. Another unsightly blemish against Nature's beauty repaired; another ugly battle scar mended.

The healing process had begun.

Adelric worked without stopping for a solid hour before pausing a moment to lean forward and rest against the end of his spade. The sun had crawled high in the mid-day sky like a brightly polished coin set against a blue backdrop as rich as the waters of Delmara Bay. If only the sky's beauty could be complemented by a comparably lush and green garden beneath it.

Adelric looked around at the job he'd done and shook his head in dismay.

He'd been working for more than an hour and all he'd been able to do was smooth out a few square yards of earth. At this rate, it would take him days to reclaim his little patch of land and bring it back to a shadow of its former glory. It was obvious that what he really needed to do was wholesale excavation. He looked at the spade in his hands, then at the hands themselves. Despite having heavily calloused palms and fingers from years of brandishing steel swords and stone battle-axes, his beefy hands were still spotted with blisters in the few places where callouses had never formed. It was a telling sign of how long he and the rest of the dwarves of Dehnlee had spent waging war rather than living in peace. He may have had the heart of a farmer, but he had the hands of a soldier.

After rubbing his tender palms against each other, Adelric gathered up his garden tools and brought them back to the house. Then, he returned to the center of his garden. As he stood there, motionless, he lifted his palms to the sun. Quietly, he began a breathy and barely audible chant.

Turning his hands over so that the palms now faced the earth, Adelric moved his hand slowly over the ground, as if spreading butter over a large and unseen slice of bread.

Several yards in front of him, the gnarled folds of earth began to move, crawling at a slow pace, but moving nonetheless.

The dog had been dead for days.

Its body was bloated, and flies buzzed around it as if too excited to know where to land. There were several wounds about the dog's head and milky eyes, and one of its rear legs bent outward at an unnatural angle. The dog had either been trampled to death by a horse or some sort of wagon. That, or else it had somehow broken its leg and starved to death by the side of the road.

It was interesting to speculate about the dog's recent history, but none of that mattered very much. Right now, the dog's body was a delicacy. Aromatic and ripened by the sun, it looked good enough to eat.

The ghoul extended the gnarled index finger of his right hand and pressed the talon-like tip against the distended belly of the dead animal.

With a quick thrust, the ghoul pierced the outer skin of the dog's corpse as if with a dagger. The surrounding air suddenly filled with even more raunchy stench than before.

The ghoul pulled his mottled gray finger away from the corpse and as he did, black liquid as thick as molasses oozed out from the hole. The liquid covered the ghoul's finger like thick, dark syrup. He looked at his finger for a moment, then licked it clean as if it had just been pulled out of a steaming plum pie.

"Mmm!" he said as he continued to lap at the finger.

The ghoul had been right to travel westward. He had smelled death and decay on the air, carried eastward by the winds, and he had followed the scent. Somewhere in the direction of the setting sun was a large number of dead—fresh and not-so-fresh. Their smell was unmistakable, as distinct now to the ghoul as fruit turnovers baking in an oven had been to him when he was alive.

If he could only find the source of the smell; the source of the death and corruption. If he could find the dead, he could feast on their bodies for days or weeks, gorging himself on the countless rotten and festering corpses, stuffing his face to his dead heart's content.

It was what the ghoul existed for: to feast on the flesh of the dead... unless that of the living was available. The ghoul sniffed at the air. Even with the stink of the dog filling his nostrils, he could still smell the pungently sweet perfume of death wafting through the air.

It was so strong that its source would have to be countless scores of bodies. Dozens—perhaps even hundreds—rotting away and sending a strong signal to the ghoul that they were just lying there, waiting to be found. However, the strength of the other smells had mixed over the course of the scent's journey from its source to the ghoul's present location. It also suggested that the source was still several days' march to the west.

The ghoul would make the trek to this land of the dead.

But first, he would eat.

And so, with slow and deliberate movements that suggested he was going to enjoy himself immensely, he reached forward, pierced the dead dog's body with all seven and a half of his fingers—the other two and a half fingers having been lost sometime around when he'd died, he really couldn't quite remember—and tore the dog's body open.

Maggots and rotting gore spilled onto the ground. The ghoul inhaled the new stench as if he were smelling a savory rack of spice-rubbed boar roasting over an open spit.

"Mmm," he said again, before burying his face—dirty yellow teeth leading the way—into the exposed belly of the canine corpse.

The garden was coming along nicely.

With the use of some simple earth magic, Adelric had been able to not only flatten the soil and remove the blemishes brought on by the war, but he'd also been able to move and shape the land a little more to his liking. And to some genuine purpose, too.

As a result, the garden had become something more than he had originally intended.

At the end of the gravel stone pathway leading away from the house, he tilled the soil to make space for a ring-shaped flower bed that would eventually encircle a patch of emerald-green grass. In the center of the grass, he planned to erect a monument to remember Evan, and to all those brave souls who had died defending the vagha from their enemies. This way, Adelric could pay his respects to his brother daily, keeping Evan's memory fresh in his mind for the rest of his life.

If other vagha wanted to share in the peace and serenity of the garden, or pay tribute to Evan, and the others who had fallen in battle, so be it. With a strong sense of purpose to his task, Adelric used what little earth magic he knew more freely to work the soil as if it were some sort of malleable and fluid-like thing between his fingers.

Such power to shape and create was a heady, almost

euphoric experience for Adelric, who was so used to utilizing his limited knowledge of magic for the purposes of war rather than harmonizing with nature. This harmony is what the gods had intended when they gave magic to all residents of Esfah.

As he moved his hands from side to side, great mounds of earth overturned and flowed as if being pushed aside by a giant farmer's plow.

Adelric moved the earth towards the back of the garden, where it piled in great, house-sized mounds. Finally, when the earth was set in place, he shaped it into a rough semicircle, which could serve as both an amphitheater for official ceremonies and other celebrations, or as a secure backstop for practice and competitions between crossbowmen and marksmen. It could also be used as instruction for visiting experts from other villages and cities.

Slightly fatigued, Adelric stopped a moment and surveyed the worked land. It had come together nicely. He knew that some of the more conservative vagha would think him a cheat for using earth magic so frivolously—moving the earth by hand was the more noble and honorable way to shape it—but he didn't much care. He was changing the landscape in order to help beautify it. What difference did it make how the goal was achieved? Besides, there would be plenty of opportunity for back-breaking labor when he planted trees and flowers and put the finishing touches on his garden.

He just wanted to get to that point as quickly possible.

After a short break, he drew a dirty, golden hand across his sweat-dampened forehead and continued on, moving stones towards the semicircular mound of earth and piling them flat on top of each other to make elevated flower boxes that would later be filled with all manner of florals and bushes.

On and on he worked, for hours without break, until at last he had completed the roughed-in shape of his garden. Although there was still much to do, in his mind's eye, Adelric could already see the completed garden in full bloom…

It was magnificent.

He stopped a moment and inhaled deeply. He could almost smell the life force of the flowers and trees and plants, aching to sprout up from the ground. He heard the buzz of future bees as they bounced about in search of tender petals and pollen.

*Soon,* thought Adelric. *Soon.*

But before that could happen, there would be many hours of arduous work. He took one last look at the garden under the fading light of day. As he did, a warm breeze blew up from the south, skimming a layer of dust off the top of the soil. Adelric watched the dust swirl and curl in eddies, then vanish as winds carried it away.

And suddenly, he realized that if his garden was to bloom and flourish, it would need a constant supply of water. Of course, he could carry buckets full of water from the spring in the center of Dehnlee, but he would hardly be able to carry enough to make the entire garden thrive.

What he needed was a stream or creek to run through the garden, carrying water to wherever it was needed.

He let out a little laugh. Easier said than done. He could move the earth effortlessly enough, but not so regarding water.

For that, he would need the water magic of a selumari—coral elves attuned to the elements of air and water. Many selumari could even breathe while immersed; Aguarehl, the fourth-born god, had granted many families such a blessing.

Anything was conceivably possible with the gods, but Adelric had his doubts. After nodding pensively and realizing that he might be unable to complete the work in the garden, Adelric turned away from it and headed towards home to consider the problem further.

Specifically, he needed to figure out a way to bring water to his garden without the aid of water magic.

Adelric knew he could find a way, but so far, the mental energies required to summon magic had him worn out. He needed to take some time to ponder it.

The selumari sailing ship eased into the vaghan docks with little fanfare.

Adelric's housekeeper, Hildegard, stood alone on the docks to receive it, her arms crossed expectantly. When the ship lashed to the dock and the gangplank lowered, a single coral elf stepped gently onto the dock. The blue-skinned elf appeared to be young, although such an appearance was deceiving thanks to the coral elves' incredibly long life span. The selumari was actually older than Hildegard, despite the fact that he looked young enough to be her grandson.

"You arrived sooner than I expected. Thank you," she said, greeting him with a handshake that she maintained while the coral elf kissed her on both cheeks.

"I came as soon as I got your message," said the elf. Then, after a pause, "How is he?"

"He's irritable and curt with everyone. He doesn't eat much, and he hasn't performed any of his official duties in days. It's understandable that he's still grieving the loss of his brother, but it's been over a tenday now and he isn't getting any better. In fact, he's getting worse…more and more depressed with each passing day.

"Losing a loved one is always difficult."

"But life does go on."

"Yes, of course."

Hildegard sighed. "Do you think you can help him?"

"I'll do my best," the selumari said with a slight smile.

Hildegard looked at the elf's grin and found it infectious. In mere seconds, her matter-of-fact attitude had softened, and her demeanor slowly became less serious. "That's all I ask," she said, returning the selumari's smile.

Without another word, they turned away from the ship and started walking towards the interior of Dehnlee.

## CHAPTER THREE

The dog he'd feasted upon days ago had sated his hunger, but the feeling of fullness inside the ghoul's belly hadn't lasted for very long. The excruciating pangs had returned almost as quickly as the meal had sent them away; ever since reawakening as an undead creature, he'd been plagued by a nigh insatiable hunger. And now, the ghoul was once again ravenous for the rotting flesh of corpses.

As he stood in the middle of a slight dip in a vast rolling plain, the scent of dead flesh hung heavily on the air. It smelled thicker and sweeter than ever. The surrounding soil appeared scarred and battered, as if a war had recently been fought. Obviously, many had died in this place, leaving behind an intoxicating mix of smells, and making the ghoul practically mad with hunger. The famished condition pulled him ever forward and would continue to do so until the source of the sweet, sweet scent was found.

He remembered being called upon as a child to escort a delivery of baked bread for a royal reception taking place in the neighboring town. As he rode alongside the baker's cart, headed to town on the morning of the royal event and laden with fresh bread, his sense of smell was tantalized by a wondrous bouquet of fragrances: broiling chicken and beef; frying eggs; simmering stews; uncorked wines; poured ales; fresh-cut flowers; powdered ladies, and freshly shaved men. The smells had been so pleasant that he'd stopped at the edge of town for a few moments so that he might breathe them all in.

Now, as a ghoul, he did the same, but with the smell of

the dead.

The ghoul sniffed at the air.

There had been plenty of morehl here. The volcanic ash of their homeland imbued their fiery red skin and gave a distinctive burnt smell to the cadavers. There were also many dwarves buried here. He thought their scent akin to freshly tilled soil.

The ghoul took another few sniffs at the air and nodded.

There might have also been a few coral elves in the mix, judging by the faint smell of water on the air, but it was different from the taint of swamp that would have indicated trogs. There were bogs not so far away, though the Boland Marsh had shrunk so much in the last several years as the morehl forces of Garnock betrayed their allies and pushed them from the region.

So many smells.

So much dead flesh to eat.

It was all so close, so very close. But where was it?

The ghoul closed his eyes and inhaled deeply.

*There!* That way.

He opened its eyes and knew instinctively that the dead he sought were somewhere over the next hill…

Just waiting to be found.

Standish worked slowly and methodically, the movements of his strong hands made with surety and without hesitation. He worked the land as meticulously as an ant might—laboring long hours and moving single grains of sand over and over until it miraculously appeared as if progress had been made.

This had always been the old dwarf's way. Even years ago, during his time as one of Dehnlee's finest warriors in the generation before Adelric's. In battle, as a sergeant in charge of a company of footmen, he had never been impatient and had never looked for an easy way to victory. As a result, he had been recognized as a hero of many battles and been decorated by his fellow soldiers on more than one occasion.

And now, long retired from duty, he busied himself as a custodian in exactly the same way. He worked the ground as best he could, tending to the bodies of the dead and making their final resting place as respectable as he was able, without concerning himself with how much was accomplished on any single day. Eventually—lo-and-behold!—everything would be completed, and the dead would be laid to a peaceful rest. And nature would be radiant in all her splendor.

In many ways, it felt the same as winning a war—one battle at a time.

Presently, the sun sank toward the City of Dehnlee and past Delmara Bay on the western horizon. Standish raked the ground between two fresh burial mounds, clearing away small rocks and clumps of earth to make sure that everything appeared neat and tidy.

Burying the dead was a gruesome job, especially for an ex-soldier like Standish, but it was an important job all the same. And while others his age thought it somewhat demeaning work for a former hero of various wars, Standish never thought of it that way. In his mind, there was no more important job than making sure his comrades in arms rested in peace.

After all, it was the least he could do for the soldiers who had given everything they had, namely their lives, during battle. Besides, if Standish had been unlucky enough to die on the battlefield, he would have hoped that his remains be treated with the same measure of respect that he bestowed upon his fallen comrades.

The official name for the graveyard was Wakefield Memorial Gardens, but Standish had never been one for pomp and ceremony. He certainly did not like fancy titles. Named within the last tenday, this stretch of land covered only a tiny corner of Wakefield Plain, barely a league north of the last and most recent battle against Garnock's invaders. It had once been the site of a terrible battle in which many vagha, selumari, and humans lost their lives. Its dead were interred here, hence the graveyard. It was as simple as that to Standish. Maybe after a few years of peace, once the graveyard had grown over with flowers and trees, he could think of it as a "Memorial Garden." But until then, it would be a graveyard, or if the sun was shining and he was in a particularly good mood, perhaps then he might upgrade his thinking to "cemetery."

He raked the earth between another two fresh plots, making the grounds presentable after the bulk of the work had been done with earth magic. Standish softly hummed a few lines from the famous epic, "The Soldier's Journey."

> *The Bright and Shining Land*
> *devours and transforms the soul*
> *and replaces the husk*
> *with a thing of beauty,*
> *a rare and wondrous being of love.*
> *The Bright and Shining Land*
> *is love,*
> *and it calls the soldier home.*

Even though "The Bright and Shining Land" of the poem referred to selumari lands, reciting the lines helped Standish pass the time, easing the sense of loss he felt in the aftermath of war. Some of the grave sites he tended belonged to old friends and relatives; two of the dead were his nephews—sons of his wife's brother.

The thought of the two young lads, cut down so recently and in the prime of their lives, deeply saddened Standish Dead at the hands of the vile morehl.

Anger suddenly boiled up within him at the thought of the red-skinned demons. To think he'd had to bury some of their dead—left behind while the cowardly lava elves retreated back to their home within the Red Rock Mountains.

That had been a true chore, but a necessary one. He'd buried the morehl wherever they were found, leaving them scattered across Wakefield Plain like the wind-blown refuse that they were: corpses in random, unmarked graves. They had no place in the Dehnlee graveyard.

Standish paused a moment to let his anger pass. Such feelings helped in the heat of battle, but were useless for tasks that required shovels instead of axes.

He patted the soil around the edges of a fresh mound and let out a sigh.

*Done.*

He got up to inspect the day's work, using the handle of his spade to help him climb to his feet. As his body straightened out, the time-stiffened joints of his legs and arms cracked and popped like kiln-dried wood. Then, once he was upright, he kept a firm hold on the spade while he assessed the day's work. He wiped dirt off his hands, passed a few fingers through his shoulder length white-streaked hair, and took a good look around. He'd managed to clean up the ground around several plots. It didn't sound like much for a full day's work, but Standish didn't care. He was an old dwarf and at his age, things took time. Tomorrow, he would tidy another few plots, and then another few, and another, until he finally finished. Then, the cemetery would be worthy of the great soldiers who were buried there; a place where all vagha could pay their respects.

All it took was time and patience.

And Standish had plenty of both.

As he collected his tools and prepared for the walk back to his home in Dehnlee, Standish reflected once more on the unfortunate location of the graveyard. He hadn't been the dwarf to make such a decision. It was important to return Dehnlee's newly fallen to the earth as quickly as possible to prevent the winds from blowing the odor of bloated corpses into town.

Still, something about the layout of the graveyard didn't sit well with Standish. The plot had long been a burial area and many morehl and other enemies had been buried in the area's northern section after the last war-torn skirmish.

The custodian twisted his lips. It wasn't right that vagha and morehl shared the same burial soil—even if they were still separated by some distance.

He'd also heard the remains of the trog village still stood in the marsh. And even though the village was abandoned and in ruin, Tarvanehl only knew what had finally uprooted the goblin infestation that Dehnlee had tried for a century to eradicate. Standish believed what he'd heard about the trogs' willingness to feast upon carrion. He didn't like the thought of goblins sneaking into the graveyard to exhume Dehnlee's fallen for their dinner tables.

If Standish had his way, the ruins would have been leveled, and all fallen morehl and trogs would have been buried under rivers of molten lava, carrying the disgusting creatures screaming and burning into the fiery depths of the Abyss itself. He took a moment to envision it, then laughed at the image of the heinous little enemies being washed away by rivers of flame. *Oh well,* he thought, *at least the morehl would be reclaimed by the earth soon enough.* Soon, they'd be little more than a faint remembrance, while the memory of the vagha will have grown larger and stronger with each passing year.

Hopefully the same would be true for the vagha and morehl who survived the war. For the stronger the vagha grew, and the weaker the morehl became, the less chance there was of war continuing between the two races.

And that would be a good thing for all.

A very good thing.

Finally, Standish collected the rest of his tools and prepared them for storage in the locker he kept on the grounds. He hummed merrily as he worked.

*The Bright and Shining Land*
*demands a courage,*
*a heart and soul,*
*from those who would live there*
*and eat its glittered fruits.*
*Few are they*
*who can love so greatly*
*they can endure the Bright and Shining Land.*

The ghoul crested the hill and surveyed the rolling, rocky land that stretched out before him.

The ground here had been recently disturbed.

Not so much disturbed by war, although there was plenty of evidence of that in much of the outlying areas, but rather by spades and shovels and picks. He could tell by the fresh mounds of earth scattered about, one next to the other.

It was an incredible sight.

The mounds went on and on, as far as he could see.

And that could only mean…

He had stumbled upon a feast unlike any he'd ever had before.

With a newfound sense of urgency, the ghoul hurried

down the slope toward the edge of the plain. There, he nearly collapsed from the joyously intoxicating stench that invaded his nose. He inhaled deeply—so deeply that his ribcage pressed hard against the mottled gray and blackened skin of his chest, opening several long cracks along the dead skin's dust-dry surface.

Without another moment's hesitation, the ghoul dove forward and clawed at the earth, slowly at first, and then with more speed and urgency, until he looked like a dog trying to unearth a bone.

And then his hands struck something.

Another hand.

The ghoul grabbed a firm hold of the hand at the wrist and pulled. It hardly moved, so he braced himself and pulled harder.

The hand finally moved as the arm it was attached to suddenly broke free. The ghoul looked at the limb for a moment with both surprise and delight. But then, his instincts took over and he feasted, looking for all of Esfah like a dwarf munching contentedly on a drumstick of roasted foul.

Standish had gathered together all his tools, glancing once more at his locker.

He looked up at the orange sky of twilight. It was clear and cloudless, meaning there would be little chance of rain. He decided to leave the tools between two plots where he'd work tomorrow.

Standish picked up the small-headed spade to use as a walking stick on the way home. It could also serve as a weapon if needed, but considering the war was over, the chances of that were slim. Still, it provided some comfort to an old warrior to be armed, however tenuously.

As he turned for Dehnlee, a cold wind blew in from the east. Standish stopped in his tracks. There was something strange about that wind. While it was somewhat cold for this time of year, that wasn't what bothered him. It was something else, something…

Standish sniffed at the air and the hairs on the back of his neck stood up on end. There was something foul on the air, carried over to him by the wind.

It smelled like Death.

Not like the deathly smell of the deceased who he'd been burying, but another kind.

Death personified…

*Living* dead.

For one of the few times in his life, Standish felt fear.

He turned for Dehnlee once more and began walking as quickly as his aged legs would carry him.

After sampling the arm and tossing aside the bones, the ghoul uncovered the rest of the body and began munching on the rest of its delicacies at his leisure. When he was finished feasting, it was well after dark and the almost-full glow of Rhaudian, the moon, brightly hung in the black night sky.

The ghoul lay back against a nearby mound of dirt and considered his options. He could rest here for the night and feast again in the morning. Then, he could repeat the process night after night, day after day, until the entire supply of corpses had been completed. Tempting, very tempting.

Perhaps he could bring a few of his fellow undead here,

too. Ghouls and ghasts—maybe a carrion crawler—for a days-long feast. It would provide companions, but to what purpose?

There were so many dead. Some great battle had been fought with the fallen recently buried. The ghoul took another look around, able to see as clearly in the dark as in the light of day. He counted the mounds in one direction and stopped at ten. Then, he counted the mounds leading off into another direction, stopping at five. Using those numbers as a rough guide, he guessed that there were twenty-five bodies buried in just this small part of the plain. Maybe even more.

Twenty-five. That was a gang. How many more might be buried further west? Or in any of the other parts of the plain? There was an *army* here, if the dead could be revived, as he had been. What a formidable fighting force they might make.

Fully trained soldiers who were already dead.

A fighting force with nothing to lose.

The ghoul laughed out loud at the thought, quietly at first, then progressively louder. It was a dry, rasping sort of laugh, with a hint of madness to it.

"Oh, wouldn't she be pleased," said the ghoul, the words sounding like two pieces of sand cloth being rubbed together. "Wouldn't she be so very pleased?"

Standish arrived at the gates of Dehnlee just after sundown. The low stone homes of the city were alight from within with hearth fires, candlelight, and the smell of meals cooking in dozens of different kitchens. It was enough to warm his heart and make him wonder what he might be having for supper.

It was comforting to arrive in Dehnlee. He had no

explanation as to what had made him uneasy on the plain. That feeling persisted even though he was so close to home.

He continued into the city, his spade *clanking* against the gray pavers set in the road. He passed few people on his way, who seemed to be in a hurry.

*Perhaps others felt it too,* thought Standish.

As he arrived at his home, a low squat house near city hall—where the most self-important of locals worked—his wife Hortense stood out front, waiting for him impatiently. "It's about time you be getting home," she said in a guttural accent that had softened with age. "I was about to send out a search party to look for your old bones."

Standish sniffed at the air, then said, "Don't tell me you've been so busy waiting for me, that you've gone and burned my supper." He crinkled his bulbous nose in disdain. It was a little game they played with each other. She'd nag him for being late, although he returned home every night at precisely the same time for years, and he'd chide her about the quality of her cooking, even though he licked his plate clean at every meal.

"Never mind that," she said, crossing her arms and waiting for him to go inside. "You'll like it well enough or you won't be eating at all this night."

"All right, then," said Standish meekly.

Hortense gave him a little grin. But as Standish approached, her smile quickly disappeared and she asked, "Are you all right?"

Standish shrugged.

"What is it? Why, you look as if you've seen a ghost…"

*Or perhaps felt one's presence,* thought Standish. But he looked at his wife and did his best to smile. "Just a cold night is all, my love. I feel it in my bones. A nice hot meal and a warm seat by the fire will do me good."

"Well, get yourself inside, then," she said, all the

playfulness gone from her voice.

Standish placed his spade against the side of his house and stepped inside.

Hortense waited for him to go in, then rubbed her hands over her bare arms.

There was indeed a chill in the air.

She went inside and closed the door, locking it behind her.

The ghoul dug up three bodies before he'd found one that was suitable for his purposes. The first two were incomplete, missing one or more body parts. That would make the journey home more difficult than it had to be.

The soldier was a morehl soldier, or perhaps more correctly, a former morehl troop. Judging by the deep color of his skin, the soldier had been dead for a tenday or two. His black hair was still quite black, although it had lost much of the shine it likely had when he was alive. The corpse clutched a rapier in the curled fingers of his cold, stiff hand. His blade was pitted up and down the side, and the tip had been broken off, but other than that, it was still a formidable weapon.

The ghoul brushed off some of the remaining earth from the body and searched the surface of the red skin, looking for the fatal wound. At first, he could not find one and mused that perhaps the soldier had died of fright. But a second, closer look revealed a small puncture just under the left breast. The opening was barely as wide as a thumb tip, but looked to run deep into the vitals.

He assumed this morehl had been run through by an enemy spear or, more likely, a sword. Dwarves, for all their lack of height, didn't much use them. The favorite vaghan melee weapon was usually the ax, and that would easily explain the missing limbs of the first two bodies.

*So,* the ghoul mused, *a war had occurred between the morehl and the vagha... and other races were present in some measure as well?* Old memories from his previous life niggled at him. He recalled scraps of his time as human, emotions mostly, and he was certain that he'd been killed during the war. Possibly the earlier days of *this* war, given how long some of them raged.

But it hardly mattered to him. Though he did vaguely wonder which side had been victorious, undead soldiers were not loyal to the old masters of their former life. The only question on the ghoul's mind was which race would make a better undead soldier: a vagha or a morehl?

He'd find out soon enough. He had a perfect morehl specimen that needed to be revived.

After giving the body a final clean up, the ghoul lifted it onto his shoulders and carried it north and eastward toward the marsh that was there. He walked deep into the fen, almost until dawn arrived. When his feet began to sink into the moist soil underfoot, he dropped the body unceremoniously onto the wet ground, where it landed with a loud *splat.*

Taking a look around, he noticed several wooden structures scattered about the marsh. Shacks, sheds, and lean-tos listed to one side or the other and all in desperate need of repair.

A trog village, likely abandoned sometime during the war. If not this most recent war, then perhaps a previous one.

That was good. A trog settlement was a sign that the forces of Death and Corruption were strong in this place—especially if the goblins had a shaman. And if the ghoul was to be successful in his little experiment, he had to conduct it here in the swamp where what little death magic he knew would have the best chance of succeeding.

After setting the corpse on its side, partially submerged in marsh water, the ghoul began an elaborate series of chants and mumblings. Combined with dramatic arm movements, he tried to summon a spell to reanimate the corpse of the fallen soldier and elevate him to the status of undead.

Several times during the process, the ghoul had to stop. Did he remember the right words? *Were there any right words?* He repeated his attempts several times.

He growled something he thought he'd heard as a child. Words once forbidden and rumored in scary stories. "…and walk the earth among us, not as one of the living and guided by the powers of nature, but as one dead, commanded by the all-powerful forces of death and corruption…"

By the time the ghoul was done, the words were little more than whispers. His throat was as dry as desert sand and as raspy as a handful of iron filings. If he had been alive, there likely would have been pain in his throat. Much pain.

He looked down at the body lying in the marsh. Nothing.

It had not moved at all, and all of his efforts seemed to have gone for naught.

He pushed at the body with the toes of his left foot, gently at first, then slightly harder.

Still nothing.

He kicked at the body and rolled it onto its back.

More nothing.

Disgusted, the ghoul knelt down in the tall grass and shook the body with both of his hands. Flecks of the black goo which leaked from the ghoul's pustules burst and splattered onto the morehl cadaver.

Still, the dead soldier refused to move.

He tried one last time, slapping the face of the corpse in an attempt to wake it from its eternal slumber and bring it back from the void.

Nothing.

The ghoul straightened up, remaining on one knee as he looked out over the land. Perhaps he'd cast the spell incorrectly, or he'd selected an unsuitable specimen for reanimation. Maybe his limited powers of death magic were too weak—he seldom used it. He hadn't been highly skilled at spell craft during life, either. Whatever the reason, it looked as if this corpse would remain dead for all eternity.

A thought struck the ghoul. *If I can't revive the corpse, I might as well eat it.*

*Yes,* thought the ghoul with a slight, but decidedly ghoulish grin. *A fine solution if there ever was one.* And so, with an ever-growing smile on his cracked lips, the ghoul leaned over the corpse and prepared to take a bite out of its shoulder.

Just then, the corpse's eyes popped open, revealing a pair of milky white eyeballs set back in its deep dark sockets. Its lips pulled back in a snarl, revealing two rows of decayed-but still quite formidable—yellow teeth.

The ghoul jerked back in surprise, just in time to avoid a swing of the rapier as it arced in the direction of his head

"You're alive!" rasped the ghoul, then giving his head a slight shake, revised the statement, "You are undead!"

The blackened leakage had absorbed into the corpse, who stood now as a fully animated zombie. It tromped across the marshy ground and strode toward the ghoul. Its movements were stiff, but that was to be expected after someone had been dead for a while. There was also a peculiar look on the zombie's face, one that suggested it was intent on killing anything and everything in its path.

It wanted to kill.

*Perfect,* thought the ghoul. He'd had such things on his mind when the minion had first arisen.

But then, the zombie suddenly struck him with its rapier,

cutting a fresh gash into the ghoul's shoulder. The zombie wasn't so perfect anymore. It needed to be controlled...

But could it be? Could *he* control it?

It was worth a try at any rate.

"Put down your weapon," wheezed the ghoul.

In response, the zombie slowly lowered its arm, then dropped the rapier to the sod.

*Close enough,* thought the ghoul and ran over to pick up the rapier. He gave the zombie a closer inspection, looking into the blank eyes that would show no fear, no remorse, no evidence of conscious thought unless its master allowed it.

It was a perfect killing machine.

She would be pleased. Very pleased.

"Follow me," the ghoul ordered.

The zombie took one step forward, then another, and another.

The ghoul walked ahead quickly, then turned around to watch the zombie catch up to him. The zombie's movements were slow and awkward, but it made steady progress.

At this rate, it would take several days to get to their necessary destination, but when they arrived, she would be pleased.

Very, very pleased.

Perhaps even pleased enough to forgive him.

The ghoul continued walking eastward.

Dutifully, the zombie followed.

# CHAPTER FOUR

"Milord."

Adelric stopped his work, but did not turn around.

"Someone to see you, milord." The voice belonged to Hildegard, soft and kind, but with an underlying strength to it.

"Tell them to go away," Adelric snapped. "I'm not in the mood for guests."

This was true. Adelric was still affected by the loss of his brother, and the last thing he wanted was to entertain visitors.

"I can't do that, milord." Hildegard's voice remained even and sure.

"And why not?"

"Because this visit was arranged several months back ...as a kind of diplomatic visit."

At last, Adelric turned around. "Like I said, I'm in no mood to entertain guests, certainly not any senile old bureaucrats." He let out a sigh. "Who was the stone-skulled dwarf who arranged this visit?"

Hildegard was silent for several seconds, as if thinking. Then at last, she took a deep breath and said, "That stone-skulled dwarf would be you, milord."

Adelric thought about that. He might have arranged the meeting himself... so much had happened in the last month that it was possible for him to forget such a thing.

"Before the war with the morehl you asked me to arrange a visit for a selumari diplomat," said Hildegard, her voice unwavering. "You felt it was important to try and strengthen the ties with our neighbors across the bay. Well, now that diplomat is here."

Adelric felt embarrassed, but wasn't about to alter his plans for the day on account of some coral elf. "Can't you get Sergeant Cadman to show him around the city, take him to inspect the troops or something?"

Hildegard's brow suddenly knitted together, and her eyes narrowed. She took several steps toward Adelric and then spoke, "With all due respect, milord, you aren't the only vagha to have ever lost a loved one in battle. Dozens of families lost husbands, fathers, and sons in the war with the morehl and they are all getting on with their lives as best as they can. Admittedly, Evan was a great warrior and a good dwarf, but he's dead now and mourning for him at length will never bring him back. Remember that *you* are still among the living and as such, you have a responsibility to them as warlord. One of those responsibilities happens to be strengthening the ties with our neighbors."

Her strong, forceful voice trailed off, and when she spoke again it was with the gentler voice one would expect from a dwarf her age. "Shall I bring the diplomat around to see you?"

She asked the question in a way that suggested Adelric had no choice in the matter.

"Yes," said Adelric, feeling like he'd just had his rear end kicked by a frozen boot.

Hildegard was right, as usual.

He knew he'd been too withdrawn of late, avoiding people and his responsibilities as warlord. He had lost a loved one, but so had many others. He expected others to carry on, but had never demanded the same from himself. Perhaps it was time to get back into the regular routine of his life. He took a deep breath and said, "I'd be more than happy to welcome this selumari diplomat into my home."

Hildegard smiled and nodded approvingly. "Very well, then. I'll go and fetch him.

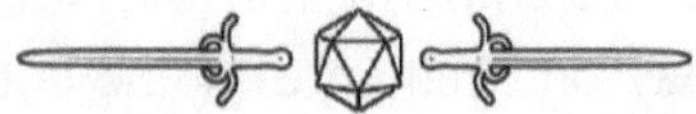

"Hullo!"

Adelric had resumed his work on the garden, but now stopped and listened carefully to the voice calling out.

"Hullo, there!"

There was something odd and familiar about the voice. He'd heard it before, but perhaps without such a cheerful timbre to it.

"I say," said the voice, closer now. "Let's not charge down the hill and dispatch but a few of those disgusting morehl…"

*What was going on here?*

"…Let us walk down there and kill them all."

The words were followed by a raucous laugh.

Adelric pondered the familiar voice. *Could it be?* Adelric turned to look, then shouted in surprise, "Dorian!"

Adelric dropped his spade and ran to greet his old friend. They came together, first simply shaking hands, then in a strong, heartfelt embrace that lifted Dorian off the ground and which Adelric seemed uninterested in releasing.

At last Dorian spoke up. "Easy, my friend," he said, gasping for air. "Or you will end up squeezing the life from me!"

"Oh, I'm sorry," said Adelric, somewhat embarrassed. He put the selumari down and fussed at straightening his tunic and cape. "I'm so happy to see you, I … I suppose I got a little carried away there."

"No matter," said Dorian, taking a deep breath and

righting the decorative, golden helm atop his head. "Better to die in the arms of a friend than in the clutches of an enemy, I always say." He finished his words by giving Adelric a firm slap on the back, perhaps as payback for the loss of breath he'd suffered.

Adelric smiled.

He had fought alongside Dorian in several of the coastal wars against the trogs, when the strength of Boland Marsh had been at its peak. They had been long-time friends ever since. Adelric had known Dorian during times of battle. He'd been jovial then, but he was even more so now. Dorian exuded an airy lightheartedness that Adelric found refreshing, especially after such a long and hard-fought war.

"What brings you here?" asked Adelric. "I was told to expect a stuffy old diplomat."

"Well, we had one of our stuffiest all set to visit, but it turned out that he couldn't make the trip so I volunteered to come in his stead."

"I'm glad you came."

"So am I."

"Now," said Adelric. "Please tell me you're here for more than just a brief visit. Tell me that you'll stay for a tenday as my personal guest."

"Well, I had planned on overstaying my welcome, but you seem to be trying to make that difficult for me," said Dorian. He paused a moment, as if considering the offer. "Oh, all right, then. I'll stay as your guest for as long as I can stand you. How does that sound?"

Adelric's smile grew wider. "Wonderful," he exclaimed. And then, as if speaking to no one in particular, he said, "You're just what I need right now."

"Indeed," muttered Dorian under his breath. He watched Hildegard out of the corner of his eye. She smiled and nodded her head, deeply satisfied that things were progressing as she had intended. She waved good-bye to Dorian and turned to leave. Dorian returned the wave, then turned his deep blue eyes onto the garden currently under construction. "I see you're trying to keep busy," he said, heading toward the garden with his blue cape rolling and cresting behind him like the whitecaps of Delmara Bay.

Adelric hurried to catch up to the coral elf, but found it hard to match the selumari's longer strides. "Yes," he said. "When I returned from the war, I found the land in shambles. We used very few earth spells in the fight, but the land here seemed to be particularly sensitive to the disturbances of the surrounding terrain. I've been working for half a tenday trying to get it righted—"

"And you've done well, Warlord Adelric," said Dorian, stiffly. It had been years since they'd seen each other last and both had acquired higher titles and ranks since. Neither quite knew how to address the other. Adelric nodded. "As well as I could. But please, just call me Adelric. I prefer not to be addressed as a warlord during peacetime."

"Very well, *Adelric,*" Dorian said with a nod, placing extra emphasis on the name. He paused a moment, then pointed into the distance. "What's that mound of earth there in the back?"

Adelric was pleased that Dorian showed interest in his work. "That will eventually be a backstop for an archery range," he said with a fair amount of pride in his voice.

"And this?" Dorian asked, pointing to a flower bed.

Adelric told him what he planned for the spot, then took the coral elf on an extended tour of the garden. He explained his plans for the rest of it and about erecting a monument to the memory of his brother.

Dorian was a perfect guest, nodding thoughtfully throughout the tour and asking questions whenever there was a lull in the conversation. Adelric couldn't be sure if Dorian was truly interested in the garden or merely being a polite diplomat, but he didn't really care. He was simply grateful the elf was there with him.

"So you see," Adelric concluded the tour. "I've shifted the land and prepared it for planting. Perhaps in another season it will flourish, but I'm still a little concerned that all my work might go for naught."

"Really?" said Dorian. "Why is that?

"Well, no matter what I plant here, the land will remain dry until I can get irrigation installed. And I don't think I'll be able to bring in enough water to keep everything alive and thriving without a major diversion from a stream ... We're uphill from the Delmara, so getting the water here might be difficult."

"Water?" said the coral elf, his pointed ears rising slightly at the word. "Believe me, water is not a problem, my friend."

"Do you think you could help?" asked Adelric hopefully.

"It would be my pleasure," said Dorian, with a wave of his hand that suggested it would be no trouble at all. "Besides, it is the least I can do in exchange for your most gracious hospitality."

Adelric nodded deeply in thanks, remembering the coral elf's skills. The warlord was merely passable at magic. Dorian, however, had actual training and become quite good at it.

"Now then!" Dorian said, removing his cape and laying it gently over Adelric's outstretched arm. "In which direction would you like the water to flow?"

Through the rest of the day, the two worked together, vagha and selumari, landscaping a garden that was worthy of both races.

Dorian was a master of water magic. He used it to create a number of freshwater springs which could later be used to feed a series of fountains. Adelric used what earth craft he had to pile rocks around the edges of the newly formed springs, divert running water through stone culverts, and feed the eventual banks of flora.

They worked in tandem—complimenting and enhancing the land and each other's magics. Finally, it became a kind of friendly competition to see who could perform the more impressive magical feat.

Adelric was severely outclassed. No matter how well he thought he performed a task, Dorian was an actual spell caster not limited to minor orisons.

Adelric didn't mind. He knew that Dorian was a class apart when they'd begun, and the results were spectacular. Had a rivalry of brute strength come up, however, Adelric would easily win the day. He was a warlord; Dorian was an enchanter, the coral elf equivalent to vaghan wizards who cast spells attuned to earth and fire, the gods Eldurim and Firiel.

The dwarf remained content to stand back and watch Dorian work his magic. Dorian moved his arms in a series of graceful arcs and flourishes designed to move the water from where it was to where he wanted it to go; it played out like a kind of dance, as if a child whirling streamers on a Turambar's Day celebration.

Finally, Adelric ceased altogether and merely watched the expert work. He clapped his hands with enthusiasm.

"Thank you," Dorian said with a bow. Together they stood and took a long, appreciative look at the work they'd accomplished. The improvements to the landscape were significant and readily apparent; a creek even babbled all the way through the garden on its way out to the sea. With Dorian's help, the garden had been transformed into a true work of art.

Dorian slapped Adelric on the shoulder and declared, "We've done well! If I do say so myself."

"It is beautiful, isn't it?" said Adelric, breathing deeply with satisfaction over a job well done. "It will do justice to the memory of my brother."

Dorian nodded. "Indeed, to all brothers of the first races."

They stood there in silence for several moments. The trogs and morehl were among the first races; only the dragons, elder monsters, and eldarim had come before, and the eldarim were a considerable mystery. Though many from the first races were content to interbreed with human-like species or follow their shamanic ways.

A voice broke his reverie. "Warlord Adelric!"

Adelric sighed. "I knew it. I've allowed one visitor in and now the flood-gates have opened." He turned around and saw Carswell Adar approaching from the north side of the house. Carswell was a few years older than Adelric, but still spry for his age. He managed to look even younger by dressing in fashionable robes of violet and blue, as well as boots edged with golden trim. But the dwarf's attention to finery didn't end with his clothing. His long, red hair flowed as if blown by an unseen wind, and his equally lengthy beard looked as if it had been brushed at least a hundred times that morning. He was even brash enough to go by two names—Carswell Adar—even though most vagha only used one outside of formal occasions.

Carswell was the master mapmaker of Dehnlee. His skills were constantly in demand on a world as malleable and as ever-changing as Esfah—and Carswell knew it. All of which didn't exactly endear him to Adelric. Of all the people in Dehnlee, Carswell was the only one required by Adelric to address him as Warlord Adelric at all times. Adelric waited for the mapmaker to join them, then made the introductions. "Dorian, this is Carswell." Adelric refused to use the mapmaker's second name. "He is Dehnlee's cartographer." He turned to indicate his friend. "Carswell, this is Dorian, a selumari enchanter."

"Pleased to meet you," said Carswell Adar, struggling to offer a hand in greeting while keeping the maps under his arm from tumbling out of his grip.

"The pleasure is all mine," said Dorian politely. "The skill of the mapmaker is one I've always admired."

Carswell smiled at that, obviously taking a shine to Dorian. "It is a fascinating profession, requiring…"

"What brings you here, Carswell?" Adelric cut off the mapmaker mid-sentence.

Carswell was a chatterbox who could talk forever if he thought he had a sympathetic ear.

"Oh," said Carswell. "Yes. I've just finished the new maps of Dehnlee and the surrounding lands. I wanted to show them to you and uh…perhaps get your approval."

Adelric looked at the mapmaker cynically. Sometimes he wondered if the dwarf was a businessman first and a mapmaker second. Carswell Adar wanted Adelric's approval so that he could sell the maps to the citizens of Dehnlee. The only maps the citizens trusted were the ones used by the warlord in times of battle. Hence, if Adelric approved a certain map, that map became the "official" map of the area by default.

It was a profitable business for Carswell Adar since the landscape around Dehnlee—indeed, all across Esfah—often changed due to cataclysmic activity. In a good year, Carswell Adar made three or four new maps and sold dozens of copies of each. However, no matter how good his maps were, no one would buy a single one until Adelric put his mark to it.

It irked Adelric somewhat that Carswell Adar had become wealthy selling maps while he—the one who effectively wielded the real power in regards to these same maps—lived a modest life. It occurred to him long ago that he could charge Carswell Adar a fee for his approval, but knew it wouldn't be right for a Warlord to profit from any aspect of mapmaking since it was in his power to change the landscape any way he pleased during times of war.

In the end, and with really no other choice, Adelric tolerated Carswell Adar, taking what little pleasure he could by sometimes making life difficult for the foppish dwarf.

"Of course," said Adelric. "Let's step into my new garden and have a look at these maps of yours, shall we?"

"Garden?" asked Carswell. Adar. His bushy red eyebrows arched in surprise. "I'm sorry, but it sounded like you said *garden.*"

"This way," said Adelric, ignoring Carswell Adar's words.

"Did you say *garden?*" repeated Carswell Adar, chasing after him.

Dorian looked over Carswell Adar curiously, then glanced at Adelric. Adelric acknowledged Dorian's glance with a subtle wink to let him know that he was just having some fun with the garrulous mapmaker.

"Yes, a garden," Adelric finally said in response. "Dorian and I have been working on it for a while now."

Carswell looked more closely at Dorian and his face began to pale. "You're a coral elf," the dwarf stated the obvious.

"The last time I checked, yes," said Dorian. "And a spell caster, too."

"And your magic is attuned to the element of—" he paused. "Is that water I hear?"

Adelric tried, but was unable to keep a smile from breaking across his face.

"Why, yes it is," he said. "What a keen ear you have, Carswell Adar. But of course, you are a mapmaker, so identifying specific geographic formations should be second-nature to you..."

As they continued toward the garden, the sound of water cascading over rocks became more distinct. It was a pleasant sound, very peaceful, but it clearly agitated the mapmaker.

Carswell Adar ran ahead as quickly as his stubby legs and cumbersome robes allowed. He stopped at the edge of the stream and fell to his knees. "No," he muttered, shaking his head slowly from side to side. *"No..."*

"Is something wrong?" asked Adelric innocently.

"When did you put this river here?"

"Fresh this morning," said Adelric. "But 1 can't take all the credit for it. I couldn't have done it at all without the help of my good friend Dorian here."

"You are too kind, Adelric," said Dorian, playing along.

"You put this river here...*today?"* repeated Carswell Adar.

"Just before you arrived, in fact," said Dorian. "But please, you flatter me by calling it a river. It is hardly a stream, and barely that."

Carswell Adar rose from the ground, allowing the rolls of maps to fall from their place under his arm. "River, stream, what difference does it make?"

"Well, a river is much wider than a stream," Adelric said, in a dead-panned voice.

"And a river carries far more water than a stream does. It flows faster, too," said Dorian. "Surely as a master mapmaker you would know that."

Carswell Adar turned. "I've just spent three days making all new maps of Dehnlee and now you've gone and put a river through it! The least you could have done was tell me."

"Three days doesn't seem like much time," offered Dorian.

"Especially since you're able to sell the maps you make

during those three days for a long while afterward," Adelric added grumpily.

"You did this on purpose, didn't you?" said Carswell Adar and poked a stubby finger against Adelric's chest. Adelric remained stolid, watching Carswell Adar's face turn from paler shades to darker hues that verged on red.

"Oh, yes. We absolutely did it on purpose," he said flatly. "You don't put a river through a garden by accident now, do you?"

Carswell Adar pressed his lips together hard enough to make them all but disappear. He took several breaths to calm himself, then opened his mouth as if to speak. Then, he hesitated.

"Yes?" said Adelric, drawing the word out as if daring Carswell Adar to speak his mind. "Something you'd like to say?"

Carswell Adar sighed deeply, as if in defeat, then quietly bent down to pick up his maps. "I'll be back in three days' time, with a new set of maps.

"I will be here," said Adelric.

*"We'll* be here," corrected Dorian, who intended to stay at least a tenday.

"Right. We'll be here."

Carswell Adar stormed off, muttering below his breath.

Adelric and Dorian watched the cartographer walk away. When they were sure he was out of earshot, they both burst into laughter.

The ghoul had been on the move for several days and nights and it seemed like he was getting nowhere. While he was anxious to get back to the castle, the zombie traveling with him had no such concerns. The ghoul marched along at a brisk pace, but had to stop and wait every few minutes to allow the zombie to catch up. Even worse were the times in which the ghoul ignored the zombie for too long. When that happened, the creature would clumsily trip over a rock, bump into a tree or simply make a wrong turn that sent it in the complete wrong direction. Then, the ghoul would have to double back and redirect the zombie, losing valuable time in the interim.

After the third such episode, the ghoul devised a solution to the problem.

Finding some vines at the edge of a field, the ghoul fashioned a hangman's noose from them and slipped it over the zombie's head. With the lasso in place, every time the zombie took a wrong turn, the ghoul felt a tug on the vine. Then, all he had to do was jerk hard on it and the zombie would stumble forward and correct its course.

It had worked well up until now; the vine was beginning to cut into the rotting flesh of the zombie's neck. If the ghoul continued to pull on it as he had been doing, he was liable to sever the minion's head from the rest of its body.

And that would render the zombie useless.

Although it went against his character, the ghoul tried to be gentler with the zombie—coaxing it along rather than yanking it. At least until they reached the castle.

"Come on," the ghoul said in a dry whisper. "Just a little further." He gave a slight tug on the vine and turned to look behind him. The vine had cut further into the zombie's neck, causing its head to loll limply to one side.

The ghoul let out a sigh, a little angry with himself for so severely damaging his prize.

"Stop!" he commanded the zombie. It stopped walking and stood erect, its arms hanging limply from its shoulders and its white eyes open and staring blankly into the distance.

The ghoul approached it and gathered up the vine in his hands. After straightening the zombie's head, he wrapped the vine around the creature's partially severed neck hold its head firmly in place. When he was done wrapping the vine around its neck, he tied it off and stepped back to admire his handiwork.

"Good as new!" he rasped.

The zombie's head still fell slightly to the right, but now, it was at least supported by the makeshift brace wound about its neck. The slight tilt of its head gave the zombie a sort of inquisitive look, as if it were wondering what it had ever done to deserve such indignation.

"Follow me," said the ghoul.

The zombie took a hesitant step. Followed by another, then another.

"We're almost there," said the ghoul, taking a few hurried strides, and then turning to watch the trailing zombie approach.

"And won't she be *pleased!*"

After an excellent supper of roasted coneys and fresh corn Hildegard had prepared—and washed down by mugs of dark mountain wine—Adelric and Dorian sat contentedly in the garden. They listened to the water stream past and watched the sun slowly set behind the western horizon.

"You should come and visit Galatea sometime," said Dorian. "I know the selumari would be honored to entertain a warlord like yourself as their guest."

"I've often thought about it," said Adelric. "I've heard that Galatea is quite a beautiful place. But I've always been so…busy."

"Oh, it is very beautiful," said Dorian. He closed his eyes and tilted his head back, guessing that folks like Adelric, who seldom traveled, must have found their own homes beautiful enough not to investigate others.

"There are gilt-edged mother of pearl towers at each corner of the city and all around are buildings decorated with inlaid coral and bits of shells taken from the depths of the seas..." His voice trailed off wistfully.

"It sounds wonderful. Different, but wonderful."

"There are those," continued Dorian, "who say that the Bright and Shining Lands the poet referred to in 'The Soldier's Journey' was in fact a reference to Galatea."

"Really," said Adelric, impressed. "I've sometimes wondered about that. Perhaps I should visit, then. Someday."

Dorian straightened up in his chair and opened his eyes. "The door of my home will always be open to you, friend."

"I will keep that in mind."

Their small-talk came to an end, with each content to sit and enjoy the splendor of their surroundings and the beauty of the sunset.

Dorian suddenly sat bolt upright in his chair. "Look at that!" he said sharply, pointing to something moving through the new grass.

"What is it?" asked Adelric, looking about as if he'd just misplaced a boot.

"I believe it's a babbit ... There!" Dorian pointed to a spot about fifteen paces away. There was indeed some movement in the grass. A ball of white fur with two short, sharply pointed ears and four short, stubby legs waddled about, probably in search of a new home.

"By Firiel!" said Adelric, with a smile. "It is indeed a babbit."

"I didn't know they were found within cities."

"Neither did I," said Adelric.

Babbits were primarily burrowing animals found mostly on the open plains, where the ground was soft and they dug comfortable homes beneath the earth. They were a little small for eating, but since their numbers on the plains were quite plentiful, they sometimes became a staple for armies on the march.

"I bet you've seen enough of them on the plains."

"Indeed, and they were quite tasty, too," said Adelric.

"I don't know what it is, but there's something about fresh babbit cooking over an open fire that puts the fight into a soldier."

"That's the effect of a full belly," Adelric laughed. "Soldiers tend not to fight well on empty stomachs."

Dorian didn't argue the point.

"Perhaps. I know I've never seen selumari troops fight so fiercely as when they've had their fill of roast babbit."

Silence burgeoned between them once again.

While Adelric would have loved to reminisce with Dorian, any talk about war only reminded him of the loss of his brother. It would obviously take time to heal the wound, regardless of all the healing magic on Esfah.

At last, Dorian broke the silence. "I'm just glad your war with the morehl is ended."

Adelric turned and regarded him.

"I know it was a necessary war," Dorian continued, "And I know that the morehl had to be beaten back. Tarvanehl only knows what might have happened to us selumari if those disgusting lava elves had been victorious. Dehnlee is the last bastion before Galatea."

The dwarf shrugged. "Garnock had no navy…and most morehl are too afraid to leave the shores far behind on what trading ships they possess. They'd never get past Delmara Bay."

"Perhaps, but if the fall of Daur-Bor-Nin during the

Dawn of War taught us anything, it is of the treachery and resourcefulness of the morehl. I was glad for dwarves as neighbors. I still am." Dorian let out a sigh. "But my impression is that your victory over them was a hollow one."

Adelric nodded, wondering if the current low in vagha morale was really so obvious to an outsider. "The cost of waging war is always higher than the end it achieves," he said. "We had peace before the war. We have peace after the war. In between, many dwarves and elves lost their lives. That is a great price to pay for something we all had before it began."

Dorian was silent, pondering the thought. Finally, he said, "Do you think the peace will last?"

"I'd like to think so," said Adelric. "But I know all too well that it never does."

Dorian said nothing in reply.

## CHAPTER FIVE

As the sun peeked over the eastern edge of Esfah and chased the shadows from the landscape, the ghoul trudged toward a distant point of northern darkness. A jagged and elongated black spot on the horizon rose up from the ground like a row of broken teeth.

The ghoul walked behind his prize and poked it in the small of its back to move it forward. But that area had soon become full of holes and so he switched to the shoulders and upper back as sticking points. Those parts held up fairly well and were likely to get the zombie where it was going in one piece.

As they neared their destination, the point of darkness became more distinct.

It was a castle—or at least it had been at one time—appearing like a silhouette against the fog-shrouded light of morning illuminated from the east.

The ghoul desperately wanted to call the castle home. Perhaps this time, with the zombie as a gift, she might let him back inside.

Then again, she might just laugh in his face, chase him away, or blast him to pieces with one of her spells.

It was hard to tell which it might be, and that's what made her so dangerous. He'd only ever known her to be this way: switching between manic modes. And the ghoul had only ever wanted to be in her presence—it had been that way in life, as well.

It was a long story…

The castle was fabled to have been built by vagha long, long ago, before the Dawn of War. That was over a half millennium ago.

Over the years it had been a home to almost all the races of Esfah and had similarly been conquered by as many. As a result, it was severely damaged—and subsequently repaired—over the course of its lifetime, especially during the battles fought for its possession. The castle's final death blow had come when it was taken by a band of firewalkers who traveled west after the fall of Sshkkryyahr the Dread on the opposite end of the continent more than a century ago.

The firewalkers had arrived from Empyreanoral on the East Coast to rescue their neighbors from the first major rising of the dead. After declaring themselves an enemy of Death, and all Malgrimm's chosen, a band of adventurers went west and claimed the castle from trogs who had let its condition fall into major disrepair.

A relatively small band, they'd made themselves comfortable and lived in the ruins of the castle for many years. The fire within their bodies scorched the castle's stone walls and left them thoroughly blackened and charred. In the end, it became a hideous structure that seemed to perfectly suit the desolate landscape surrounding it.

Some of those firewalkers remained even now, as thralls of the woman who had conquered it: an undead queen named Renata. She'd been a human and a magic-user before Death's power claimed her, and she had lost her final skirmish with a band of marauding trogs. But Malgrimm resurrected her, transformed her into a heucuva: a fiend of black magic. A spirit of the damned trapped within a sepulcher of rot who used illusory magic to appear as beautiful as ever…or even more so.

As a heucuva, Renata made herself queen of the dead before finding the castle ruins. She'd proven herself capable of raising corpses to her cause through some mysterious, magical means which the ghoul did not understand. She'd repaid the empyreans for their actions during the fall of the Obsidian Grotto so long ago in one glorious night, killing the firewalkers as they slept and raising many to her cause.

The filthy black stones of the castle seemed to suggest that the castle itself was dead, its life sparks extinguished long ago by the ravages of war. The castle had died a thousand violent deaths and had then been purged of any vestige of life by the cleansing power of Renata's black flame when she claimed it a half decade ago. It was the perfect place for a heucuva to practice her death magic. Its very appearance scared away any who ventured close enough to observe its new inhabitants.

Renata had slowly amassed an army to fill her home, occasionally leaving the walls in search of warm bodies which she could convert to fill her desires. She often disguised herself as a woman in distress, a ruse that honorable warriors fell for every time.

And when she had enough strength, she revisited her wrath upon the trogs of Boland Marsh, nearly eradicating their kind in one glorious night. The ghoul had been there to witness it. That was where he'd found Renata, whom he had loved since before he'd been reanimated in whatever shallow grave had birthed him. He lived with her in the castle for several months, watching her revive more and more undead until she was able to live in luxury with their countless numbers—servants to do her bidding. He found himself more than deeply in love with the dead spell caster, but also jealous of her power.

Renata knew as much and saw only envy. Never his adoration. Her magic was far more potent than he had imagined it to be and would never attempt an uprising against such raw power. Still, in a fit of rage, she banished the ghoul. Banished him instead of obliterating his body, or torturing him, or chaining him to a wall for all eternity. She'd simply cast him out for the rest of his days. Such was a punishment worse than any other for poor Peregrine.

The ghoul realized how devastating her sentence had been, a calculated move by the mad queen of the damned. And so, he wandered the face of Esfah, searching for something that would convince her to allow him back into the castle—and her presence.

And now, at last, he had the gift.

And she would welcome him back inside.

With open and deadly arms.

Despite Peregrine's slow pace, by mid-morning, the ghoul was close enough to see the individual stones and blocks that made up the ruins of the castle. Such detail was difficult to see at the best of times. The castle had a range of two basic colors, black and dark black, and unless you were mere paces away, the entire structure looked like a single, continuous piece of onyx.

As the ghoul and the zombie approached, several skeletal creatures walked the perimeter of the ruins. Renata often forced the same undead to wander the grounds, moaning in agony for months until total collapse. Peregrine once saw one of them try to break the heucuva's control and run screaming toward the moat. Of course, the moat had dried up ages ago and as a result, the skeleton threw itself into the deep ditch where it smashed apart. It reassembled itself with inky, black tendrils that reassembled joints, and clawed its way back out before starting the whole process over again.

Why Peregrine's zombie seemed devoid of will, but

Renata's horde contained some mental faculties and autonomy remained a mystery. The ghoul assumed it was tied to magic under the creator's command or the crafter's method of reviving.

As the ghoul and the zombie approached the entrance gate, a dead trog cackled about the end of Esfah. One half of the trog's head had caved in, but the creature looked to be strangely at peace, as if suffering from madness.

The ghoul turned away from the goblin, pushed the zombie in the direction of the castle's entrance, then used the hilt of the zombie's rapier to knock on the charred wooden gate. As the two waited for a reply, a skeleton rattled past and threw itself over the edge and into the moat. When it hit bottom, there was a loud crack as its bones smashed apart. Still, it managed to right itself and begin crawling up the steep dirt wall.

Peregrine wondered if this was the same one from his memory. If so, it had been trying to destroy itself for months to no avail. Renata would never allow her slaves to willingly leave. Autonomy or not, some things she had put limits upon…Though she did not seem able to control Peregrine.

Just then, a small door opened at eye level.

"Yes?" hissed the voice from the other side of the murder hole.

"I'd like to see Renata," said the ghoul.

"And who are you?"

"A ghoul," he said. "A ghoul who has traveled many tendays for the privilege of an audience with his queen."

"What is your name, ghoul?"

The ghoul let out a dusty sigh. This was the point where the door usually ended up being slammed in his face; he had made three previous attempts. "My name…is Peregrine."

A slight rasping sound came from the other side of the door as the gate-keeper laughed at the mention of his name. "You don't give up, do you?"

Peregrine ignored the question. "I must see her."

"You've been banished," said the gatekeeper. "I've been instructed by Renata to never admit you to the castle."

"But that was two years ago."

He paused on the interior of the door. For those minions with lesser vestiges of mind left to them, the passage of time meant nothing. "It makes no difference to me."

The gatekeeper was suited to such a single-minded task. To him, a command given a century ago by his creator remained as fresh as if given a minute ago. That was why the zombie he'd brought with him would make such a good soldier. It would only have to be instructed to kill once and it would continue to perform that task until it was no longer able—a maintenance-free killing machine.

If only he could show her.

"I've come such a long way," said Peregrine.

"I have my instructions," the gatekeeper said without pity. "You cannot enter." The sliding view hole began to close.

"Wait! Wait!" said Peregrine. He understood the gatekeeper could not be convinced under any circumstances unless Renata desired it. Peregrine offered to sate a desire. "I've brought a gift for her."

The tiny door slowed on its track, hesitated a moment, then opened again. The gatekeeper poked its head through the opening and looked at Peregrine with two milky-yellow eyes. "What sort of gift?"

Peregrine realized that he'd found his way in. The ghoul brought his zombie front and center, and brushed some of the dust and dirt from its head and shoulders. "A zombie," he said. "A new soldier for the queen. One of many I could give to her … If Renata might only let me in."

The gatekeeper stared a moment and said, "Just a minute." His face disappeared behind the closed and locked door.

Peregrine stood patiently before the gate, confident that

this time he would be allowed inside and given an audience. While he waited, the skeleton ran headlong into the moat, again. It landed upon a large rock embedded in the moat floor and the skull shattered on impact, breaking at the base. The scattered bone fragments twitched in the dust for a few seconds, then finally came to rest as the dark tendrils relented and turned to a dark wisp of smoke and evaporated.

Watching the episode, Peregrine wondered if the skeleton had' hit the rock on purpose, finally discovering the way to end its miserable existence.

The door in the gate suddenly popped open. "You may enter," said the gatekeeper.

"Wonderful," said Peregrine, trying to run his fingers through his heavily matted gray-black hair. The portcullis beyond him rose. In addition to the gatekeeper, two guards waited for him. It occurred to Peregrine that they might try to snatch the zombie away from him and then let the gate fall, so he wrapped his arm around the zombie and held the rapier at his side—not exactly at the ready, but ready enough to strike if the need arose.

All the residents of the castle tried to please Renata. One might attempt something rash.

"This way," said the gatekeeper, which he realized had once been a *female* coral elf who, judging by the condition of her skin, had been dead a long, long time. Probably much longer than Peregrine; Renata may have reanimated her from the castle's crypts, which she'd emptied on the first night when she took the location from the empyreans.

Peregrine and the zombie followed her into the castle with the two guards taking up the rear. Behind them, the gate fell with a re-sounding crash.

For a moment, Peregrine wondered if, now that he was inside, he would ever be allowed to leave of his own free will. It sounded crazy, but that was Renata's way. Unpredictability.

One of the things that made her so dangerous. Even before death, it was part of why the easily predictable Peregrine had loved her so.

"Wait here!" said the gatekeeper.

Peregrine nodded and watched the selumari disappear down a hallway. Then, he moved the zombie over to a stone bench set against a wall. Together, they sat down and waited.

The end of the tenday with Dorian arrived, and Adelric decided to visit the plot where Evan was buried. He'd finally felt some semblance of peace approaching and the dwarf hoped this might solidify it.

"If you'd rather not go with me," he told Dorian, "I'll understand completely. I don't want to darken what has so far been a pleasant visit."

"Nonsense, Adelric," said Dorian. I am here to acknowledge Galatea's debt to those who have fallen in defense of our homelands, but I am also a friend. Either provides plenty of reason to go with you."

Adelric smiled at that. "I'm glad you feel that way, Dorian." He paused, then said, "We better be on our way."

The sun shone brightly, making their walk to the memorial a pleasant one. On the way, the two friends chatted about how magic, weaponry, battle tactics, and strategy had all changed over the years.

"They say trade has never been higher for this eldrymetallum stuff," Dorian said. "Rumor is that they found a lode of it on the slopes of Karakto and that the gnomes are fashioning all sorts of wonderful things from it down in southern Charnock."

"Bah," said Adelric. "I ain't never seen a gnome. I barely believe they exist—I think it more likely they're made up to sell some fancy forge's new blades. But no matter what new-fangled weapons these folks devise, nothing takes out an opponent quite effectively as a sharp blow to the head."

"Indeed," laughed Dorian.

By the time they reached the plain, they found several other vagha already there and paying respects to their family's fallen. As they approached the graveyard, its superintendent came out to greet them, an old dwarf named Standish.

"Warlord Adelric," Standish said, shaking Adelric's hand more vigorously than his graying hair suggested was possible. "This is both a surprise and an honor."

"How have you been, Standish?" asked Adelric. "Are you keeping well?"

Standish placed his hands against his lower back and grimaced slightly, giving Adelric an idea of what he could expect in fifty or more years.

"'A tenday ago I felt a chill, as if the very Death Bard of Dereh'Liandor were planning on dragging me away. But the feeling went away the next day and I've been feeling good ever since."

Adelric smiled and took a look around. "You've done a fine job here, Standish. You've reason to be proud."

"Thank you, milord. Thank you very much."

Dorian made a sound just then, as if he were having trouble clearing his throat.

"Oh, yes," said Adelric. "Where are my manners? Standish, this is Dorian. He is an enchanter from Galatea, and a very good friend of mine."

The two exchanged short bows.

"Pleased to meet you, mister Dorian."

"And I you," said Dorian with a nod.

"Uh, Standish," Adelric said, interrupting the

pleasantries. "I'm here, of course, to pay my respects, but also to visit the grave of my brother, Evan. Can you tell me which one is his?"

"I think so," answered Standish. "He's in the northwest corner. Two down from the top and three from the left."

"Good, good," said Adelric. "If you'll excuse me now, I'd like to spend a few moments alone with…" His voice trailed off as if he were suddenly embarrassed by what he was saying.

Standish put up a hand. "No need to explain," he said. "I understand completely. I know you and your brother were very close."

"Thank you," sighed Adelric, relieved. He turned to look at Dorian.

"Go ahead, Adelric," said Dorian. "I'll wait for you here."

Adelric nodded. "Thank you."

"You're welcome," said Dorian. "Take as much time as you need."

Adelric turned stiffly and left.

Renata's ancient gatekeeper returned sometime later. "Renata will see you now," she said, pointing down the hallway from which she'd come.

Peregrine and his zombie stood up and waited for the gatekeeper to lead the way. But she did not. Instead, she and the guards returned to their posts back at the entrance gate, leaving them to make their own way into the throne room.

They headed down the hallway the gatekeeper had indicated. Together, they turned the corner. Peregrine felt suddenly overwhelmed by the carnival-like atmosphere that permeated Renata's court.

Although the room was massive, it stood crowded with undead, who each kept busy with their own gruesome tasks. Every one of them hoped to catch the eye of the fickle queen and earn her approval, just as she'd urged them to when she reanimated each of them. The end result was only confusion and chaos.

Nearby, a one-armed dwarf stoked a fire which burned brightly, but did little to rid the castle of its constant chill. The dwarf fed the fire with wood, but also tossed in parts of undead bodies which had fallen or broken off due to decay or injury. Burning flesh gave the room a distinct odor that Peregrine knew pleased Renata.

Through a broken doorway leading out onto the balcony, two morehl attempted archery practice. The balcony was rather long, so it was possible for them to stand at one end of it and fire upon a target on the opposite side. Neither hit the target: an old, portly vagha with a distended belly they expected would burst if their aim proved true. But the dead were lousy shots. Reanimated bodies could rarely match the dexterity required to properly loose an arrow.

Peregrine walked deeper into the menagerie. An elderly human woman walked the floor with a broom and dustpan, collecting broken fragments of the walking dead for the one-armed dwarf at the fire.

And finally, closer to the throne, a long-dead minstrel plucked a dissonant harp with several missing strings, entertaining Renata with a song.

> *I am the wound and the knife!*
> *I am the blow and the cheek!*
> *I am the limbs and the wheel—*
> *The victim and the executioner!*

The song was no "Soldier's Journey" but Renata seemed to enjoy it. So much so that she hardly noticed when Peregrine and the zombie entered her court.

Peregrine waited until the undead minstrel finished serenading the heucuva, who sat upon her blackened chair radiating beauty, which even he knew was no more than skin deep. Peregrine didn't mind the wait, however. He was enthralled—happy just to look at Renata, the queen and commander of an army of the dead.

Renata wore a robe studded with fine gems and crystals; it belonged to the former owner of the derelict castle. When the heucuva had claimed it, she claimed all its possessions as well, hoarding it to herself as an elder dragon might collect treasure.

She was a beautiful woman, or more correctly, had *been* a beautiful woman. He remembered her from life, how she had been tall and muscular and her long dark hair had flowed down her back in braids like corded lashes. Now, even though she was dead, she retained her beauty through the dark magic of Malgrimm, the Death god.

Renata's skin had grayed somewhat, mottled and patchy in places, but still appeared smooth and unbroken. Her hair, long and flowing, had remained virtually unchanged, although she sometimes decorated her locks in iron-tipped braids and used them as whip-like instruments. And her eyes.

Best of all were her eyes. Even though the whites had yellowed, her pupils had remained the same emerald green as they had been during her lifetime.

They were the only thing of color in the entire castle, and they were stunning to behold.

They were also the thing that held control over her undead legion. One look into her vibrant green eyes and the undead were virtually bound to her will. The minstrel finished his song, and Renata clapped appreciatively. "That was nice," she said, her voice high-pitched and raspy. "But I've heard that song before. Next time I want to hear something new, understood?"

The minstrel looked around and grew more pale, if that were possible. He gave Renata an exaggerated nod. "I understand."

"Very well, then," said Renata, flicking her hand in his direction as if she were brushing away a piece of dirt.

The minstrel bowed deeply, then walked away, already strumming his instrument and trying out words for a new song.

With the minstrel gone, Renata's attention turned to Peregrine and the zombie. What had been a smile on the heucuva's face suddenly vanished, replaced by a sneer.

Peregrine tried not to notice her disdain. Instead, he stood tall and brought the zombie to the former amazon queen. Before he could say anything, Renata began to laugh. It was a mocking, hurting sort of laugh that caused even the undead to feel a sharp pain deep in his heart.

"What is this ... *thing?"* she asked.

The commotion that had been going on since Peregrine entered the throne room suddenly died. All the undead turned toward Peregrine, anxiously awaiting his answer to the vexed sorceress queen of the damned.

Peregrine looked at the zombie and had to admit the creature hadn't traveled well. His head lolled to the side and the constant prodding at his back had left him little upright support, causing him to sway like a tree in a windstorm. Perhaps if he had been a more powerful spell caster, Peregrine wondered, he might not have needed the help in steering the creature.

Still, he was on his feet and able to hold a rapier and that's all that was important right now.

"It's a gift," Peregrine said, standing taller after saying the words. "A gift of a zombie for you."

Renata laughed again, her mouth opening wide, revealing two rows of teeth that she'd somehow been able to keep shining white. They were a terrifying sight, especially in combination with those emerald green eyes. "This is what you thought could persuade me to allow you back into my midst? This..." She shook her head and let out a short laugh of disgust.

"I found this one in a graveyard several day's journey from here. The grave site is huge with dozens of bodies scattered about, most of them buried just below the surface. He was still quite fresh. A recent war ended...vagha and morehl, I believe."

The assembled denizens of the room suddenly grew excited over the prospect of an ample supply of food. A murmur rose among them.

"Silence!" commanded Renata.

The throne room fell quiet. She turned to Peregrine, once more shaking her head. "I already have plenty of zombies like that—and most are in better shape. What possible need would I have for such a decrepit creature as that?"

"I'd like to show you," said Peregrine. "If you would only allow me to demonstrate."

Renata appeared intrigued by the unexpected bit of entertainment. "Very well, then," she said. "Show me!"

"I'll need a volunteer."

A ghoul dressed in a tattered red tunic stepped forward, limping badly on a severely deformed leg. "All right," said Renata. "You have your volunteer. Now what is it you want to show me?"

Peregrine put the rapier in the zombie's hand, then went up on his tiptoes to whisper in its ear. "Kill."

Almost immediately the zombie moved, lunging forward and running the unsuspecting ghoul through with his rapier. It had been enough to end the ghoul's existence by severing its head, but the zombie did not stop there. In another series of quick movements—quick, at least, for the zombie—it cut the ghoul into six neat pieces, leaving the head, torso, and all four limbs piled in a heap on the floor. Then the zombie returned to a standing position, as if awaiting for its next command. As a precaution, Peregrine took the rapier from its hand. "Well done," he whispered, even though he knew the kind words would mean little to the zombie.

The silence in the room continued, until some of the undead began to laugh at the fallen ghoul, realizing he'd unwittingly volunteered to be slaughtered.

"Quiet!" Renata shouted, and her voice pierced the air like a dagger.

A moment later, silence returned.

She leaned forward on her throne, as if to move closer to Peregrine without getting up. "And there are more of these?"

"Dozens more, maybe even hundreds," Peregrine said, his gritty voice sounding more than a little excited at the prospect of being allowed back into the castle. "My guess is that there was a major battle fought in the area and many of the dead were buried wherever they fell."

"An entire army," she mused.

"Two of them, actually," reminded Peregrine. He shared many memories with the queen and knew that many occupants of the back castle were her former subjects who had served in the Gwich'in—subjects who, like Peregrine, were not trained as warriors—the humans who had never qualified for the amazon caste.

"Soldiers … just waiting to be resurrected." Renata got up from her throne and moved slowly toward Peregrine. "Waiting to fight another day."

As she approached Peregrine, his cold, dead heart felt a flutter of apprehension. Excitement that bordered on arousal. But fear of Renata's fickle, violent shifts in mood soon took control of his deadened heart.

She stopped in front of the zombie and looked it over. "Give it the rapier," she said.

Peregrine had an idea what she had in mind—she wanted to test the zombie by having it attack her—and wanted no part in helping harm her. "No…"

"I said, give it back its rapier!"

Peregrine still didn't want to do it, but he knew she might strike him down if he refused her a second time. Reluctantly, he placed the rapier in the zombie's hand.

"Good," she said. "Now, tell it to kill."

Peregrine hesitated momentarily. After a second, he nodded, rose to his toes, and whispered, "Kill," into the zombie's ear.

As before, it lunged at its target. Renata was quicker than the previous ghoul had been—and also aware that an attack was coming. She was able to move out of the way in time. The zombie swung its rapier, but once again, the heucuva avoided its blow.

The zombie continued hacking and slashing, and after a while, instead of moving out of the way, Renata stood still, defending herself with her magic.

Each time the zombie swung its rapier, she put up an arm and deflected the blow before it made contact with her. She measured the strength of the minion's fighting ability. Judging by the smile on her face, she was pleased.

Still under Peregrine's compulsion, the zombie tried a quick combination, swinging left to right, then quickly moving the blade before it completed its arc. The sudden change in movement caught Renata off-guard. While she deflected the blade in time, the rapier sliced through the little finger of her left hand, cleaving it cleanly off at the third knuckle.

The throne room fell silent as everyone watched Renata's finger soar through the air.

Peregrine instructed the zombie to stop, and the rapier came to rest at the creature's side.

Renata looked at her left hand curiously. She clenched

and unclenched her hand, making a fist and measuring the effect the lost digit might have on its operation.

Peregrine trembled in fear.

In the meantime, the elderly woman with the dustpan scuttled into the center of the throne room and swept up the errant finger, then turned for the hearth.

Finally, Renata looked at Peregrine and the zombie. A black fire burned beneath her emerald eyes.

Peregrine feared the worst.

"Excellent!" Renata wailed. "Absolutely fantastic!"

Peregrine let out a dusty sigh.

"And you say there are more of these...soldiers who were trained in life and might be suited to an army. How many more?"

"More than I could count."

"Wonderful," she said, and wrapped her arms around herself in a kind of content hug. "Take me there immediately." She put him down and looked up at the dim light shining through one of the many holes in the ruined walls. "Imagine an army of the dead marching across the face of Esfah. Destroying everything in its path, adding to its ranks with every battle, and growing stronger with every fight." She placed a hand to her cheeks, as if to steady herself against the headiness of the moment. "Undead...and unstoppable."

As he watched Renata consider the possibilities, all Peregrine could think about was the fact that she'd hugged him, and that maybe, just maybe, she'd forgiven him.

"I've been waiting for an opportunity like this since my death," she said.

The undead in the throne room fixed her with rapt interest.

"Now I have it," Renata said, her raspy voice little more than a whisper. She touched her hands together and separated them; thin and sticky trails of black, like foul honey, strung together like a gooey web between them.

Peregrine regarded the stuff curiously, knowing he had seen it before. *Was it before my death, when I was a mortal?* He remembered the odd hut above the Trent River, but little more.

Renata's words broke his reverie; there was *no before*, only an eternal future alongside his undead queen.

"It will only be a matter of time until all of Esfah is mine."

## CHAPTER SIX

Both Adelric and Dorian woke up with the morning sun.

"What's on the agenda for today?" asked Dorian as they ate the breakfast Hildegard had prepared.

"Well, there's always more work to be done in the garden," said Adelric cheerfully as he pecked at oatmeal, fruit, and cheese.

Dorian looked disappointed. "We've done enough work on the garden already, I think. Besides, you have to give it a chance to grow and let nature take its course. After all, nature's balance is delicate enough already, you don't need to go trampling it into the ground by fussing over it like an old maid." And Dorian crossed his arms.

Adelric laughed. "Relax. All I said is there's always work to be done on the garden. If it's not done today, it can easily wait until tomorrow."

Dorian nodded in silence.

"What I actually had in mind was a visit to Carlin Park. It's where our soldiers train for battle and new recruits are educated."

"Are they training now?" asked Dorian.

"Of course," said Adelric, trying a spoon of his oatmeal and finding it too dry for his liking.

Dorian passed him a pitcher of milk. "But your war with the morehl is over."

"For now, at least, yes, the war is over. But there's always need for a well-prepared army."

Adelric poured the milk, but the pitcher proved top heavy. "Oops!" He spilled too much into his bowl.

Dorian smiled.

"That's the trouble with oatmeal," he said. "Too little milk and it's too dry, too much and you've got a mess."

Adelric nodded, feeling very much like a schoolboy being lectured by his mother.

"So your entire army is constantly training for battle?" Dorian asked.

"No, not all of it," said Adelric, leaving the oatmeal to sit and slicing a piece of cheese from the large wheel on the table. "But there are always new recruits who need to be trained. Young vagha are eager to learn the art of war, but we do keep a core team of soldiers constantly at the ready, in addition to the city guard, our constabulary force. They can fight, of course, but their focus is far different from a military one."

Dorian nodded.

"Our army is filled out with a reserve corps: residents of Dehnlee—butchers, cobblers, wheelwrights, and blacksmiths. Everyone of age undergoes training a few days each month so that in the event of war, they can be called upon to defend the city as soldiers."

"An interesting way to organize."

"We've learned that citizens die the same as soldiers," said Adelric. "Might as well equip them to be useful if the regulars falter. We always keep a number of professional soldiers as a core that can be reinforced within days, or sometimes, mere hours after the outbreak of war. Citizen soldiers are what helped us resist Garnock."

"That's very different from the Galatean forces."

"Really? I would've thought our organization the logical system."

"I suppose it's logical," answered Dorian. "But we

Galateans have been somewhat spoiled by the location of our city. But with Diamantia to the west of us and strong ties with Xlinea to the south and you at Dehnlee across Delmara Bay to the east, we've never really had to prepare for large-scale war. Certainly we've aided our neighbors in battle, but we've been insulated enough that our military has never been a patriotic imperative."

"But what if your allied vagha or humans were overrun by the morehl or goblins? Surely there must be a plan for the defense of your city?"

"Oh, I'm sure there is, but I've never seen it. It's never been an issue…out of sight, out of mind, I guess."

Adelric's eyebrows arched in surprise. While the selumari lived on coastal lands and were quite powerful on or near the sea, to not keep an active strategy for defense of the city was pure folly. Dorian winked at him, and it suddenly struck Adelric that Dorian might be having fun with him. Of course there was a strategy for the defense of Galatea, and part of that strategy was keeping its details a secret—even to friendly neighbors.

"You selumari are a sly and cunning race, aren't you?"

"That we are."

"Then I am glad that we are allies."

"As am I," said Dorian. Then after a pause. "Galatea is quite well fortified and an invading army—of any race—would likely find it difficult even getting near the gates of the city."

"I was beginning to suspect as much."

"I'll gladly give you a tour of Galatea's defenses when you visit."

"I'll take you up on it," Adelric said. "But for now, since you are here in Dehnlee, how would you like to accompany me to Carlin Park?"

"I'd be delighted."

As Adelric finished the fruit and cheese on his plate, he

remembered his bowl of oatmeal. The oatmeal had dried out while they had talked. He pulled the bowl close and tried to push a spoon through it. The spoon barely made a dent on the surface.

Suddenly, Adelric wasn't all that hungry any more.

"Shall we go?" he asked Dorian.

"Lead the way."

Carlin Park looked very much like the military encampments Dorian had participated in during wartime.

Upon entering the gates, the two visitors came upon a large stone building that housed both soldiers, as well as various weapons and supplies. Further along were smaller stone structures designed to act as barracks. There were ten such buildings on either side of the camp. If more space was needed, temporary shelters were stored in the main buildings, which could be erected to host more trainees.

Further along were many clearings used as practice ranges for bowmen and other tactical drills.

And finally, at the far end of the camp was a long stone structure partially open at one end. Their stable housed the army's ponies and the giant lizards they bred for battle. There were spaces in the stable available for mammoths, but the vagha of Dehnlee were currently without any. Mammoths were expensive and a point of ride among dwarves. Unless Dehnlee could purchase some from another vagha army, they would have to find and capture a mated pair in the wild; the temperamental beasts typically proved too difficult to tame for use, but their eventual offspring would be suitable. Dehnlee was years away from using woolly beasts since their last one died early in the fight against the lava elves.

As Adelric and Dorian walked through the compound, they passed many soldiers. The bearded troops saluted as they passed.

"Morning, Warlord Adelric!"

"Morning," replied Adelric, returning each salute. "As you were."

They eventually stopped at a clearing to watch two young trainees practice hand-to-hand fighting. Both were squat and muscular dwarves who appeared evenly matched. Their axes sliced through the air with power and authority, but their blows crashed loudly into the heavy shields held tightly in their left hands. There was a kind of rhythm to their battle, a sort of *clunk-clunk, clunk-clunk* that echoed through the clearing.

After watching the two combatants for some time, Adelric interrupted them by pointing to the dwarf on the left and saying, "Give that one a rapier!

The two dwarves stopped fighting and nodded to Adelric. One of them put down his ax in favor of a morehl blade.

"In addition to being practiced in vagha fighting techniques," he explained to Dorian. "They are also taught how to use the weapons of their opponents. Not only does it give them an idea about their opponent's tactics, but it also enables them to pick up an opponent's weapon if theirs ever gets lost or damaged during a battle."

The two dwarves squared off again, this time more cautiously as the ax-wielder treated the pointed tip of the rapier with a respect that he hadn't shown the ax.

And then, they were once again fighting hand-to-hand, their blows banging out a different rhythm this time—*clunk-thud, thud-clunk.*

"Very impressive," said Dorian. "And all vagha are so trained?"

"Yes, all of them."

They watched the two dwarves battle for another few moments, then moved on. "Carry on!" barked Adelric, to ensure the combatants didn't stop their training in order to salute him.

"What's over there?" asked Dorian and pointed to a group of dwarves standing in a circle.

"Ah," mused Adelric. "Something you might appreciate."

Just then, someone called out, "Warlord Adelric! Warlord Adelric!" Adelric turned and spotted Sergeant Cadman hurrying over from the main building. He stopped and waited for the young dwarf to come near. "What is it, Sergeant?"

"I wasn't informed you'd be visiting today," Cadman said, the inflection in his voice suggesting he felt slighted by the oversight.

"Sergeant Cadman, allow me to introduce you to a friend of mine. This is Dorian, a selumari enchanter who is visiting with me for a few days. I am giving him a very informal tour of the camp. Nothing more."

"Pleased to meet you," said Dorian, shaking hands with Cadman. "The camp here is quite wonderful."

"Thank you," Cadman said to Dorian. The sergeant turned to face Adelric. "Informal or not, all visitors—especially warlords and selumari enchanters—must make their presence known to the Sergeant-in-Charge before entering the grounds."

Adelric knew Cadman was right, but he wasn't about to admit it. "Consider yourself notified, then," he said, staring down the young dwarf with a look of mild annoyance.

"Very well," said Cadman meekly. "And if you could, warlord, please let me know when you leave."

"I'll do that," said Adelric, saluting.

Cadman returned the salute, then turned and walked off.

"Charming young dwarf," said Dorian.

"He's a good soldier," said Adelric. "But a bit of a rules

stickler if you ask me." Adelric turned to Dorian. "Being a soldier in any vagha army requires tenacity, wisdom, and self-control. Cadman has the first and the last in spades. Unfortunately, wisdom is something he can only acquire over time."

Dorian peered at his friend as if he knew something brewed beneath the surface.

Adelric took a breath and considered why he'd neglected to follow protocol. "Perhaps I'm growing tired of being a soldier and living by so many rules."

Dorian nodded as if he understood. "We were heading that way," he said, pointing to the nearby circle of dwarves.

"Ah yes, right. Follow me."

A lightning bolt struck Renata's castle many years ago, and the flames destroyed fourteen of her minions. The former firewalkers—once elemental beings of fire and air transformed into wraiths and specters by the heucuva's power—had kept the flame stoked ever since, perhaps as an homage to the fading memories of their former life.

Their meager coals now fanned to flames as the dead empyreans worked hammer-lengths of iron into curved blades and quenched to harden. Skeletal drones worked them to a razor's sharpness on circular lava rocks spun by morehl artisans who knew best the ways of hot rock and steel.

Finally, with blades sharpened to deadly edges, they were attached to long poles made from the hardest woods of the nearby forest. The forge churned out simple scythes: implements of harvest with a keen edge to gather in sheaves of grain or flesh.

The denizens of Renata's castle did not require fancy swords or finely crafted flintlocks. They had no dexterity to wield bows. They were a brute force of replenishable bodies and did not need high craftsmanship. Only additional weapons, which were reproduced quickly and cheaply, and could kill as effectively as the next.

Many of Renata's soldiers already possessed weapons they brought with them when they left the grave, but at least as many possessed items in total disrepair as none at all. The new but crude scythes would outfit those soldiers.

An undead weapon crafter hefted a freshly completed scythe and motioned for the next minion in line. The zombie moved hesitantly, as if it feared the former firewalker and the deadly weapon it held at the ready. Nevertheless, the zombie moved front and center, stopping several paces away.

Without warning, the crafter brought the scythe to waist height and swung it in an arc from right to left as if he were working a wheat field's harvest. The scythe cut the zombie down at the thigh, severing both legs, hacking through bone and cleaving flesh. The creature fell to the floor and landed with a dull thud.

The wraith nodded approvingly at the effectiveness of the weapon, then checked the sharpened edge of the blade for any marks or defects. Satisfied it was well made, he turned and placed it against the wall, then headed back to the hearth to begin fashioning another.

The zombie groaned, collected its legs, and held them close to its body as it crawled back into the shadows, searching for tourniquets and stakes to fashion splints so the unstoppable soldier could reconstruct its destroyed legs.

Until its head was separated from shoulders, the thing was bound to its master. It would do whatever it took to fulfill Renata's commands.

Adelric and Dorian approached the cluster of assembled dwarves. They remained quiet so as not to disturb their activity, although that became increasingly difficult. Especially since a small knot of idle soldiers had begun following them around the camp, eager to see what the warlord and his guest had planned. Nevertheless, they did their best to remain inconspicuous as they watched the vaghan soldiers in training.

There were eight vagha gathered around in a circle, five males and three females. Seven of them were dressed in flowing blue-gray robes while the eighth, obviously the leader of the group, was adorned similarly, with his robes also trimmed in gold.

"These are our theurgists, the magic-users," said Adelric. "They gather together in small groups and practice their craft under the guidance of the thaumaturgist." He indicated the dwarf in the gold-trim.

Dorian nodded in understanding. "Now this," he said, "is the kind of training I'm more familiar with."

They moved to the outer edges of the circle and watched the dwarves conduct mystic exercises. In the center of the group sat a large, heavy stone twice the size of the nearest dwarf. As the training session continued, members of the circle took turns changing the shape of the stone, first by using a spell to transmute the rock into mud, then using their individual creative talents to sculpt the softened mud and clay into some recognizable shape. Then, they changed it back into a boulder.

The theurgists were quite good at their task and the stone constantly shifted shapes.

A sword…

A shield…

A tree…

An ax…

The flow of the shape-changing slowly shifted to produce likenesses of the potential enemies of the vagha.

A goblin…

A firewalker…

A lava elf…

At that, they stopped the exercise, leaving the form of their most recent enemy cast in the stone.

"Excellent!" cried Dorian, clapping his hands. "Absolutely magnificent!"

"Yes, quite excellent," echoed Adelric, pondering if a statue of his late brother could be made by such a process. He decided to call on these crafters later.

The theurgists, who up until now had been totally taken in by their exercise, turned to see Adelric and Dorian standing nearby. "Warlord Adelric," said the thaumaturgist, an elderly vagha named Ruskin. His bright red hair rose up from the top of his head like wildfire and his long matching beard flowed down over his chest to a point near his waist belt; both shifted into gray at the tips the further the manes grew from Ruskin's face. His eyebrows were bushy, but the brown eyes beneath them were both warm and friendly.

"We were not aware of your presence, but we're glad for it just the same."

"That's all right. I much prefer the anonymity," said Adelric, stepping forward. "Allow me to introduce you to my good friend, Dorian."

The magicians paused, awaiting further information.

"Dorian is a selumari enchanter."

"Dorian?" said Ruskin wistfully. "*The* Dorian?"

Dorian nodded.

"We've studied many of your known feats."

"You flatter me," said Dorian.

"And you honor us with your presence," replied Ruskin. He continued hurriedly, "Please, would you honor our circle by joining us?"

Dorian smiled from ear-to-ear. "It would be my pleasure." He moved forward and joined the circle as its ninth member. After a brief moment, the stone again shifted and changed its form, running through the same series of basic shapes, each one now somewhat more refined.

When it came time for Dorian's turn, the stone formed the shape of a morehl who held a flint-lock pistol in his right hand. The pistol was pointed skyward in a triumphant pose, and there was a decided sneer on the figure's face. Instead of continuing the exercise, Dorian cast a spell that set the stone shape atop a tiny disc of water.

Adelric wondered where the water had come from, since the terrain of Carlin Park was dry and rocky. He had to conclude that Dorian had conjured the water out of what moisture could be found in the cool morning air.

Quite impressive.

But Dorian wasn't done yet.

After a moment to steady the statue, Dorian turned slowly to the left. At the same time, he forced the water to drill a passageway up through the rock to the tip of the figure's upturned pistol.

At last, water began to squirt out of the morehl's pistol, making the usually deadly fiend the subject of much laughter.

"Your reputation does you no justice," said Ruskin.

"You're too kind," said Dorian diplomatically. "You see, the power to move water is nothing on its own. You and your earth magic gave my water magic some context."

The thaumaturgist flashed Dorian a smile, proud of the shape they'd made.

## CHAPTER SEVEN

The undead crept across the terrain like shadows across a graveyard. They followed Renata's pet for several days' walk from the castle, crossing many leagues. Walking tirelessly, they strode freely through the blackness of night and the heucuva summoned a chalky sort of haze to mask their presence during the day.

Peregrine showed them the way, riding in tandem with Renata on the back of one of her great skeletal steeds. The huge strides of the nightmare beast—a former draught horse—bounded over the plain. It ran past the lines of the undead, which made their way south and a little westward to help with the wholesale excavation of Renata's new army.

"There!" said Peregrine, pointing at the scattered mounds that spotted the ground. "I feel some of them there. The dead are strewn across this plain in shallow graves."

Renata pulled back on the reins, and her steed snorted a scream of terror as it came to a stop on the rocky ground. Within seconds, Renata slid off the animal and stood with her hands on her hips, scanning the landscape for bodies.

A look passed across the heucuva's face, the shadow of a memory. Something about the long-since abandoned battlefield hinted at memories from her prior life—flashbacks that she couldn't quite recall. They haunted the dead as much as the undead haunted the living.

Behind her, Peregrine struggled to free himself of the knobby backbones of the steed, getting first an arm, then a leg, caught between the protruding ribs of the animal's belly. Eventually he fell to the ground, hitting his head on the earth and tearing a flap of hair away from the side of his scalp.

He got up slowly. By the time he got to his feet, many of the slower undead had arrived on the scene. "This is much like the place where I unearthed the zombie," he said.

Renata turned in a slow circle, mouthing something silently as her mind pieced together the implications. *This was the edge of where a large war had been fought… and she'd had a part in it years prior.*

"There's another body buried there, see. And another one there, and there," Peregrine stated, pointing.

"Yes, I see," said Renata.

He pointed to the places where the unliving creatures were to begin their excavation. "Start here! You, there!"

Obeying, one of the zombies sunk a spade into the ground, pushing it hard with a kick of its foot. Another swung a pick deep into the soil. The implement made a loud crunching sound, sounding like the breaking and snapping of bone.

"Stop!" shouted Peregrine, diving to the ground and clearing the earth away with his bare hands. In minutes he'd uncovered the upper portion of a dead morehl. Its head had been cleanly severed from the rest of the body and made useless for their purposes.

Renata stepped forward and came to a stop by Peregrine's side. He inhaled deep, intoxicated by her smell.

"They're no good to me chopped up into little bits," Renata said, striking the zombie who'd done the damage. "Use your hands if you have to, but I want them all excavated intact!"

The rest of the zombies simultaneously dropped their tools and fell to their knees. Slowly, they clawed at the earth with their hands and carefully uncovered the awaiting dead.

"What should we do with this one?" asked Peregrine, holding the head of the lava elf by its thick mat of hair.

"Feed it to the ghouls," she said.

Peregrine tossed the head aside, and a pack of ravenous dead immediately set upon it. "Fat, my sweets!" cried Renata, letting out a laugh that cut like a dagger. It was a terrifying sound, even for the dead.

The excavation of bodies continued through the night.

After a dozen bodies had been reclaimed, Renata attempted to revive them one-by-one.

She had done this before. But she had no true method.

After taking several moments to prepare, she cast a spell over the body of a trog. She waved her hands back and forth over the body, mumbling a string of words under her breath.

And nothing happened.

She tried a different spell, changing the direction of her hands and the timbre of her voice.

Again, nothing happened.

Looking flustered, but still keen on making the operation work, she turned her attention to the body of a wolf which the trog had ridden to both their deaths. If she couldn't revive its rider, then at least the wolf could serve in her army.

She cast a series of spells, retrying what she'd tried previously. And still, the dead did not stir.

Peregrine watched Renata's spell-casting with great interest. At first, he was surprised that she also had trouble awaking the dead. After all, the powers of a heucuva were far superior to that of a lowly ghoul, and as far as he could tell, she cast each spell correctly. But as Renata's revival spells continued to fail, Peregrine grew more and more concerned—not for the dead, but for himself. For if she could not revive a single corpse, she would be furious with him...*He* was the one that led her onto this errand.

He tried to envision what the full force of Renata's anger might bring upon him, but knew that no matter how hideous a fate he imagined, it would pale in comparison to what she would actually do to him.

For the first time in Peregrine's unlife, the recurring nightmare he had about his personal obliteration at the hands of some obscure monster did not seem like such a bad way to go.

Renata was presently working on an unearthed morehl who had likely been fighting alongside the trog. While Peregrine couldn't say for sure what the creature's role had been in the army, he recognized it was probably little more than a simple foot soldier—an unremarkable fighter in part of a much larger horde. But despite casting several spells over the lowly specimen, Renata's death magic had the same effect it had on each of her previous attempts...

Which was none at all.

Peregrine grew terrified now; he physically shook in anticipation of the blow he was sure was coming. He knelt down and did his best to cower beneath the protective cover of his outstretched arms.

Renata approached him slowly, like a cat preparing to pounce heavily upon an unsuspecting mouse.

"Where did you revive your zombie?" she asked him, placing a finger under his chin and lifting it up so she could affix him with her mesmerizing eyes.

Peregrine was still terrified knowing full well that his undead life could be terminated at any moment. He trembled at Renata's touch, unable to answer the question. "I, uh ... I..."

"Look at me!" Renata said, driving the tip of her finger through the skin beneath his chin, hooking it sharply around his jawbone, and back over his lower teeth—much like a fish caught on a hook. She jerked his head upward until he had no choice but to do as she said. He opened his eyes and looked at her.

"Where?" she repeated.

"There's a m-marsh in that d-direction," he said. His words sounded slurred thanks to the intrusion of Renata's finger in the underside of his mouth.

"Why didn't you tell me that before?" she asked, removing her finger so he could answer her more clearly.

"Your magic is so much more powerful than mine. I didn't think it would matter."

She smiled at that, and Peregrine couldn't be sure if he had flattered or offended her. When she did nothing to him, he continued, "It's a large swamp. And there looks to be the remains of an entire trog village there, likely abandoned years ago. I brought the zombie there thinking the decay of the swamp might help me revive it."

"And did it?"

"You saw the zombie."

She looked at him suspiciously for several moments. "You know, Peregrine, it's not wise to withhold such vital information from me. You might think it makes you more valuable to me, but all it's done is wear down my patience and bring you closer to my wrath."

"I swear, Renata. I thought your powers would be enough to revive them. But if I was able to revive a zombie in the swamp imagine how strong your magic will be there."

She considered the point, and another smile broke over her face. It was obvious his words delighted her. She looked down at Peregrine, and her smile suddenly vanished. "Move the bodies to the marsh."

"As you wish."

"Use the steeds if you have to, but I want them all out of the ground and in the swamp by sunrise. If not, I will hold you personally responsible, Peregrine." She bared her teeth menacingly. "And believe me, I'll make you pay a price if you fail me."

Peregrine looked deeply into the heucuva's green eyes and almost felt his still heart pound out a beat. *At last,* he thought. *She's giving me responsibility, a position of power, a chance to prove myself.*

Renata turned away without another word and watched the exhumations closely. Hundreds had already come up from the soil, and they'd finally unearthed additional corpses: humans. A smile and a warm familiarity washed over the undead spell caster.

*She might make me pay a price if I fail,* thought Peregrine, *but if I make her proud, she'll reward me.* There was only one reward the ghoul truly wanted.

By the time the first sliver of yellow-white sun crested over the eastern horizon, all the bodies had been exhumed and transported. They were now laid out in neat rows at the edge of the marsh a league west, where the trickles of the Trent River, dammed up by some creature up river, fed into the marshes.

As the hours of darkness waned and Sol's burgeoning light threatened to cast light upon the ghoul's hellish operation, Peregrine revived a few of the dead at the edge of the marsh. They helped with the excavation of their brethren. The move had made a big difference in the night's work, quickening the process by almost half.

Now, as the morning's light began to cast shadows beneath the bodies of the dead, Renata toured the marsh, investigating Peregrine's handiwork like a general might inspect an honor guard.

He had lined up the dead according to species.

Here were three rows of morehl with thirty to a row, and there were two lines of trogs with just as many in each line. There were also a few dead beasts: two horses, as well as the wolf Renata had failed to revive earlier. In various states of decay, nearly twice as many humans as their enemies lay in tighter rows to accommodate their size. Further back stood a cluster of newly made zombies that Peregrine had reanimated in order to help with the dig. They stood obediently at attention, awaiting instructions from their master, Peregrine.

"Wonderful," said Renata, stepping back from the rows of corpses. "You've done an excellent job of amassing my army."

Those laid to rest with their weapons still kept them; Peregrine had assumed they'd have trained with whatever was found nearest them. Any others found without them would be armed with scythes.

The heucuva cast a suspicious eye towards Peregrine's corps of utility workers. Unlike the others who would soon be revived by Renata, these zombies would be forever loyal to Peregrine—the one who had brought them back from the dead. Together, they made up a small troop that could protect him from the undead woman who he both needed and feared. Loved and loathed.

"Look at them, dead yet ready to fight," she hissed.

"They're ready when you are," Peregrine said with a dramatic bow.

"So many to pick from," she said, excitement obvious in her raspy, gravel-throated voice.

"Whichever one you like. They are all yours to command."

"Yes, they are, aren't they," she said, moving forward. "This one first!"

She pointed to a trog in the center of the outermost row.

"Be my guest!" said Peregrine with a dramatic bow.

Renata cast the spell and waved her arms. She paused, as if remembering something. She removed a vial of black liquid from her breast pocket and drank from its contents. She seemed to radiate with a fell light and her eyes turned black like polished onyx.

She reached out her hand instinctively and a wispy black tendril shot from her finger like a vaporous water spell cast by a selumari enchanter. Almost immediately, the trog's eyes opened to reveal empty sockets where insects had devoured the eyes. The vacant orbs glowed red and another second later, it slowly rose from the ground.

Renata let out a sharp, maniacal laugh, then quickly moved down the row.

One by one, the dead awoke.

Any vehicle with wheels had long since decayed beyond use back at Renata's castle. Every wagon eventually used to feed the dead firewalkers' flame. However, the undead had fashioned a sled which her untiring minions loaded with crude scythes and pulled across the Wakefield Plain.

Because of muscle memory earned in life, the newly created soldiers required no training. All they needed was instruction. A single order to kill turned them into single-minded berserkers: killing machines intent on completing their task.

Renata barked orders as if she were an amazon queen rather than an undead mistress who lorded over a pile of ruins, assembling her small army. Peregrine beamed, but caught the eye of the heucuva. There was still little matter of Peregrine and his team of zombies.

Renata had watched him revive them, fully aware that they were loyal to him rather than to her, and Renata was ever the jealous type. She decided to allow it to speed up the exhumation process, but also because she felt that Peregrine deserved a small command in her army as a reward.

She watched him for a few moments as he tromped through the swamp. Peregrine excitedly poked at something with a stick in the marshy slop. He held the poker to his nose and sniffed whatever he'd found before giving it a lick.

Renata turned her attention back to the army. She was concerned that she might have made a mistake. She hadn't been able to control Peregrine—she hadn't created him—and Peregrine was more ambitious than the rest. He, and his minions, could refuse an order, unlike her other mindless drones. She knew there was nothing she could do about them now other than treat them as a part of her army; a part which just happened to be under Peregrine's command. That meant she would have to trust him.

Peregrine had come alongside her as she turned her thoughts inward.

"Is this all there is?" Renata asked, scanning the army that had swelled to several hundred. It was a boon, but she could not let him know that she found the dusty remains and decayed corpses satisfactory.

"No. There is so much more. I found my zombie further south of here, below the edge of the Boland Marsh. There is a fresh graveyard near the most recent battle site from this war. Many bodies…far more than we've revived here."

Renata licked her lips and touched a hand to her breast pocket, where the black liquid rested. She did not understand it, except that it amplified her powers immensely, and that she'd drank most of it. The liquid grew like a yeasty dough, replenishing itself, but that took time.

Peregrine grew suddenly brave and took Renata by the hand. He took her deeper into the slop, where he'd found a roiling mass of the ichor and stirred it with a stick. Something in it called out to them, much like the hunger deep inside each of the undead beckoned them to feast upon the flesh of all others.

Renata squealed and plunged her hands elbow deep into the goo. In heaving glops, she devoured the stuff like a bear set upon a honey pot. Once finished, she turned to Peregrine. "With this, we could create an army of darkness that covers the world. And to what purpose?"

Peregrine offered, "To feast. Take and eat. And to increase in strength always. Below the marsh lies the graveyard, but between it and the sea lies a dwarven city, filled with the meat of the living."

Renata inclined her head. She hissed, *"Yes.* We move again to claim the residents of the grave ... And then— we surround the vagha against the sea and we feast."

She barked a simple command with a guttural screech and focused her dark will. Moments later, the fiendish army turned and plunged through the marsh, heading ever southward.

## CHAPTER EIGHT

Standish whistled to himself as he walked. The warlord's selumari friend had taught the tune to him after visiting a couple days ago. The dwarf liked traditional vaghan songs, but he prided himself in his eclectic tastes and that he knew a few coral elf tunes.

By the time Standish reached the cemetery, the morning sun had grown considerably warm. He decided it best to work quickly before the heat became unbearable and forced him to quit early. Today, he planned to set tombstones, a physically strenuous job that would likely prove a challenge to his aged and tired frame.

After he picked up his tools from where he'd left them between the two plots, he placed a large water-resistant cloth on the ground, which he would later use to cover the tools. That done, he carried the tools to the first plot, set them down, and continued to the row of tombstones leaning up against one of the larger plain oaks.

There were four of them lined up against the tree—delivered yesterday by one of the stonecutters in Dehnlee. More of the stones would be delivered each day until the cemetery was completely outfitted. The tombstones were large and quite elaborately decorated, with battle axes, swords, and crossbows, depending on what sort of specialty the deceased had earned in the military.

In addition, all the tombstones stood adorned at their pinnacle with the symbol of the vaghan community—a multifaceted stone encircled by a ring of flame.

Standish was glad that the stonecutter could only produce four tombstones per day, as four was just about as many as he could erect in as much time. If they delivered any more than he could handle, people might begin wondering about his ability to do his job.

He paused a moment to read the inscription on the first tombstone, which had been written by the dead dwarf's family.

*Here lies Footman Burgess,*
*Who died on Wakefield Plain,*
*But he did not die alone,*
*On that fateful day,*
*Before he was struck down,*
*Fighting morehl and goblins grey*
*He took six of the fiends with him,*
*And held many more at bay.*

*Beautiful,* thought Standish, *and it's got a kind of lilt that fits the selumari tune I'd been whistling an hour ago.* Footman Burgess would be proud of the epitaph. He bent forward to lift the tombstone and noticed something peculiar. Standish stood upright and sniffed the air. It was the same sort of smell that he'd sensed many days earlier, yet it seemed stronger.

It smelled like Death.

Standish turned and walked about the graveyard, sniffing the air. It wasn't coming from anywhere close by, since he made sure all the casualties had been properly interred before they turned ripe. No, this smell came from further away—from somewhere across the plain.

Perhaps in the north, or to the east.

He took a moment to ponder that thought and wound up making an unsettling connection, turning his eyes in the direction of the Boland Marsh, which had been silent for far too long. He'd assumed the trogs had abandoned it to fight east with their morehl allies, but goblins were often known to have a pungent, sickening stench.

Still, this smell felt different. Standish swallowed. He did not like the dark place where his mind went.

He worked feverishly into the hot part of the day, constantly wrinkling his nose with disgust from the fetid wind blowing in off the northern marshland. Still, he hoped the nagging in his gut was nothing more than an active imagination, and he dared not dwell on it too deeply.

Maybe the sweltering heat had fermented the worst of the bog muck. Maybe a large creature died in the fens and *that* was the odor. Regardless, with the unbearable heat of the day looming, he'd be home early and hopefully the next day would be better.

Time had drawn near for Warlord Adelric and Dorian to part company. He had stayed long past his originally intended tenday, but Dorian had other diplomatic duties to attend to in his home country.

Several folks in Dehnlee absolutely refused to let Dorian leave without arranging a proper send off. That evening, as the sun began its descent over the waters of Delmara Bay, a crew of dwarves threw a banquet in Dorian's honor. It took place at the largest meeting room in the town hall. It was a relatively small gathering, with only a few dozen people in attendance. But all the most influential citizens of the city were there, including Warlord Adelric. Sergeant Cadman and several of the other leaders of the vagha army arrived along with Carswell Adar, who presented Dorian with a recently revised map of the city. Magdeline Borden, mayor of Dehnlee, gave Dorian a token gift and Hube Herbert, Dehnlee's master forger, gifted Dorian a specially made ax. It featured a detailed inscription on its shiny head to commemorate both Dorian's visit and the victory of the vaghan forces at the Battle of Wakefield Plain.

Dorian was quite taken aback by it all and admitted as much when he was asked to make a speech at the conclusion of the elaborate meal. His hosts even tried to cook selumari delicacies like spiced shellfish, squid, and boiled kelp weed over skate.

Although the seafood paled to that prepared by selumari cooks, Dorian was flattered by the valiant attempt and made sure to smile at those around him as he ate.

It was not surprising that, when he began his after-dinner speech, Dorian addressed the vagha cooks before all others. "Never have I had such wonderful cooking so far from my elven homeland." All of which was true. "My compliments to the chefs!"

Dorian looked around the room. "Friends," he paused to let the word sink in. "When I came to visit Warlord Adelric, I feared that I might have been intruding. After all, I had arrived shortly after a dark day."

Dorian flashed a knowing look at Hildegard, who sat two tables to his right. "I came at a time when so many of you had recently lost so much." A moment of silence stretched between them to honor Adelric's younger brother Evan. "And I was quite uncertain about what type of reception I would receive. After all," Dorian's voice suddenly became more jovial, "I'd heard that the warlord can be quite a curmudgeon on even the best of occasions."

Dorian turned to Adelric, smiling. He raised a glass of wine to his friend and the room resounded with the sound of good-natured laughter.

"But contrary to my fears, my friend did not chase me away. Instead, he welcomed me into his home with open arms and invited me to stay for as long as I wished." Another pause, this one to allow the vagha to feel good about their hospitality.

"So, for the past few tendays, I have lived under the same roof as the warlord and had the chance to meet so many of you. Some at length, and some in passing. I admit I had a most wonderful time—in fact, I regret that the time has come for me to leave your fine city."

"You will come again?" called out Magdeline Borden, who had expressed increasing diplomatic and trade relationships between the two races when they'd met four days ago.

Dorian nodded. "For over the course of the last few days, I have come to realize that the hospitality and generosity I received from Warlord Adelric is not an exception when it comes to the vagha race, but rather, it is the rule. While in Dehnlee, I have felt like a citizen of this splendid city."

The attendees offered him their applause. Dorian let it go on for a short time before putting up his hands in an attempt to restore silence. Slowly, the noise died down.

"The importance of this is obvious to me, as I'm sure it is obvious to each of you. If a selumari can be made to feel so comfortable among the dwarves then maybe—just maybe—the other races of Esfah: humans, firewalkers, other races yet undiscovered, and even the trogs and morehl might all some day be able to live together in peace and harmony. It is my grand dream that someday, all the races of Esfah will co-exist in a world that has advanced beyond war. And it all starts here, with the bonding of the first two races, the vagha and the selumari!"

The room erupted in further applause as the dinner guests all rose from their seats in a standing ovation.

"Thank you," Dorian said softly, bowing graciously. "Thank you very much."

Peregrine and his cadre of minions arrived at the edge of the Dehnlee graveyard in the middle of the night. He sniffed and looked around, verifying he was in the right location from his memory. He rode one of the skeletal steeds in Renata's service.

Renata approached with her army in tow, climbing the gentle grade of the vale that sloped down and away from the cemetery. She left her minions behind her, riding upon her tireless, undead horse. It trotted at a slow and purposeful gait.

Peregrine watched her coolly, noticing how bright her emerald green eyes shimmered beneath the light of the moon and stars.

Before she could arrive, he reached beneath his mount and took out a bundle from inside the steed's ribcage. The bundle held six scythes, each one virtually identical to the ones given to the zombies of Renata's army. Identical, except for one small detail. The steel used to make these scythes had been specially tempered, making them twice as strong as the scythes wielded by the rest of the undead army.

Admittedly, it was a small improvement over the other weapons and would make little difference in a fight against a coral elf or dwarf. Should his zombies be pitted against Renata's, it might give them some small advantage against their foes.

Peregrine loved his mistress. He even knew that he had died in her service—even if he couldn't remember the specifics of it. He was not so stupid to think otherwise.

"All finished?" Renata asked as she crested the ridge to find him outfitting his zombies with weapons. Until now, they'd carried none.

"All done," he said and smiled, then realized it was somewhat out of character and turned that smile into a grimace. "Your army is fully armed. Armed and dangerous."

"And ready for battle?" Renata asked. She sniffed the air. "I smell flesh in the distance. Dwarf meat."

"There's one good way to tell if they are battle-ready."

"Battle itself?" she mused.

"Actually, I was thinking more along the lines of a test."

"Yes," she hissed. "A test."

Peregrine pointed and his minions exhumed several second-grade bodies from a mass grave and brought them to Renata for reanimation. She was only too happy to add to her army's ranks, although the bodies were each missing one or more vital parts. As a result, they wouldn't prove much of a match for the fully armed and fully limbed zombies of her army, but they would nevertheless provide some measure of the undead's fighting ability and strength.

Peregrine picked a zombie at random and set him up inside a ring of soldiers. He took the first of the newly revived corpses and gave it a rapier. The zombie had trouble with the weapon; it was missing an arm and half of its left foot, and therefore had a hard time keeping its balance. Nevertheless, it took a fighting stance and looked as if it had once been a formidable opponent.

The scythe-wielding former trog seemed to handle the reaping blade as if it had been revived with all the required skill to wield it. With a deft hand, it spun the scythe menacingly in front of its body like a blade in a windmill, then whirled the scythe in a horizontal arc, as if cutting rows of wheat or stalks of corn.

Renata snickered at the zombie's adeptness with the weapon. The zombie and the scythe were made for each other. "Begin," she cried, and watched the demonstration.

The scythe-wielder moved forward to attack. The other

zombie raised its rapier in an attempt to defend itself, but the scythe moved with too much power for the sword to do much good and batted it aside. The scythe whirled and arced, knocking the morehl blade free and slicing the newer zombie's head clean from its shoulders in one smooth motion. The head landed with a thud, rolled a few feet, then stopped dead in the dirt. A second later, the reanimated body buckled at the knees and fell forward—dead once more.

With no enemy, the scythe-wielder stood still, almost at attention, with the weapon held close to its body. The blade curled over its shoulder and the gore-stained tip pointed backward.

"Idiot!" screamed Renata, striking the zombie on the back of the head with an open palm. "You didn't have to destroy it! I could have used that zombie for something."

Peregrine stepped forward. "It was given the order to kill, so that's all it knows how to do," he reminded her. "That's what makes zombies such good soldiers."

Renata remained silent, thinking about it. She and Peregrine had each resurrected creatures to the unlife. Some in the heucuva's macabre court had more will than others, and she began to connect the dots. Unless she granted her minions free will at their creating, they were perfect slaves. For her, they would walk through flames without hesitation if she desired it.

Her mouth turned from a frown to a smile—an evil, malicious sort of grin. Renata stared at the headless corpse. "I want to see it again."

Peregrine motioned and his loyal troops dragged another partial body forward. This one was missing half of its abdomen and parts of both arms below the elbows.

Renata dabbed a glob of black necralluvium onto its forehead and breathed onto it with a lusty kind of voice, saying, "Rise. Rise and kill."

The creature pushed himself off the ground with his

broken stumps. It moved towards the zombie, who held its scythe. Steel glinted in the moonlight for a moment, then came the sound of the blade slicing through air. Then through flesh.

The armless drone groaned as the blade cleaved through spine and flesh, breaking it in two. Using its stumps, it dragged itself towards its enemy with unrelenting desire. Finally, another blow hacked its head from its neck, destroying the thing completely.

After a moment of pregnant silence, all that Peregrine heard was Renata's maniacal laughing. She stared at the dismembered corpse.

Renata's cackling finally muted, she commanded. "Do it again!"

Dehnlee's post-banquet celebrations went long into the night, and Adelric and Dorian awoke early the next day with a somewhat painful throbbing in their heads. Dwarves knew how to celebrate in excess.

But as much as they both wanted to spend the morning recovering from the previous night's revelry, Dorian couldn't hold up his ship's departure any longer. They left Adelric's home without eating—neither of them could think of stomaching food—and they walked the short distance to the vaghan docks on the shores of Delmara Bay. A selumari sailing ship awaited Dorian's arrival.

It was a pleasant morning; the cool dew gave everything an invigorating freshness. By the time they arrived at the docks, their hangovers had mostly subsided.

"Tell me, Dorian," said Adelric. "Did you really mean what you said about the races of Esfah living together in peace and harmony—I mean *all of* the races?"

"Yes, of course," answered Dorian. "I wouldn't have said it if I hadn't meant it. I'm an enchanter, not a politician. I don't have to say things for other people's benefit. I only have to speak the truth."

Adelric laughed. "Do you think we will see such peace in our lifetime?"

Dorian looked at Adelric with an expression of sadness on his face. "I'm afraid not," he said. "Nor will our sons, nor the sons of our sons. But still, I hold out hope that the future will bring peace to the people and stability to the land. It's inevitable. It has to be if life is more powerful than Death."

Adelric nodded. It was inevitable, but he was sorry that he wouldn't live long enough to see it. As they crested a slight hill on the path, the selumari ship came into view. It was a large ship, bigger than anything Adelric had ever seen and dwarfed by the few vagha ships that were berthed near it on the water or at the docks. Dwarves were not widely regarded as sailors and their boats were more like skiffs than ships.

Dorian's ship sat proudly among the others. Its hull was almost completely white, as if it had been carved out of pearl and pieced together like a mosaic. It had two sails, the masts of each also white, that rose up from the deck like a pair of ivory towers. Even though the sails themselves were furled, it was obvious to Adelric that they were made of the highest quality. The ship was awe-inspiring, and it furthered Adelric's resolve to visit Galatea at the first opportunity.

"Ah, the *Atalante*," said Dorian, a bit of wistfulness to his voice even though he'd seen the ship at anchor countless times. "They must be eager for my return."

"Is this a special ship?" asked Adelric, feeling almost foolish asking in the glow of the incredible brightness shining off the ship's hull.

"It is the finest ship in Galatea's fleet."

"It looks as if it might be the finest in *anyone's* fleet."

Dorian nodded graciously. "That's kind of you to say. For a water ship, it is very fine. But we also have one that can take to the skies: a coral airship."

Adelric's eyebrows rose. "That must be a sight."

"Indeed it is."

The two of them fell silent a moment, as if they'd exhausted all the small talk they could manage, and now the inevitable was upon them. It was time for Dorian to say goodbye. But it was Adelric who spoke first.

"I want to thank you, friend Dorian," he said. His voice nearly cracked. "I truly appreciated the extended visit. The time we spent together made it that much easier to deal with the loss of my brother."

"As long as I haven't helped you to forget him," said Dorian.

"That could never happen. His memory will live with me forever."

"Good," said Dorian, placing a hand on Adelric's shoulder. "For if we remember the horrors of war, then we're likely to have fewer battles in the future."

Adelric nodded, and the two came together in a long embrace. When they parted, the dwarf felt compelled to speak. "I will miss you my friend."

They came together in a second embrace, this one longer than the first. "I am sure we shall see each other again, and likely sooner than the time between our last encounters."

And then at last, Dorian said goodbye and Adelric watched his friend walk down the dock and board the *Atalante*. The ship cast off minutes later, and then, with Dorian waving from the ship's bow, it pulled away from the dock, turned effortlessly from port, and began its journey across the bay to the city of Galatea.

Adelric remained on the dock long after the ship

disappeared from view.

CHAPTER NINE

Standish hadn't attended the banquet held in the selumari's honor. Even still, he'd gotten a poor night's rest as revelers coming home from the party kept him up half the night with their incessant merriment.

*You'd think the coral elf had won the damn war for them the way they were carrying on,* thought Standish as he trudged into the graveyard to begin his day's work.

Although it had rained during the night, his tools were still safely stowed where he'd left them, and with the cloth still bundled around them, no doubt remained clean and dry. He unwrapped them and laid them out before him like some healer might do with his instruments before a delicate operation.

"Healer Standish at your service, boys," he mumbled as he selected a long-handled spade from the pile. He let out a soft laugh and shook his head. "Silly old dwarf," he said. "Better get to work before you waste any more time daydreaming."

He turned to the day's line of tombstones. There were five there this morning, laid out last night after Standish had left early. One more than there'd been yesterday. *The stonecutters must be getting quicker,* he thought. Either that or they've started cutting corners on the work.

The simple thought of it enraged Standish to no end. He hurried to the row of tombstones and examined them in detail. If any one of them was less than perfect, he'd cart it back into town and tear a strip from the master stonecutter's hide.

But no matter how closely he looked, he could see no flaw in the work. They were all precisely cut, suitably adorned and worthy of heading the grave of a heroic vagha soldier.

"Very well, then," he said. "If they can produce five tombstones in a day, then I'll set down five in a day as well."

With that, he spit into the palms of his hands and rubbed them together, eager to get started on the day's labor.

But then, he heard a sound.

He stood upright and listened carefully for it. He was sure there had been no one else on the plain with him this morning, though there might have been someone following him from some distance behind. He turned around, scanning the surrounding area slowly, but could see nothing out of the ordinary.

"Silly old dwarf," he said again and picked up the spade with both hands. He chided himself for yesterday's superstitions. The air smelled as foul today as it had then, but he'd already made up his mind to ignore it, and so it bothered him less.

He was about to start digging when he heard it again. It was a dry, rattling whisper, like someone walking through a pile of autumn leaves. Yesterday's smell suddenly assailed him. It grew stronger, so pungent that Standish could almost feel it hanging on the air like smoke.

It was the smell of Death.

He stood up, trying to convince himself that all was well with the world and that he was merely going senile. That was when he saw them.

Two undead soldiers slowly making their way toward him.

As he caught sight of them, the first thought that crossed the old dwarf's mind was that he had somehow desecrated a couple of graves and these two living dead had risen up to exact their revenge upon him. But as they neared, he came to realize that these two were undead trogs, not vagha.

And that made him feel even worse.

"Tarvanehl, have mercy on my soul," he whispered as he grabbed the spade firmly in his wide-spaced hands.

The zombies continued moving toward him, their stone axes raised in preparation for battle.

Before they got too close, Standish shortened his grip on the spade and swung it in a wide and deadly arc. The blade of the shovel sliced through the tattered rags of the first zombie, then cut into the midsection of the second. A wound opened up in the zombie's abdomen. Innards spilled out of the walking corpse, but still it moved forward, its ax raised even higher.

Standish recovered from the swing by widening his grip and holding the spade before him like a staff. With movements that might have made a younger dwarf envious, he blocked several of the two zombie's blows with the sturdy hardwood handle, then countered with quick jabs of the shovel's blade. He connected with each of the zombie's legs, cutting deeply into the dead flesh, but failing to hobble either of them. The blows merely staggered them, and moments later, they were able to continue their attack.

"Filthy, maggot-infested vermin," Standish cried, as he desperately blocked a series of ax blows.

The zombies were slow and if there had been only one of them, he might have been able to defeat it, or perhaps hold it off. But there were two of the nasty things and Standish had his hands too busy with defense to even consider mounting an attack.

Still, he fought bravely, and at one point managed to cut one of the zombie's ax-wielding arms from its torso. "Hah!" he shouted breathlessly. "There's plenty of fight in this old dwarf yet!"

But even as he spoke, the zombie bent down and took

the ax out of the dismembered right arm with its left hand. Then it rose up and resumed the attack as if it had merely dropped its weapon on the ground rather than the arm holding it.

The sight of the one-armed zombie approaching after he was certain it had been disabled was too much for Standish to bear. He continued to battle bravely, but much of the spark was gone from his fight. And, as if a reflection of his resolve, the handle of his spade had been whittled down to half its width by the continuous blows from the two zombies' axes. Three more blows and it cracked in two, leaving Standish with little more than a pair of sticks to defend himself with.

The dead trog's first blow hit him in the shoulder and knocked him to the ground.

Before the second blow crushed his spine, Standish managed to impale one of the zombies with a length of the spade's handle. Putrid gray liquid oozed from the zombie's wound, but the creature did not cry out. It simply continued to fight as hard as ever, bringing the ax down onto Standish's skull and ushering the old dwarf's world into utter darkness.

Renata inspected the ground beneath her feet. It appeared soft and wet from the previous evening's light rain and looked more like swampy fens than the fertile plains Wakefield was known for.

Renata had watched the grass wither beneath her feet wherever she went, as if bowing to Malgrimm's presence. She fingered an old wound upon her chest where a bulge in her breast had sealed over with pallid skin. Beneath it, a hard mass festered. The darkhold gem her master had placed inside her darkened the land wherever she went. Its power through her had swelled the fetid marsh where long dead trogs once practiced their devotion to the god known as Death.

The heucuva felt her dread lord's desire blossom warmly in her chest. Her purpose was to sow chaos upon the plains and devour the living. Eventually, the marsh that expanded with her power would overtake the entire peninsula.

And then…

Day by day, it would continue to grow. Tenday by tenday, city after city would fall to her undead hordes. Month by month, entire mountains would turn to mire. And year by year, the seas would dry up like old bones, on and on until all of Esfah was recast as a planet-wide festration: the perfect home for Malgrimm. A place where he could walk freely and where the other gods would be forced to flee.

In another day or so, it would begin in earnest. She would harvest the Dehnlee graveyard for its supplies and then scrape Dehnlee off the map.

"Renata!"

She stopped her scheming for a moment and turned to see who it was. Peregrine approached with a pair of zombies in tow. One of them had lost an arm and carried it, while the other dragged a fresh body behind it.

"What is it?"

"The two scouts 1 sent out on patrol have returned," said Peregrine. "With another corpse." He directed the zombies to leave the body with them.

They unceremoniously dumped it there and then turned to rejoin the other troops. The one-armed minion replaced his arm at the socket, where the ragged flesh reached out to rejoin the missing limb with tiny tendrils of black ichor.

"A dwarf," said Renata nonchalantly. "And an old one at that."

"Yes, but he's an excellent fighter. He took one of the zombie's arms off with a spade before they were able to kill him."

"Impressive," said Renata. "He will make a fine addition to our army."

"Yes, he will fight well for you," said Peregrine, wondering if she had tested his ambitions by saying *our*. "But that's not his real significance."

"Oh?" She rubbed her hands together, clearly intrigued. Peregrine had proved his worth as of late and she would hear him out. "Tell me."

"Apparently, this dwarf's job was tending to the vagha graveyard," he said. "The other bodies we've harvested were from the defeated forces of morehl and trogs. He has been burying the fallen dwarves…"

"More soldiers for my army?"

Again, Peregrine nodded. They had already established that.

Renata chuckled sardonically.

"But it's more than that," Peregrine insisted. "If they are still burying them, the dead are greater than we anticipated. The city is ripe for our arrival."

A smile spread across the heucuva's face as she lifted the newly turned vagha zombie to his feet. "Join the others," she commanded.

The zombie turned and went to join the ranks where one of Renata's lesser generals waited to place an unblooded scythe in the still-warm zombie's hands.

"Excellent," she hissed, thinking about the flesh they would soon devour and the panic they would strike upon the Wakefield Plain. Malgrimm would be pleased with her.

Her army would grow larger with each battle, and every opposing soldier that died would be revived to turn against his or her former comrades. The thought of using an army's own fallen soldiers to crush it made her wriggle with glee.

Peregrine watched Renata's eyes as they sparkled with

glee and the festration around her increased. Grass turned black below her and crumbled to dust as if she radiated entropy.

"Soon," she said. "Very soon. Begin harvesting our new bodies."

The bow of the *Atalante* rose sharply as it crested a wave, then drove back down for the water's surface, cutting into it like an ax into wood.

"The seas have grown rough," Dorian said to the captain of the *Atalante*, a tall coral elf named Ageeus.

"Nothing this ship can't handle."

Dorian nodded but said nothing. Surely the ship could withstand much rougher seas than these, but the suddenness of the storm seemed unnatural, somehow. The enchanter sensed a kind of magic in the sudden turn.

"Have there been storms on the bay in the last few days?" asked Dorian.

"None that I've seen," said the captain.

"What about on your way back over to retrieve me?"

"As smooth as pearls."

A splash of water hit Dorian in the face as the ship crested yet another wave. There could only be one answer. Whether the sudden chop was caused by terrain upheaval elsewhere on Esfah or the sudden unnatural shift in weather, magic was certainly involved. Regardless, since the waters of Delmara Bay were so affected by it, the changes had to be occurring somewhere nearby.

Dorian walked toward the stern and gazed off the rear of the ship, looking out over the white-capped waters at the City of Dehnlee. As he watched it growing smaller and smaller in the distance, he wondered if everything was all right in the home of his friend Adelric.

It sounded crazy, but something in the pit of his stomach told him that maybe it wasn't.

Hortense fussed over the dinner table one more time. The elderly dwarf woman decided to place a heavy earthenware bowl upside down over the food piled onto the plate, to keep it warm.

It was a futile gesture, she knew, for the food had been served over an hour ago and was already stone cold. But she was beside herself with worry, and the simple attempt to maintain a sense of order felt comforting to her. She adjusted the cutlery yet again, then let out a sigh.

She moved over to the window that overlooked the street. Sol hovered just over the lip of the horizon, as if it were aware of her dilemma and trying to remain in the sky as long as possible before disappearing from view.

*It wasn't like Standish to be late,* Hortense thought.

In all her years of marriage, she had never known him to be late for supper. Even when the vagha were at war and he was a soldier in the warlord's first regiment, he'd manage to get back in time for a meal. He valued his time at home and absolutely cherished their time together, especially now that they were both aged and their lives were slowly coming to an inevitable end. If he was unable to return from the cemetery, it could only mean that something had prevented him from returning. Something was wrong.

But what? What could happen to an old dwarf tending a graveyard to stop him from coming home at night? Maybe he'd just stopped for a drink somewhere, or for a chat with an old friend.

*Yes, it must be something like that,* Hortense told herself, lying to cover her true fear.

She let out a little laugh, chiding herself over how silly she'd been to worry.

He'd likely be coming down the street at any moment, no doubt whistling a merry tune. Standish did love his music.

She went to the front door, opened it, and stepped outside to wait for him. The sun finally gave up and descended rapidly beneath the horizon.

As she looked down the street, she thought she saw him approaching. As she watched with desperate hope, the movement of shadows turned out to be a pair of young lovers out for a twilight stroll. The sight of the two dwarves walking arm-in-arm reminded her of another time, long ago, when she and Standish had gone on such walks. The thought made her heart feel heavy.

After fighting off a shiver brought on by the sudden coolness of the night, she chewed on the tip of her thumbnail, a habit she'd quit a century ago.

*What could have happened to him,* she wondered.

Without attempting to answer the question, she returned to the kitchen and put the food back on the stove so it would be hot when he came through the door. After all, it just might help if he had something nice to come home to.

## PART TWO

Dhanriath peered out from under the cloak of an invisibility spell he projected via magical means. Nekarthis paid his protégé little attention. He spent much of his time writing observations in his books.

"How many years have we watched? How many more do you think it might be?"

Nekarthis spoke calmly, "Patience, Dhanriath. You are black shara, like me. Time is a lesser concern than the demand for knowledge."

Dhanriath tightened his lips and turned back to watching. He'd been waiting for those infected with the necralluvium to act on some impulse for ages now. Beyond Peregrine's late-night wanderings, there had been very little happenings worth holding his interest.

And now? Finally, they were on the move—and they couldn't move fast enough for the eldarim's sake.

"Patience and knowledge," Nekarthis whispered. Our order has always horded these virtues. They are our weapons, setting the stage like a fulcrum so that we may move mountains with one tiny push. We possess more of either than any enemy, and by their power we shall claim Esfah … When the timing is right, we shall strike, but not sooner."

Dhanriath nodded and swallowed.

Nekarthis turned back to his notes.

## CHAPTER TEN

There was a series of knocks at the door.

"Warlord Adelric!"

The voice was that of a woman, and quite frantic.

"I'm coming, I'm coming," Adelric mumbled under his breath as he slowly threw the covers off. It wasn't the first time he'd ever been roused from a peaceful sleep by a knock at the door, but it was certainly unexpected considering that peace had finally come to the vagha of Dehnlee.

He blinked his eyes open and noticed that the room was dimly lit, as if whoever was at the door had waited until sunrise to start knocking—and just barely, at that.

The knocking continued, growing louder and more urgent with each passing moment.

Adelric looked for his housecoat, but as the pounding on the wooden door continued, he decided it might be better to forego formality and answer the door dressed in his bedclothes.

"Warlord, are you there?"

"Yes, by the flame, I'm coming," he replied as he hobbled down the hallway, his bare feet chilled by the cold stone tiles of the floor. He undid the latch and threw open the door, speaking before the door was even open. "What is it?"

He found an old dwarf woman standing there, her hand poised to rap her knuckles against the door yet again. Her eyes were wet and red, and her clothes looked disheveled, as if she'd been wearing them throughout the night. But despite her ragged state, there was no mistaking the pattern of whitish gray streaking through her long red hair—it was Hortense, the wife of Standish, the cemetery keeper. He'd known her and Standish for many years.

The moment she set eyes on Adelric, the woman burst into tears.

"Hortense," said Adelric softly. "Please come in."

She stepped inside the house, still weeping. Adelric placed an arm on her shoulder and led her into the reception room, just off the entrance hall.

"What is it?" he asked as she sat down. "Tell me what's wrong."

"It's my husband, Standish," she said between sobs.

"What about him?" Adelric said, already thinking he was going to be an arbiter in some sort of domestic dispute between husband and wife. As warlord, that duty sometimes fell to him, especially for the higher ranked military men. But Standish had retired from service some years ago…

"He didn't come home last night."

"Enjoying a night of revelry?" offered Adelric with a polite smile, even though that sort of conduct was uncharacteristic of Standish.

"You know he's not partial to drink or revelry, milord."

"Of course," said Adelric, now feeling somewhat embarrassed about having made the suggestion.

"It's nothing like that at all." She rubbed a cloth against her eye to dry it, then shook her head. "He didn't come back from the graveyard last night."

"Has he ever done this before?"

"No, never," she said. "He's always come home. Always." She began to cry once more, muttering into her cloth between sobs. "What would I do with myself if something has happened to him? I'm too old to start my life over again, or live the rest of it alone."

Adelric hoped there was some simple explanation for

Standish's whereabouts, but knew from experience that the disappearance of a former warrior on the plain could just as easily be the start of a very serious problem—not only for Hortense, but for all of the people of Dehnlee.

"Have you looked for him in the city?"

"Yes, milord. I've already been everywhere I thought he might be, but I didn't check… " Her voice trailed off.

"The cemetery?"

"No, milord. I didn't want to venture out there alone, especially at night in the dark."

"And you won't have to now that it is light out," said Adelric. "I'll send out a pair of scouts immediately. If he's anywhere on the plain, they'll find him."

"Thank you, milord."

Warlord Adelric dispatched two of his best riders to the plain. Darton and Borvis were also professional soldiers.

"What do you think we'll find there?" asked Darton, a stocky dwarf with short-cropped hair and a neatly trimmed beard that ringed his mouth in a circle of red.

"My guess is we'll find old Standish lying between two plots and sleeping off the effects of a full wineskin," answered Borvis. He was the elder of the two riders and the leader of this expedition. His long hair blew wildly in the wind, and his beard swept up and over his shoulder, flickering behind him.

"I hope you're right," said Darton.

"Me too," said Borvis. "Me too."

They spurred their ponies to a gallop and surged ahead. It was not a far distance to Dehnlee's memorial cemetery, perhaps a league to the ridge where the raised peninsula of

Dehnlee sloped down and onto the Wakefield Plain.

When they arrived at the graveyard, Standish was nowhere in sight. As they scanned the horizon, the two scouts could barely see anything through a heavy mist that hung on the morning air like a gray pall.

"I don't like this," said Darton.

"No, neither do I," said Borvis, a chill evident in his voice. "It doesn't look right, does it?"

"We better comb through the graveyard."

"I think you're right."

They turned their ponies and let them amble through the Wakefield Memorial as they searched for signs of the old superintendent.

"Standish!" cried Darton, cupping his hands around his mouth.

"Standish, are you here?"

Borvis took a deep breath and nearly gagged on the stench wafting through the air.

"What is that foul smell?" asked Darton, as he put a hand over his nose and mouth to keep from retching. They knew it wasn't the fetid odor of trogs; as career soldiers, they'd know that particular stench anywhere.

"It smells like Death," said Borvis, taking another sniff. "Like long decaying, putrefying, and rotting corpses."

"But the bodies were all properly buried," said Darton. "I know. I helped Standish bury many of them myself."

The process couldn't be to blame. At least in the first couple days after the war, the military had helped get a head start on the project and interred two thirds of the bodies under Standish's direction.

"As did I, but look at the plots. None of them have been disturbed." He tried to peer through the thick mist, but could not see far. "At least, not the ones closest to Dehnlee, anyway."

"So where could the smell be coming from?"

"I don't know. But if we find the source of the smell, I'm sorry to say that we might end up finding Standish as well."

Darton was silent, his eyes sweeping the ground as if in sorrow.

"We best start looking for him," said Borvis, getting off his mount. Darton also dismounted, and the two led their ponies to a nearby tree. Borvis secured the animals to a sturdy branch, and Darton ventured out in search of Standish.

The mist hanging over the plain was beginning to burn off from the warmth of the morning sun, and already, the two soldiers were able to see further. But they were more interested in the land nearby. If Standish was anywhere, then it was likely he would be somewhere in or around the graveyard.

"Perhaps he's fallen into a hole?" Darton suggested optimistically, though it would not explain the odor.

The stench that had first stung their noses and made them choke had dissipated somewhat, or perhaps they had just become more accustomed to the smell. Either way, it became less of a nuisance and they were able to function without being constantly reminded of it.

As Borvis finished up securing the ponies, Darton called to him.

"Borvis, over here," he cried.

Borvis was off and running.

He joined Darton seconds later in the middle of the graveyard where Standish's tarp lay open. The old dwarf's tools lay scattered about the ground. Darton held up the spade end of the shovel Standish had used to defend himself, inspecting the jagged end of the broken wooden handle.

Borvis took a quick look at the broken tool and then at the ground nearest their feet. "From the way the earth is turned up, there looks to have been a struggle."

Darton turned the broken spade over to examine the shovel end. Something dark stained the metal, something that almost looked like dried blood. He brought it closer to his face and sniffed at it. "Ugh!"

"What is it?" asked Borvis.

"Smell this." Darton held the shovel up to Borvis's nose.

*"Fweh!"* Borvis gagged and pushed the end away from his face. "It's that same rotten smell."

"What do you think happened to him?"

Borvis looked at Darton, shrugged his broad shoulders and said, "I don't know. Some kind of creature, perhaps? Esfah is a large place and none of us have seen all the elder monsters. Perhaps it's something we've never cataloged or seen before."

Darton set his jaw and muttered, "Whatever it is, then, let's hope it's more friend than foe."

After dispatching Borvis and Darton to the plain in search for Standish, Adelric remained in Carlin Park, helping the other officers with contingency plans. If Standish's disappearance turned out to be more than just some old dwarf's folly, then the citizens of Dehnlee would need to be mobilized, either for war or for defense. Adelric hoped they didn't have to prepare for either, but they needed his experience despite.

Besides, nobody else needed to know he was running his troops through anything more than a training maneuver. Deep down, a painful disquiet stirred in Adelric's gut. None of this was like Standish. And the retired soldier was too old to get into too much trouble on his own, but too young to die of old age.

After considering every possible explanation for Standish's disappearance, Adelric found himself dwelling on what he thought was the most unlikely scenario of all—that Standish had been killed in a deliberate attack.

Murder, perhaps?

Adelric knew it was a preposterous assumption. After all, Standish might have simply lost his way, have fallen and hit his head, or been attacked by a wild animal. But while all those were perfectly reasonable explanations, something told Adelric they were off the mark.

Way off. And Adelric's gut had never steered him wrong before.

But worst of all for Adelric was the knowledge that his own personal fighting spirit was gone. For the first time in his life, he was not excited by the prospect of a skirmish.

Never before had he felt apprehension about possible battle. Never before had he dreaded fighting another war, even with all these possibilities. First and foremost, no one truly knew what had happened to the trogs of the northern marshes, and Adelric wondered if Standish's disappearance might be somehow related.

Perhaps it was time for him to step aside—to allow Sergeant Cad man the chance to prove himself a leader. Armies needed new blood to invigorate them, and Adelric felt that his blood was becoming a rather ancient vintage.

Yes, he decided at last. Whatever this trouble turned out to be, it would mark the beginning of the end of his military career.

It was time to pass on the torch.

Darton and Borvis continued to search the graveyard for any sign of Standish, but found nothing.

There were several sets of footprints and much disturbed ground. That was curious to be sure, but both knew that ground work was ongoing about the site. And the skids that looked like dragged areas might have been due to moving fresh headstones, which they knew were arriving almost daily.

After searching every inch of the graveyard, the two scouts split up, expanding the area of their search. Borvis checked the area north of the graveyard and Darton examined the lands to the east of it. Truth be told, they had long ago given up on finding any further trace of Standish, but they had to be thorough in their search, for Adelric would ask many questions and neither of them wanted to answer with the words, "I don't know."

"Borvis, I've found something!" cried Darton.

For the second time that day, Borvis found himself running to join his younger partner, and wondering why *he* never found anything of importance.

He came upon Darton standing with his legs apart and his hands on his knees. He bent over the ground as if examining something slithering through the grass

"I think I've found the source of the stench," said Darton.

Borvis joined the younger scout, then took up a similar pose. At once he saw the curious thing moving across the ground.

"It's an arm," he said, both in recognition and astonishment at the sight.

The arm was black and gray, with dark bruises and open wounds running up and down the dead flesh. Only four fingers remained on the hand. Despite the gruesome appearance of the limb, its mere presence paled by what it was doing there on the ground.

It was *moving.* All on its own.

Its fingers opened and closed as it inched its way over the ground.

Then, the arm bent at the elbow to cover a larger

distance—no more than a few cubits—before using its fingers in a slow, spider-like crawl.

"Incredible," sighed Borvis.

"Have you ever seen anything like it before?"

Borvis shook his head. "Not in all my years." He paused a moment to think. "I've heard stories, but…"

"But what?"

"I never really believed them to be true."

Darton waited for an explanation. When one wasn't forthcoming, he prodded Borvis. "Never believed *what* to be true?"

"This arm," he said. "It belongs. Excuse me, *belonged* to a zombie."

"A zombie?" cried Darton. "You mean, like—"

"Yes," Borvis nodded. "There are undead among us. They say that the dead rose first, much further south in Charnock before the breaking of the Gods'own, the Champions of the Gods. And then again they rose on the East Coast, prompting the firewalkers to reveal their existence when they rescued the selumari there. They say there were some even in the fall of Karakto."

"But where are they now?"

The soldiers stood and watched the arm a moment. It crawled eastward towards the plain. The scouts looked up and across the land.

"To the east," guessed Borvis, looking westward and spotting a pile of rotted corpses that had been cut into various pieces. Black blood and withered grass marked the north-most ridge of the cemetery, where the mass graves of the enemy soldiers had been placed. The dirt there was recently disturbed, as were many of the vaghan burial sites—the implications were dire.

Darton nodded. "I'll go have a look."

The *Atalante* pulled into port at Galatea. A dozen people waited on the docks to greet it. Some were family and friends of crewmembers, some were dock workers, and some had just wandered down to look at the boats.

Dorian barely noticed them. His attention still firmly fixed on the waters of Delmara Bay and the City of Dehnlee beyond.

*There is something going on,* he thought. He could feel it in the pit of his stomach.

It was a strange feeling, and reminded him of the stories he'd heard about people being able to predict the weather or the success of harvests by the pain they felt in their bunions. He'd always dismissed such stories as coincidences or wishful thinking, but not anymore.

He knew there was something dire happening somewhere.

But what?

And *where?*

"Excuse me, Dorian," said the gentle voice of Captain Ageeus. "Would you care to grab lunch? There are a few members of the Galatean administration hoping to speak with you about how your trip went, diplomatically speaking, that is."

Dorian nodded. "I'll be there in a minute."

Darton headed toward the ridge that marked the northeast part of the cemetery, creeping quietly in the interest of stealth. The distance to the top of the hill wasn't very far, and the ledge wasn't too terribly steep.

As he reached the crest of the hill, Darton crouched down and then crawled the last few feet to the top. Once there, he pulled a shiny brass long-look from his waistband, extended the instrument to its full length, and used it to scan the rest of the plain.

Over to the left of him was a cloud of mist, similar to the one they'd seen upon their arrival at the graveyard.

Near the mist ambled a number of upright figures, lurching and stumbling aimlessly about—either in a series of meandering circles, or continuously rocking in place—but never getting anywhere. Their bodies looked cadaverous, and their walks stilted, as if what limbs they had were stiff and unbending.

As if they were *dead.*

Their sheer numbers meant that all the graves must have been emptied. Graves where dead trog and morehl soldiers had been buried. "This is bad," muttered Darton under his breath. "Very bad."

The realization hit Darton in the gut like a mailed fist. The dead army was moving slowly towards Dehnlee, skirting around the ledge of the plain and resuming the route of attack that had nearly arrived at the doorsteps of the vaghan city years ago.

Without another moment's hesitation, Darton packed up his long-look and hurried down the hill as fast as his short legs would carry him.

"Come here, you disgusting, rotten, maggoty piece of

filth!" said Borvis, who followed the path of the dismembered arm as it trekked across the ground.

Borvis grabbed a few tools from where Standish had left them and was now doing his best to scoop up the arm without touching it.

While he and Darton planned to give a full report to the Warlord, their story might sound ludicrous without any physical evidence. Hence, Borvis needed the arm. In addition, the arm might prove useful for experimentation. That way, they could figure out how to best kill these nasty, savage things and devise a plan from its effects.

Borvis stalked the arm cautiously, wrinkling his nose at the awful smell.

Although there was little danger of the arm physically hurting him, it was still dead—had been for a long time—and probably carried countless diseases. The thing could easily end up killing him indirectly if he wasn't careful.

Borvis tried to brush the wriggling hand into a wide-mouthed shovel using a hand rake. It sounded like a simple enough operation, but accomplishing it wasn't so easy. To Borvis's surprise, each time he moved closer to the arm, it suddenly changed direction and speed-crawled away from him. Although the arm had no eyes, or ears, or any other senses of any kind, it was as if it could still sense his presence and his intention.

"Come to papa, you festering, rancid, foul and putrid piece of meat." The arm scurried away, flipping and flopping over the ground like a fish out of water. "Not to worry my decaying little limb, I don't want to eat you."

Borvis suddenly shuddered at the thought.

After several unsuccessful attempts to capture the arm, Borvis moved in front of it so that he was positioned between the arm and its ultimate eastern destination.

He decided that he would let it approach, then hit it with

the shovel to stun it for a few moments while he scooped it up with the rake and shovel. Then, it would be a simple matter of transporting the arm to his waiting pony and transferring the arm into one of his saddlebags. After that, it would be back to Dehnlee for an audience with the warlord.

Borvis raised the shovel over his shoulder and prepared to deal the arm an immobilizing blow.

He tensed, waiting…

And felt something push him from behind.

Borvis flew through the air, landing face-first on the ground. He was dazed momentarily, but still retained the presence of mind to roll to the right.

An axe head sliced into the ground mere inches from where his head had been moments before.

He rolled twice more, then looked up. To his astonishment, he found two undead beings standing over him. One was a trog, a despicable creature even in life, and the other was a *vagha*. One who seemed more dignified and imposing.

Borvis almost let out a laugh at the irony of the situation.

They had found Standish!

Unfortunately, Standish was dead—or undead—to be precise.

But the moment of irony was fleeting. Borvis had no time for bemusement. The two zombies set upon him immediately, the expressions on both their faces savage and hostile.

Borvis threw the hand rake at the dead trog. Its three sharp steel tongs pierced the creature's chest and stuck there. But while such a wound would have disabled a normal opponent, the zombie simply pulled the tool from its body—taking with it a large clump of gray-green flesh—and held it menacingly in its hand, ready to use it against Borvis.

Borvis rose to his feet, the shovel still in his hand. He

also had an ax tucked in his waistband, but that weapon would allow the dead things to get closer than he liked and allow their weapons to become effective. He decided to use the shovel for now. If it couldn't kill them, then at least it would keep the zombies' weapons out of range.

Where was Darton?

"Darton!" Borvis cried. "Come quick, I need you!"

The two zombies flailed as they pressed upon him, but he managed to keep them off by poking at them with the blade end of the shovel.

Borvis laughed; it didn't seem too difficult to keep them at bay. At this rate, he could remain safe for quite some time. At least until help arrived.

What was taking Darton so long?

"Darton, over here!" he cried out again.

The two zombies lunged for him, but once again, he was able to hold them off with the shovel. "You'll have to try harder than that, you disgusting pieces of—"

Borvis's words were cut off by a sharp blow to the back of his head.

He felt a burning pain shoot through his upper body and when he looked down, he saw the tip of a scythe blade jutting out from his shoulder. The shovel was jarred from his hands, and he fell heavily to the ground.

Blood pooled beneath him—red blood that didn't smolder in the air—and he knew it was his own.

There was a tug on his shoulder and the scythe blade yanked free in a moment of blinding pain. He looked up into the rotting face of a third zombie, ready for another blow. The scythe blade arced toward him, and Borvis just managed to pull out of the way. He drew his ax, even though he knew its handle was woefully short to fight the scythe-wielding zombie.

He stepped back, avoiding another strike, and stumbled over something on the ground. It was the arm, still making its way eastward.

Borvis reached down, picked up the arm and held it by the hand. He began swinging it like a mace. He managed to club two of the zombies—including the former Standish—in the head. But the bony end of the arm had little effect against the enemies who corralled him within their midst.

Out of breath and at the point of exhaustion, Borvis took a final look around. More of the undead creatures had arrived, about five or six , and still more approached.

He raised his weapon again, but before he could strike a blow, multiple hands seized him and began ripping, tearing, pulling him apart.

As his blood flowed more freely onto the plain, Borvis had two final thoughts.

*What happened to Darton?*

*And I hope he got away…*

Darton could hear some sort of commotion in the distance. It sounded like a fight.

He quickened his pace.

As he neared, he heard more noises. It sounded as if Borvis called out his name, then cried for help, but the words had been too faint to be certain. Darton grabbed his ax as the eastern edge of the graveyard finally came into sight.

Where he found a sight that stopped him dead in his tracks.

Five zombies, each armed with scythes, huddled around something on the ground. At first, Darton thought they had resurrected one of the dead vagha soldiers, reanimated it, and added it to their ranks.

But as the collected zombies slowly parted, Darton was hit with the awful, gut-wrenching truth. The thing in the middle of the group was Borvis, and by the way he'd fallen to the ground when they let him go, he was already dead.

Darton slumped to the ground, then found cover behind a rock where he watched in horror as the zombies mulled around Borvis's body, poking at it with their fingers and sniffing it with their half-rotted noses.

Blood trickled from a wound in Borvis's chest and his helm had been caved in, suggesting the same was done to the skull beneath it. A look of desperation had frozen Borvis's face—no doubt he'd put up a good fight against the five of them—but his eyes were mercifully closed. At least his soul wouldn't have to witness the mockery being made of his flesh. And, for whatever it was worth, it appeared that his death had come quickly.

Darton sighed. *Small consolations,* he thought.

As he watched one of the zombies grab a tuft of Borvis's long hair in order to drag him back across the plain, Darton felt his blood boil at the sight of his long-time friend and battle-mate being treated with such disrespect.

He vowed then and there that he would not rest until every last one of the vile creatures was destroyed.

*But how do you kill something that's already dead?*

He gritted his teeth at the thought. Whatever it took to kill them, he vowed not to rest until it was done to every last one of them. But revenge would come later on the battlefield. For now, his job was to get back to Warlord Adelric in Dehnlee and warn him of the approaching invaders.

He remained crouched behind a rock to watch Borvis being dragged away. Then, when there was enough distance between him and the zombies, Darton ran across the graveyard to the waiting ponies.

Darton quickly untied his pony and left in such a hurry

that he didn't even untie Borvis's pony. He felt bad about it, but Darton refused to stay a moment longer in that cursed place.

Before he rode away, he took one final look behind him.

The zombies were nearly out of sight, their images obscured by the cloud of smoke-like mist that drifted across the plain.

"Don't worry, Borvis," he vowed. "They will pay for your death a hundred times over!"

The zombies disappeared far behind him on the plain."

Darton took a deep breath, and rode hard all the way back to the city, aiming straight for Carlin Park.

## CHAPTER ELEVEN

The doors to the war room burst open. Darton ran inside. He was out of breath, his clothes disheveled, and his face pale, as if he'd lost most of his blood on the ride over.

"Warlord Adelric!" he cried. "An army approaches!"

The assembled dwarves looked at the scout with a mix of surprise and fear, then made a spot for him at the edge of the table. The scout sat down and took several moments to catch his breath.

When Darton had calmed and seemed able to speak, Adelric questioned him. "What of this army?" he said. "What have you seen?"

"Standish..." he began, still winded.

"—did you find him—"

"—is he all right—" the questions came too quickly for Darton to answer.

Adelric put up his hand to silence the others.

"Yes and no," said Darton. "Yes, we found him, but no, he's not all right."

"What happened to him?" asked Adelric, who had made it clear he would be handling the interrogation from this point on.

"He was killed by zombies—"

Several of the dwarves in attendance gasped or muttered *"What?"* beneath their breath.

"There are undead on the plain, apparently coming from the northeast. They must have come upon Standish when he was working. They killed him."

"Are you sure of this?"

Darton nodded.

"How do you know?"

Darton took one final, deep breath. "I know because he was one of the undead that killed Borvis." Darton slumped forward in his chair and the room erupted in a cacophony of voices, all wanting to know what in Tarvanehl's name was going on.

Slowly, Darton told them what he'd witnessed. He told them of the disturbed graves, of the stench wafting across the plain, of the arm found crawling over the earth on its own accord, and of the undead who brutally killed Borvis and dragged his body away.

"There were too many of them," said Darton. "I couldn't have done anything for him, and besides that, he was already dead..."

Adelric placed a hand on Darton's shoulder and gave it a gentle squeeze.

"All right, young warrior," he said. He turned to two of the other dwarves in the room. "Take him to the barracks and see that he gets some rest."

"Yes, milord," they answered in unison.

Darton got up to leave the war room, but before he left, he turned and looked at Adelric with an expression of sorrow. It barely masked the rage and anger that roiled there.

"Don't worry, Darton," Adelric said, before the young scout had a chance to speak. "You will have the opportunity to avenge Borvis's death. You have my word. We will not leave you behind when the fighting starts."

Darton nodded, then left the room with the two dwarven escorts.

After he was gone, the war room went silent for several minutes. At last, Sergeant Cadman spoke, "What do you think it means, milord?"

"I think," said Adelric cautiously, "that there is an army amassing on the plains, the likes of which we have never seen before."

The room fell once again silent and remained that way for a long, long time.

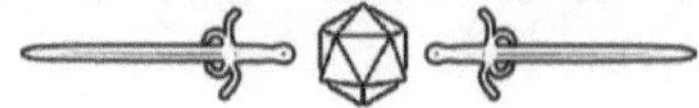

Adelric stood at the window of the war room that overlooked the grounds of Carlin Park, watching the army gathering into ranks. They were good, strong warriors, but the looks on their faces told him they were weary. It was too soon to fight again. They needed rest, time to enjoy the peace they'd so bravely fought for. Time to plant crops and make baby dwarves. Time to remember why fighting was sometimes so necessary.

Although he would never let such an emotion show, Adelric was terribly worried over this latest turn of events. He had wanted to begin sharing some of the responsibilities of leadership with Cadman, but he didn't see how that was possible when none of them knew much about this new and terrible enemy.

Had it been a marauding band of morehl, or an army of trogs, he could have easily told Cadman to take charge and lead the vagha forces into battle, but this? If what Darton had said was true, then this wasn't simply another battle. It was a nightmare come to life.

Hopefully, the battle wouldn't last long.

To that end, Adelric had called for Carswell Adar to bring him his most recent map of the lands surrounding Dehnlee. Perhaps it might help in their fight. That way, they could know where the undead had originally come from and what—if anything—was the source of their power.

Carswell Adar entered the war room slowly, a single map tucked under his arm. Gone were the flamboyant robes and the haughty air.

He knew the vagha prepared for war and conducted himself accordingly.

"I have the map you asked for, milord," he said, and lay the roll on the long stone table in the center of the room. When the map was completely unfurled, he took four flat and polished stones from his pockets and set them over the corners to make sure the map wouldn't curl.

Adelric and the others in the room looked at the map in silence for several long moments, while Carswell Adar stood by, anxiously awaiting their comments and questions.

"What's this?" asked Adelric.

"What's what?" asked Carswell Adar.

"This!" Adelric jabbed the tip of his index finger against a section of the map. *"Here be Dragons?"* he said, a slight fluctuation in his voice. "What is *that* supposed to mean? "

Carswell Adar cleared his throat and said, "I don't know."

"What!"

"It means, *'I don't know.'"*

"How can that be?"

"I don't know what's there," said Carswell Adar, sighing as if in apology for letting the warlord down. "Few who've ventured that far east of Dehnlee have ever made it back alive. And those who have returned have simply said that bad and evil things lurk there. That's hardly enough for a mapmaker to draw out an area so I designated it an uncharted region that's best avoided. Hence, 'Here be Dragons!'"

"Wonderful," said Adelric, unable to keep the sarcasm from his voice. Privately, he thought, *now at least I know where this strange army comes from.*

Renata, Peregrine, and two dozen undead soldiers moved silently through the graveyard, inspecting the terrain.

"There are more dead bodies here," said Peregrine. "Vagha soldiers, no doubt. Many of them laid to rest reverently."

Renata looked giddy with excitement. "More dead," she laughed. "More loyal soldiers." She inspected a few of the corpses that Peregrine's minions pulled from their dirt wombs. Many had been buried in their armor, which would only further Renata's purposes.

She turned her gaze, studying her surroundings as if she suspected something was wrong but hadn't figured out what.

"What?" asked Peregrine at last. "What is it?"

"Over there!" She pointed to the spot where Borvis's pony was still tethered to the tree."

"It's the pony belonging to the dwarf our patrol brought back."

Renata was quickly on the move, headed toward the animal, her eyes scanning the ground as she moved.

Peregrine followed, wondering what she was looking for. As he neared the tree, it became obvious to him. There were many hoof prints on the ground around the tree, some even outside the ring created by the tether.

Searching around the tree, it became clear that two ponies had come from Dehnlee, but only one remained, meaning a second soldier had ridden back to the city to warn the citizens there of the undead presence.

They had lost the element of surprise.

"There!" Renata said, pointing to a set of tracks leading away from the tree.

"l see it," answered Peregrine, turning back around to face the graveyard.

"Start digging them up!" he commanded the troops. "Quickly! As many as you can."

The undead soldiers quickly dug up the graves of fallen vagha. In no time, there were dozens of bodies piled onto the back of Peregrine's cart drawn by a skeletal steed. "What do you want me to do about the pony?" asked Peregrine.

"Kill it," Renata growled. "Feed it to our army to stoke their hunger."

A zombie nearest it swung a scythe with a curling sort of motion so that the sharp point of the curved blade pierced the pony's body just behind the front flank.

There was a sharp crack of bone, the pony whinnied, and blood began to flow along the length of the wicked blade, spinning off the end connected to the handle and falling to the ground like rain. The animal staggered once before falling with a thud, the heavy impact with the ground causing the beast's final breath to discharge from its lungs in a whoosh.

The zombies nearest the dead animal moved closer with ravenous intent.

And feasted.

Preparations continued on the grounds of Carlin Park, with Adelric and his officers trying to find out more about the enemy they would soon face.

The door to the war room opened once more and the scholar and chief librarian, Kelda Whare, entered the room with several large tomes.

Adelric had asked her to find anything she could in reference to the undead. Although the vagha of Dehnlee had never confronted such a foe, perhaps some of the volumes in the shared vaghan histories made some reference to them.

Kelda was an elderly looking dwarf, although no one was sure how old she really was. She had served as scholar and chief librarian under three different warlords and that was almost the same as having the position since the beginning of time. Hence her input and advice on matters was not to be taken lightly.

She dropped the books on the table in the center of the room and nodded to the dwarves in greeting.

"Thank you for coming so quickly, Kelda," said Adelric.

"It's always my pleasure to serve, milord."

"Have you found out anything about these undead creatures that Darton claims to have seen?"

"He's seen them all right," said Kelda, her eyes widening as if to say, *Don't make the mistake of doubting the soldier's words again.* "And since he's seen them, it's a good chance they've seen him. And if that's the case, it is likely they are headed toward Dehnlee."

"Do you have some references?"

Kelda nodded, pulled one of the leather-bound volumes toward her, and opened it to a page marked by a red ribbon. "This is from the third volume of the shared histories," she said, as she rested a pair of small lenses on the bridge of her wrinkled nose. "It comes from the account of a dwarf named Almen, who observed them far south of Dehnlee in Charnock, across the bay."

She looked down at the book, cleared her throat with a cough, and began reading:

"There is no racial name for the undead. They are simply the bodies of those killed in battle, bloodless yet restored to some hideous semblance of life by the powers of Death." She paused and looked up a moment, perhaps to see the reaction of those in the room, before continuing,. "They are experts with death magic, drawing magic from only their one god, Death, much like an acolyte who has forsaken all other gods." She cleared her throat and then read Almen's account of hacking a creature down. It had kept coming for him. Coming even after its legs had been chopped off. Writhing after him in pursuit, even after its arms had been severed.

Several whispered mutterings floated around the room as the dwarves realized how dangerous this opponent could be.

Once the voices died down, Kelda read on, "They moved slowly, but their toughness made them formidable. I fought against my friend, Keddel sa'Ginner of clan Nervin and was forced to chop off his head. Keddel had been our best marksman, but he lost that skill when the black power took him—yet it gave him the unnerving strength and the determination to kill all that he loved. The only way we found to effectively deal with the army was massive amounts of fire. They fought even as they burned; they fought until they'd turned to ash and finally collapsed."

She stopped reading and looked up.

"Is there anything else?" asked Adelric, hoping to find an easier solution on how to defeat them.

"I'm afraid not," said Kelda.

"It's not much to go on, is it?" said Adelric.

"No, it's not," answered Kelda. "But when you defeat them, I'll be able to add the newfound knowledge to the shared histories for the benefit of future generations."

Adelric found her confidence flattering. He only hoped it was merited. "Will you keep searching the histories for more?"

She flashed him a look of irritation and Adelric realized he'd offended her by suggesting there might be some reference in her collection that she did not know about. Still, she answered him politely, bowing deeply as she spoke, "Of course, milord. I will continue to look, but I make no promises of finding anything more."

"And neither do I ask for any," he answered humbly.

"It's too bad they've been alerted to our presence," said Renata as she rode the skeletal steed toward their base at Boland Marsh. The *new* Boland Marsh. Something in Renata's person resonated with the place where goblins had once worshiped the Death god. The marsh had spread, stretched, as if reaching out to rejoin the festration that went wherever the heucuva did.

The new bog now stretched from the long-time stronghold of the deceased Boland goblins to the edge of the plain where Renata's army of the dead stood and waited for her command.

"We could always turn the army in another direction," said Peregrine, riding alongside Renata on a skeletal beast of his own. "There are morehl in Garnock and humans in Xlinea. Neither of them seems aware of our army's existence." He paused a moment to see if Renata commented on his reference to the army as "theirs," but Renata said nothing, seemingly preoccupied with other matters. "We don't have to attack the vagha if you think the cost would be too high. Now that you have ascertained its purpose, we could wait for the perfect timing—think tactically."

Renata laughed at that, a mocking sort of laugh that made Peregrine feel small and silly. "You fool. You're talking as if you command a living, breathing army. These soldiers are already dead. What do we have to lose by sending them against the best that the vagha, or any race, has to offer?"

Peregrine remained silent, still smarting from her insulting laughter.

She answered the question for him. "Nothing." She grinned. "We have nothing to lose, because they are already dead."

"Then why the concern over them knowing we're here?"

She took a moment to consider the question. "If they know we're here, what should our strategy be? Success is a foregone conclusion, but how can we be sure to kill as many as possible before the cowards escape?"

"If you're not worried about casualties," Peregrine said. "Your strategy is simple; send all of them in at once."

Renata narrowed her eyes to slits as she stared in the direction of Dehnlee. "That's what I planned to do." The heucuva steered her rotted beast towards the city, intent on taking it around the steeper slope that led over the graveyard. She knew her zombies and animated skeletons would fare better through the gentler grade, where the vagha had fought the morehl nearly a month prior. They would use the same route—a road that led directly to Dehnlee's eastern doorstep.

"The troops are ready for your inspection, milord," said Sergeant Cadman.

Cadman stood in the doorway of the war room, his armor polished, and his helm pulled tight against his skull, ready for battle. He looked eager to confront the enemy and anxious to repel the invading hordes.

Adelric was familiar with that look, and the feeling that went with it—a willingness to take on the world with the belief that you were utterly invincible no matter what the circumstances. He'd had it once, long ago. But years of war and devastating personal loss had dulled it--erased it from his emotional repertoire. Adelric was still warlord, still in command, but if the truth be told, knowledge of this loss was partly why he knew he must soon give up that title.

"Very well, sergeant, I'll be right there."

Cadman went back outside to await Adelric. In the meantime, the aging warlord hitched up his waistband, adjusted the ax therein, and gently placed his horned helm upon his head. He took a breath and went outside to inspect the troops.

The sun was shining brightly overhead, and it seemed a day better suited to a picnic than the start of another war. After one last adjustment to his breastplate, he walked onto the grounds where Sergeant Cadman waited.

"Since we aren't sure exactly where these undead soldiers will come from," said Cadman. "I decided to split our forces into two groups."

Adelric nodded. "Tell me what you had in mind."

"These soldiers," said Cadman, indicating the larger group on the left, "are probably the stronger of the two. They have the most battle experience and are all well-rested."

*An important consideration,* Adelric noted.

"I suggest you take them as the forward army, milord," Cadman said, knowing he would be given the task of leading the other group while Adelric led the campaign. "I can make do with the others, and can offer reinforcements from their ranks if you need them. Otherwise, we will divide our attention in the rear by blocking any attack on Dehnlee and attempting to find an angle to flank the bastards."

Again, Adelric was impressed with Cadman's assessment of the threat. The only way they could overtake the city was if they broke through the forward army's ranks. That made it important that the campaign army have the best soldiers and leadership the vagha could put forth. Cadman's second army would provide a secondary line of defense and identify the weakest place to insert themselves into the fray. This tactic would also give them the greatest impact.

"I want you to lead the campaign," said Adelric, placing a hand on the young sergeant's shoulder.

Cadman's jaw dropped like a stone. He tried to speak, but no words came out. "I'm getting old, sergeant, and a lot of the fight has gone from my aging bones." He smiled. "You, on the other hand, are young and eager…Right now, while you're looking forward to a fight, I want only peace."

Cadman's eyes swept the ground, as if he were embarrassed by the thread of truth in Adelric's words.

"It's nothing to be ashamed of. I was the same way at your age, and you will be the same way at mine. I guarantee it."

Cadman dropped to one knee. "I'm honored, milord. I won't let you down."

"You don't have to worry about letting me down, just don't let down the vagha under your command. Treat them with respect and value their lives. If you do, they'll fight for you to the last swing of an axe."

"Thank you, milord," Cadman said, rising.

"Don't thank me," answered Adelric. "Not yet. You might want to curse me when it's over."

Cadman smiled, then turned to the group of soldiers on his left. "Let's move out!

## CHAPTER TWELVE

Sergeant Cadman had the forward army on the plain by mid-afternoon. Sol shone brightly in the cloudless sky and a warm breeze blew. It seemed a shame to waste such a day on battle, but Cadman knew that the better the conditions were, the better it was for his army. Inclement weather, with plenty of rain and fog, and muddy ground beneath their feet would only favor the undead.

When the army reached the graveyard, Cadman broke off from the main force and rode to inspect the grounds. Sure enough, the invaders had dug up many vagha soldiers and carted them off to either eat them or make them into undead creatures, turning them against their own kind. He had no idea which. As unsavory as the former thought was, he preferred it to the latter.

Cadman brought his pony to a pause and looked down into one of the gaping holes that had been left after the graves were emptied. He shook his head in dismay. He'd wanted to lead for a long while, but of all the campaigns to be given a command, why did it have to be this one? He looked into the empty grave for several more seconds, his gaze drawn down into it as if it were the void itself. And then, he let out a little laugh. *Careful what you wish for, Sergeant Cadman,* he thought. *You just might get it.*

"Sergeant Cadman!"

The voice came from some distance away.

"Sergeant Cadman!"

Cadman turned to see his footman, a gray-eyed young soldier named Flynn, running across the plain toward him.

"What is it?" asked Cadman as Flynn neared.

He was pointing eastward even before he'd stopped running and tried to speak before he'd caught his breath. "Just… o-over … that—" He paused to take a few deep breaths. "There's a line of u-undead approaching the city. Eastern road, same route as Garnock took."

"How many?"

"We saw them through a long-look so it's hard to say." Flynn gulped hard. "But it's a lot."

Cadman took a deep breath and clenched the reins tight in his fists. "All right, then," he said with a nod. "Let's go show these undead how unwelcome they are on the Wakefield Plain."

The vagha army began to fan out in preparation for the inevitable battle. They arrayed themselves so that the strongest soldiers had support from the troops with crossbows. Adelric took the remainder to form a buffer between the battlefield and the City of Dehnlee. Cadman had decided the missile troops would be firing first since they knew the undead had no range weapons. That meant the bowmen could fire at will without fear of retaliatory fire. That knowledge alone had done wonders for the army's morale.

But the sweet-smelling afternoon turned sour as the smell of death wafted across the plain, hanging on the air like a pall. The vagha fell silent when the stench stung their noses. Any smiles they had turned into stern grimaces.

The expressions on the front-line soldiers' faces changed once more, this time to masks of horror, as they saw for the first time the soldiers that made up the abominable army.

There walked a former goblin with its chest torn open and its rotting black heart dangling from the wound by a few gray-green arteries. Here was a long-dead lava elf walking with a severe lurch; one of his feet missing above the ankle. Next to that moved another morehl with half its stomach cut away, leaving one side of its spine exposed—no doubt the work of a finely honed vaghan ax.

It was an unbelievable sight.

Every one of the undead soldiers, every last one, had suffered some violently fatal wound. Yet here they were, moving toward the vagha. Walking across the battlefield as if they were merely wounded and making their way home after the war.

What worried Sergeant Cadman most was their eyes and their mouths. The eyes of each of the undead were simply glazed over balls of pure white with their mouths hanging open. Agape, the corners of their mouths pulled back into rictus grins that exposed rows of filthy, yellow teeth. The horrifying smiles never wavered, never changed, and likely would not ever, even while they fought the fiercest of battles with the vagha.

Cadman realized that his task was even more formidable than he'd first imagined. In addition to the large numbers the undead army possessed, they possessed a potent weapon: terror.

Pure and simple.

As Cadman looked away from the approaching army, he glanced at the faces of his soldiers. They all wore masks of horror, with their eyes opened wide and their mouths hanging open in silent screams. They had never seen anything so ghastly in their lives, not even in the heat of the bloodiest campaigns.

Cadman only hoped that they would be able to overcome their fears by the time the close up fighting began. If not, his soldiers might as well already be dead.

"Fire when ready!" Cadman commanded his

crossbowmen.

Almost immediately, the sharp twang of the crossbows rang out, and the battlefield was filled with the sounds of steel-tipped quarrels slicing through air.

Bolts streaked forward and hit their marks.

A zombie stumbled backward and fell on its back, clutching the shaft that had impaled its body. A second zombie was struck in the face, the arrow catching its open mouth, tearing its lower jaw from its face and embedding itself into the soft part of its neck. It fell to the ground.

Other zombies were hit, one after another—this one in the chest, that one in the shoulder, this one straight through the heart, another in the throat. On and on it went, with wave after wave of arrows *singing* through the air until each of the crossbowmen's flights had been exhausted. The soldiers on the front line looked out over the battlefield and saw their undead counterparts scattered about, appearing as if dead.

Helms flew into the air as the vagha army erupted in a raucous cheer.

But then, the undead rose up from the ground and began to walk once more, arrows jutting obscenely from their bodies, either whole or broken off at the point of entry as if the usually deadly projectiles were nothing more than simple annoyances.

The triumphant cheer died down as quickly as it had begun, and the battlefield filled with the sound of helms being secured and melee weapons being drawn. "Steady dwarves," ordered Cadman, his own hand shaking slightly with fear. "They may be undead, but we're sure they can still be killed."

But as he drew his ax from his waistband and guided his pony into a position to lead the vagha forces in a charge, Cadman found himself wondering exactly how to do that.

Renata rode atop her skeletal steed. The heucuva crested a hill where she could watch the initial engagement and join her minion, Peregrine, from that vantage point.

"How is our army doing?" Renata asked.

"Passing their first test," answered Peregrine. He gazed across the carnage and laughed contentedly.

There weren't as many undead soldiers as Cadman first feared. As he headed across the battlefield toward them, he realized there were scarcely more than a few dozen of the things waiting for his troops. Surely a portion of his army could defeat this ragtag collection of soldiers?

The sudden realization gave him hope. *Maybe this was all their numbers?*

He spurred his pony in the ribs and charged into battle, his ax at the ready. His companions in the cavalry raced behind him, ready to do some damage. About halfway to the enemy, he chose a suitable target. It was the lead zombie, a former morehl lumbering across the rocky ground with its rapier held out. Cadman approached the zombie from the opposite side as its sword arm and hoped to strike quickly, planning to mortally wound it on his first pass.

*Mortally wound it?* thought Cadman as he neared his prey. Not only did these bloodless creatures need to be killed in radically different ways, but the language used to describe their destruction needed to be rethought as well. Perhaps after it was done, the battle scholars could take up the task. For now, simply killing it before it killed him was all that mattered.

And he *would* kill it.

The pony acted oddly, with a strange kind of lilt to its gait. Cadman gripped the reins tighter, assuming that the beast feared the paranormal enemy as much as the dwarves did.

Cadman's pony took two more strides and suddenly he was upon the zombie, staring the stinking, rotted corpse in the face. With a swift swing of his arm, he brought his ax down onto the zombie, striking it squarely in the shoulder just below the neck. But the ax lodged between bones and as Cadman rode past, the ax handle remained where it was, ripped from his hand by the momentum of his pony.

After taking several strides to recover, Cadman looked back and saw the zombie continuing on, the ax still wedged in its shoulder, its rapier still raised and ready for battle.

"By the flame!" he cursed.

He glanced around, realizing he'd ridden right into the midst of the undead… where he planned to be. But in his plans, he still had his ax.

Darton had originally been assigned to the rear army. But although he could have used the rest, something burned deep inside of him. Darton traded places with a younger recruit, a newly-wed dwarf who had a bride to think about. The pair gladly traded posts.

Instead of guarding Dehnlee with the rest of the secondary army, Darton now found himself on the plain with the vanguard, more than eager to sink the blade of his ax into the rotting flesh of the invaders who had killed his friend and partner.

Darton had his ax drawn and at the ready, long before the call for battle was made. And when Sergeant Cadman called the order to charge, , Darton was the second to race across the battlefield and engage the enemy. First behind the Sergeant's small cadre of pony-riders.

He looked for the biggest target he could find. Darton confronted what looked to be a former goblin, although he couldn't be sure since most of the creature's face had been torn away, leaving the black splattered ivory of its skull exposed around the nose, cheek and forehead. The trog's normally ochre-hued blood had turned black, much like the reds of the dead human, morehl, and vagha. Simply looking at the enemy's disgusting visage was enough to make him want to kill it. Knowing that its kind had killed Borvis made it that much easier.

Darton attacked the zombie like a dwarf possessed. His battle ax whirled and chopped, swung and hacked. His first blows opened flesh, but did little to dissuade the zombie, though the action spilled its innards out and onto the ground.

The stench was palpable and nigh unbearable. He continued to strike at his enemy anyway, cutting it down at the knees as he might a tree, then taking swings at the zombie's rotting trunk.

Even in the midst of this brutal punishment, the undead soldier was able to swing its scythe and catch Darton in the upper thigh. He yelped in pain. It felt as if a red-hot poker had just jabbed into his flesh, but still, Darton continued the fight. It would take more than a mere flesh wound to stop him from killing these unsightly creatures.

He continued hacking away without pause until the enemy soldier lay in pieces before him.

Still, some of the dismembered pieces fought on, clawing toward him and trying to bring the scythe to bear.

In a fit of rage, Darton hacked and chopped until the once undead soldier was nothing more than a mottled gray and black stain on the rocky battlefield.

At last, he'd killed it.

And when he was done, Darton placed his hands on his knees and gasped for breath; his lungs heaved as if he'd just run across half of Esfah. How much energy had he expended in order to kill this one undead soldier?

Far too much.

So much that he was barely able to lift his ax.

He looked up and saw the battlefield dotted with dozens of the undead. Darton felt a strange sense of doom fall across him like a shadow.

The battle was fully underway now, and Cadman knew he had only a slim hope of getting back among his own troops.

As he turned to ride back across the battlefield—and hopefully retrieve his ax along the way—a sharp blow to the head knocked him from atop his pony. He braced himself for the hard landing he expected, but he was surprised to find that the ground was soft and wet. It even broke his fall.

Cadman looked up to see his pony galloping back towards Dehnlee, kicking up moist clods as it went. The spongy clods explained the mount's odd behavior; it was struggling to run upon the terrain that was slowly melting to mire. He turned his attention to the approaching enemy.

More and more of the fiends moved into view from around the hillock. There were all sorts: former goblins with stone axes, undead morehl with deadly rapiers, and several long-dead vagha approaching on shambling gaits. All consigned by the forces of Death to kill their own kind with no say in the matter, save the look of sorrow in their milky white eyes.

Though he'd lost his ax, a dwarf was rarely disarmed. Instead, Cadman pulled a dagger from his waistband. It was delicately balanced, easily concealed, and ideal for close hand-to-hand combat…or as an emergency weapon.

He had used it in battle only once before, when he and a goblin shaman had stumbled into a sink hole in the middle of the battlefield. Cadman surprised him by running him through with the dagger before he had the chance to cast a spell. Ever since, it had always been on his person, even when he was asleep. Without that dagger, he probably would've died.

Now, Cadman held the dagger before him and challenged the nearest opponent. As the first zombie approached, Cadman feinted left, then thrust to the right, catching the zombie off guard.

He jabbed at the zombie's partially exposed heart, stunning the creature before slashing it across the throat. The zombie fell, but Cadman had seen enough to know that the zombie's demise was only temporary. He quickly ran past the fallen creature and prepared for the next.

This one, like the first, was an undead goblin. But unlike the first, its right leg had been shattered by some weapon in its former life. It limped pitifully, moving with unrelenting fury all the same. Cadman watched it approach. Just as it came within striking distance, he darted behind it and stabbed it at the base of the skull, severing its spinal cord and causing it to topple like a crosscut maple.

As he watched it hit the ground, Cadman spotted the first of his victims slowly try to rise. He realized that the zombies weren't exactly formidable *fighters*. One-on-one, they could easily be taken down by any healthy vagha.

With the second fallen zombie lying at his feet, Cadman looked around the battlefield and saw that other soldiers were realizing the same thing he was. The zombies were easy to down, but nearly impossible to keep there.

It was quite possible that the vagha could keep the zombies at bay indefinitely, but they would eventually die of exhaustion in the process.

Cadman saw a clear path across the battlefield and took it. No longer afraid he'd be caught, he jogged back to the forward scouts he'd joined for the initial skirmish. When he hooked up with his clustered soldiers, he sent a messenger to bring up more forces.

Perhaps additional troops could turn the tide and overwhelm the slow-moving shamblers with the strength of vaghan steel.

"Estimate?" Renata barked.

"S-several hundred dwarves in the vanguard," Peregrine stammered.

Renata grinned wickedly from her perch where she watched the battle unfold. The fools brought their full army to bear and wasted their strength upon the trickle of minions she sent in to soak up the dwarves' vigor.

The enemy was stretched out with much space between them, moving more slowly than the regular zombies, but not quite so sluggish as to be useless.

"They do not see it, Peregrine," she cooed, congratulating herself for her brilliant tactics. "They will burn themselves out before realizing that all is lost. They think these paltry offerings are my real army."

She'd been sending in a paltry force to bait them into engagement and tire their forces with the expendable zombies who could soak up damage like a sponge. Renata cast a glance behind the hill where she'd hidden thousands of her loyal minions. They had yet to be noticed, and her distraction had worked perfectly.

Cadman's reinforcements helped for a while.

As the vagha army swelled in numbers, the dwarven soldiers beat down the undead. But the vile creatures continued to reassemble themselves. Cadman also noticed that two more arrived from over the hill whenever they managed to kill one.

It wasn't long before vagha soldiers began to fall from exhaustion.

Darton was the first.

How he had been assigned to the front army, Sergeant Cadman couldn't be sure, but it was no surprise that he was the first to fall. The soldier had been a wild thing on the battlefield, single-handedly killing off multiple enemies and—savaging them completely. He hacked them into such small pieces that they could never rise up again. But at what cost had those kills come?

Darton was wounded, slight wounds to be sure, but one could never guess about infection. Dwarves had died from mere scratches under the best of circumstances. There was no telling what would happen to a wound inflicted by a weapon wielded by something that was dead. And even without his wounds, Darton could no longer fight. He had expended so much energy killing a meager handful of opponents that he was unable to lift his ax, and likely wouldn't be able to do so for days to come.

And now, other dwarves were falling. Taking other soldiers out of the fight as they dragged their fellow vagha off the battlefield. The advantage the dwarves held upon the arrival of the reserves had slowly whittled away.

Sergeant Cadman considered his options.

He could, of course, bring in Warlord Adelric and the rest of the vagha from the second army, but that would leave Dehnlee undefended. It would show the warlord that he was unable to win a battle on his own. He could use magic against them, but he would have to surrender ground to do so, yielding the field while he pulled his troops to safety. He bit his lip.

Sergeant Cadman knew there was only one option left available to him: the arcane one. His mind strayed back to the account presented by Kelda Whare. *The southern dwarves had used fire to some success.*

"Footman Flynn!" he called.

"Yes, sergeant," came the reply as Flynn appeared before him.

"Gather the magic-corps," he said, almost as if in defeat.

Flynn let out a sigh and said, "Yes, sergeant."

Ruskin, the thaumaturgist who led those with arcane abilities, arrived not long after. At Cadman's direction, Ruskin conjured elemental forces, summoning fire from the forges of creation, and launched a fire bolt across the battlefield. It squarely struck the closest zombie in the chest. It stumbled momentarily and then continued walking. After a few paces, the thing's flesh burned off as the corpse fully immolated. Several paces later, the thing collapsed into a heap of charred bones.

"Fire," said Cadman. "Firiel's kiss is the answer." He looked sidelong at Ruskin.

The old thaumaturgist looked winded and returned a skeptical look. "I don't think you know how much energy that takes," Ruskin stated and pointed at the hordes stretching across the plain. "And that was only one of them!"

Cadman shook his head and locked eyes with the old spell crafter. "Fire is the answer...lots and lots of fire."

A knowing look lodged in Ruskin's eyes. A look that imparted both understanding, but also a dose of abject terror. He knew what Cadman was really after.

It was a strange feeling for Warlord Adelric—to know that war was raging and not be on its front lines. He could sense conflict in the distance. He couldn't exactly explain how he knew, but he had a definite feeling that the fighting was fierce and would endure for some time.

As he walked the line of soldiers set up along the eastern perimeter of Dehnlee, he almost felt like running to the battlefront. He wanted to swing his ax one last time and feel its blade against his enemies, cutting flesh and breaking bone.

Almost, but not quite. If Dorian's visit had reminded him of anything, it was that peace meant quelling that impulse. While battle was in his blood, the exhilaration he felt while engaged in combat wasn't enough to overshadow the sense of loss he experienced when one of those under his charge fell. That wouldn't happen anymore; not now he'd passed the torch to Cadman.

If Adelric was needed, he would rise to the call and fight alongside Sergeant Cadman as hard and as long as his aging bones allowed. But if he had his choice, he preferred to have Sergeant Cadman win the battle without him. If he never laid eyes upon one of the animated corpses Kelda Whare had told them about, all the better for him.

Which made him wonder…

He turned to the east, felt the sun's rays shining warmly on his face and helm, and scanned the horizon for a sign of how the battle went, but couldn't find one.

Ruskin's magic-users gathered atop a hill where they had a vantage of the vale below. Together, they tapped upon their innate mystic abilities and conjured a corporate pool of magic. Functioning as one, they delved into a distasteful form of magic. Wyrm craft was largely looked down upon because of its penchant for raw, destructive power. Magic was typically surgical in its precision, but dragon summoning flung open the gates to chaotic forces of elemental magic.

Word quickly spread through the ranks that a fire drake was on its way.

Sergeant Cadman had considered the risks of calling a dragon so close to the city. There was no guarantee that the summoned dragon would attack only the opposing army, or that it would attack them at all. Given the nature of the undead, he found the risks acceptable. If all went according to Sergeant Cadman's plan, the vagha would be able to slip away from the battlefield while the undead were left standing out in the open: a prime target for the drake's fiery breath.

And so, with the battle still raging on the plain, the theurgists completed the spell to summon a fire drake. Somewhere in the distance, under Ruskin's command, a fire drake emerged into being.

Whether or not dragons were living creatures was open to debate. Regardless, they were a terrible elemental force of nature. Much like a raging fire, the elemental dragon would attack and burn indiscriminately, serving no master. Not even the vagha who had brought it into the region.

When the magic-users finished their summoning ritual, they remained still and silent, listening to the wind for the beat of dragon wings. While others watched with naked eyes shaded from the sun by cupped hands, Sergeant Cadman scanned the clear blue sky with his long look. Not surprisingly, it was he who first caught sight of the winged terror.

And what an awesome sight it was.

The drake appeared as a magnificent crimson beast, with great bat-like wings and short muscular arms ending in long, slender hands. They featured talons rather than fingers. But as impressive as its arms and wingspan were, its head was by far its most terrifying feature of all. Its long snout ended in a hooked point, capped by two flaring nostrils that seemed to glow orange red with each great breath it took. Further back from its maw were a pair of angry eyes that burned with a white-hot intensity that could blind those foolish enough to make eye-contact with the beast. From the back of the drake's head grew a pair of long, thick, and slightly curved horns. These horns rose up from a sort of thorny crown of jagged spikes and looked as if they could impale any lesser beast with a single flick of its head.

Cadman was so enthralled by the sight of the drake that several seconds passed before he sounded the warning to his soldiers on the battlefield.

When he realized his mistake, he quickly pulled the long-look from his eye and began waving it frantically over his head. He turned toward the battlefield and called out as loud as he was able, "Fire drake from the north!" The dwarves on the battlefield paused a moment, breaking off their fight to look in Cadman's direction.

"Fire drake on the way!" he shouted, placing his hands around his mouth so his voice would carry better. "In from the north! Run for cover!"

The vagha soldiers suddenly turned from their opponents and fled the fight, scattering in all different directions and one-by-one disappearing from sight. It was an odd spectacle, like the scurrying of spiders and other creepy crawlers at the first hint of light.

As the vagha soldiers ran for cover, the undead meandered about with nearly aimless purpose. Each of them looked about, almost dumbfounded; with their enemy suddenly nowhere to be seen, they floundered, directionless.

Cadman could hear the drake's wings slicing through the air and knew it was time that he too dove for cover. But as he headed for shelter, he noticed several of his soldiers still searching for somewhere safe to hide. They sprinted from point to point on the battlefield, only to find there was nowhere to go. And they had to hide. Nothing attracted dragon fire quite so well as one who fled the field.

One soldier in particular caught Cadman's sight. A footman ran frantically toward an outcropping of rocks on the outer edges of the battlefield. He was almost to safety when the drake suddenly swooped down upon him and dumped a blast of its hot breath. The flames fulminated him as he ran, incinerating the poor soldier with draconic fury.

The dwarf continued running, his body a mass of flames. After staggering a few steps, he fell to the ground in a ball of fire that consumed him like tinder wood.

Cadman's heart fell into the pit of his stomach. The drake continued over the battlefield, scorching and burning indiscriminately, attacking undead and vagha alike. The only difference was that the undead were easy targets, standing out on the open plain, while the vagha darted from refuge to refuge. Many found shelter enough to hide completely from view.

In seconds, the entire battlefield had been scorched by the drake. The undead soldiers burned brightly. As the methane and other gases created by the decomposition of their bodies burned in flames, they flickered in all the colors of the rainbow.

Cadman watched for another few seconds, then found himself having to dive for cover behind the base of a large rock.

As he hit the ground, he felt his body buffeted by a great gust of wind; a blast of heat like a worked forge followed it.

Searing heat.

Hotter than he could ever imagine.

It lasted only a few seconds, but they seemed like an eternity.

Then, suddenly, all was quiet.

And the warm summer breeze felt like ice against his skin.

"They've summoned a dragon," said Renata, from atop her steed, where she remained well back from the battle.

"What color is it?" asked Peregrine, desperately searching the sky but unable to locate it.

"Red," said Renata.

"A fire drake."

"Yes," hissed Renata. Then she let out a laugh. "They must be desperate."

"Should we summon a black dragon? I would love to witness a dragon battle."

"No," snapped Renata.

"But—"

"I said no!"

Peregrine opened his mouth to speak, but decided better of it, and closed it again without saying a word.

And then, Renata and Peregrine watched as their forces were wiped out by the drake. The zombies were incinerated en masse by its hot, angry breath.

The drake made several passes over the battlefield, leaving behind lumps of smoldering heaps that had once been undead soldiers. The beast's wake turned the battle-field black with ash.

"Well," said Peregrine. "That battle's over."

"Yes," said Renata. "Now, we wait and give the stupid dwarves a chance to celebrate their victory." She said the last word as if it tasted bitter on her tongue.

"And then what?"

"And then, we take it away from them." She grinned wickedly. "By bringing in the real army."

Silence followed the fire drake's final pass over the battlefield.

It swooped down one last time, then streaked skyward and headed into the distance as Ruskin and his dwarven casters used their same magic to repel the beast, sending it into the distance to some other land.

The surviving vagha soldiers crawled out from under their rocks, crags, and whatever other sanctuary they had found. They looked around, spotted the scorched earth, the charred and smoldering bodies of the undead, and shouted a cheer.

"Hurrah! Hurrah!"

Sergeant Cadman took in the scene. From what he could tell, almost all of his soldiers had survived the attack. Most of the casualties were minor, with few exceptions. If the casters still remained strong enough, they could use those same arcane abilities to heal the wounds of their countrymen.

The sergeant started down the hill toward the battlefield to better assess the damage. At the base of the hill, he was met by Footman Flynn, who survived the attack unscathed.

"Report!" ordered Sergeant Cadman.

Flynn took a breath, coughed on the smoke that still hung heavy over the battlefield, and then made his report. "It looks as if we lost thirteen, Sergeant. All of them were too far gone to revive."

Cadman sighed, feeling the loss of his fellow soldiers like a heavy stone on his chest. He wondered if that feeling would ever go away, or if it would continue to gain weight until he ended up like Warlord Adelric—left without the heart to do battle any longer. He could scarcely imagine it.

For the first time, Cadman began to understand how someone like the warlord could get his fill of war.

"Very well," said Cadman at last. "Get a detail together to transport the bodies back to the graveyard."

Flynn nodded. "Yes, Sergeant!"

"Is there anything else?"

"We counted the bodies of the undead. We think there may be more."

"A couple of escaped and charred zombies shouldn't pose too much of a problem."

"No, Sergeant," Flynn said, the words coming slowly this time, almost in hesitation.

Cadman recognized the change in the footman's voice and felt compelled to inquire about it. "Is something wrong?"

"It all seemed too easy," Flynn stated. "The numbers don't add up."

Cadman's first reaction was to shout out, *Too Easy!* but he knew that winning any battle while only suffering minor casualties was indeed a battle quite easily won. He thought about the comment for a moment—as he knew Warlord Adelric would have done in this situation—then decided to ask further questions of the footman. "What makes you think it was too easy? What do you mean about the numbers not adding up?"

"Well, we summoned a red dragon. The obvious thing that our enemy should have done was summon a dragon of their own to negate it. A black dragon would have fought a red drake."

Cadman nodded. "Yes, go on."

"Well, they didn't summon one. Instead, whoever is leading this undead army just let them get wiped out. Who does that…and *why*?"

Cadman considered this, his stomach turning. Flynn was right. The dragon had been unopposed, and since it must have required a considerable amount of magic to create such a large army of undead soldiers, the ability to summon a black dragon would surely be within the enemy's power.

Whoever the enemy was…

"Yes," said Cadman. His stomach continued to sour as he thought about Flynn's words. *It doesn't add up.* Cadman bit his lip as he wondered, *how many vagha died in the war against Garnock? We didn't see so many in this skirmish—and how many trog and morehl casualties had fallen on the plains? Surely there must be more enemies somewhere.*

Flynn nodded to Cadman, then turned to collect the bodies of those who had fallen in the attack. He hadn't gone a half-dozen paces before a call came from one of the soldiers. He had been sent out in pursuit of the undead who might have gotten away.

"Sergeant Cadman!" cried the soldier, waving his arms frantically over his head.

"What is it?"

The soldier hesitated, looked back across the plain, then simply said, "You better come here!"

Cadman set out across the battlefield and then up the hill to where the soldier had been positioned. Even before he reached the crest of the hill, he had his long-look out and extended. By the time he arrived at the top, he was out of breath and found it hard to hold the long-look steady.

But it didn't matter.

Steady or not, he could see it clearly.

It looked as if the earth flowed freely, like molten black lava wound across Wakefield Plain. At first, Cadman thought it was some sort of terrain movement, like the odd spreading of marsh. But then, he extended the long-look to its full length, and for the first time in his life, he felt his knees go weak with fear.

It wasn't terrain movement at all.

It was a troop movement.

Scores of zombies marched westward. Thousands of them, moving in a ragged, yet fluid line, like a swarm of ants crawling toward a drop of honey on the kitchen floor.

But there was no honey on this trail.

This trail led directly to the battlefield, where an army of vagha soldiers waited—thoroughly exhausted and vastly outnumbered.

## CHAPTER THIRTEEN

With their wounded gathered, the vagha forces in the vanguard regrouped and Sergeant Cadman led them away from the battlefield. It wasn't a retreat—they had won the battle after all—but rather a respite that would give them time to reorganize, assess their position, and develop a new strategy to attack this second encounter.

Judging by the distance the undead army was from the battlefield, it would likely take several hours for them to reach a critical engagement distance—the point at which they had to fight them or risk them pressing into the city. By then it would be dark. That was likely a tactical move by whoever, or whatever, controlled the fiendish forces.

Sergeant Cadman made sure the wounded were taken care of, and that the rest of the troops had enough to eat and drink, before leaving the forward army to report to Warlord Adelric. He was no doubt eager for news of the battle.

Footman Flynn accompanied Cadman on the venture. He decided on a small party for several reasons, not the least of which was that he fully expected the warlord to strip him of command for his poor performance on the Plain. Cadman didn't want any more of his soldiers to witness that kind of catastrophe. Whatever fate awaited Cadman, he remembered the very real threat approaching Dehnlee; one that had to be met as quickly as possible. Cadman only cared that it was dealt with effectively and swiftly.

Riding hard, Cadman and Flynn were spotted well

before they reached the outer walls of the city's defenses. As they approached, a trio of riders came out to meet them. When they finally met up with the riders, rather than give polite greetings, their faces contorted into looks of disgust.

"And a hello to you, too," said Cadman sarcastically.

"Greetings, Sergeant," said the lead rider, taking a breath through his mouth. "We don't mean to be disrespectful, but there's a foul stench about you."

Sergeant Cadman sniffed at his arms, but could smell nothing out of the ordinary. That didn't mean he didn't stink, however; his nose had gone blind to the stench of the undead. He looked over at Flynn and realized that not only was he filthy from a roll through the dirt during the worst of the fighting, but that he'd also been splattered with flecks of rotting flesh and decaying gore. The smell of the undead had become *their* smell, too, and it would take some time yet before they were rid of it.

"Better get used to it," said Cadman. "There won't be any avoiding it in the next couple of days."

The riders from Dehnlee looked none too happy at the prospect, wrinkling their noses at Cadman and Flynn as they turned to lead them into the city.

Sergeant Cadman and Footman Flynn entered the war room, where Warlord Adelric and several top officers waited. The room grew silent as they entered.

Cadman looked at the warlord's face and tried to read it, but it remained as impassive as the stone wall behind him. He couldn't be sure of his fate, but he suspected the worst… surely he already knew of the casualties and the rash decision to invoke dragon magic.

"Sit down," said the warlord.

Cadman pulled a chair away from the table and sat. He was unsure if he should speak, but decided it best to remain quiet until Adelric spoke first.

"Well," sighed Adelric. "What happened?"

"I was forced to summon a drake. I remembered Kelda's report that fire was—"

Adelric raised his hand to cut Cadman off mid-sentence. "I saw the drake in the sky," he said. "That was the end of the battle. I want to know what happened at the beginning."

Cadman nodded. He swallowed to moisten his parched throat and gave a full report. When Cadman finished, Warlord Adelric said nothing for a long time. Instead, he rubbed his aged hands together and interlocked his thick fingers as if contemplating the sergeant's fate. Finally, he looked over at Cadman and sighed. "I'm satisfied that you did everything you could under the circumstances," he said. "It was a bold and dangerous move to summon a fire drake and should only be used as a last resort. But from what you've told me, it sounds as if it was your only chance to end the battle, given the knowledge that you had at the time."

"It was, milord," Cadman said. "And thank you."

Warlord Adelric pretended not to hear. "Just don't make dragons a regular part of your arsenal. They're too unpredictable to be summoned on anything remotely resembling a regular basis. Especially so close to home."

His voice had a hint of a scolding tone to it.

"Yes, milord."

"Now, about this approaching army of the dead. If it's as big as you say, there's little point in sitting back defending Dehnlee when we'll need everything we have to meet it on the plain."

Cadman was struck by the warlord's choice of words. If he wasn't mistaken, he'd said, "We'll need everything we have," as if inferring they would be commanding the combined army together—almost as equals—even while the warlord moved up to the front as the highest-ranking officer there.

When Cadman failed to comment, Warlord Adelric prodded him with a question. "What do you think?"

Cadman nodded, still somewhat stunned. "Yes, absolutely."

"Good." The warlord nodded. He raised his head to address the others around the war room table. "Prepare the troops. I want to start moving in twenty minutes. Send word to every dwarf with any training and skill. Citizen soldiers are being called up to duty. This new threat is too large for the regular military to handle on its own."

Several of the soldiers got up from the table without saying a word, then hurried out the door to carry out their orders. Once they'd left, Adelric turned to his advisers, especially to Cadman. "Now," said Warlord Adelric in a low and serious tone. "You've faced the undead in combat. Besides calling in another fire drake, how do we kill them?"

"I don't know," said Cadman with a slight shake of his head. "I really don't know.

Warlord Adelric nodded slowly in understanding. "That's just what I was afraid of." He absentmindedly thumped the book he'd borrowed from the aged librarian and hoped that, like the southern dwarves, they'd figure something out.

The rear army was on the move within the hour. Warlord Adelric and Sergeant Cadman led the procession, bringing fresh troops to the front while there was still some daylight left.

With the sun slowly descending, surely no army would be reckless enough to attack the dead at dusk? No, the enemy would wait until morning; they would have to retreat precariously close to the city.

Wearied soldiers tried to wash the stench of death from their bodies. Many of them had a meal of coneys and beans while scouts kept a close eye on the movements of the undead in the east.

As Adelric and Cadman made plans, a scout named Assandro hurried to meet them. "You have something to report?" asked Cadman.

"Yes, Sergeant," he said. "They seem to have made camp for the night."

"What do you mean, 'seemed to?'" asked Adelric.

"They just stopped where they were. No fires, no meals … It doesn't even look as if they'll be sleeping. They're just …standing there."

"They probably don't need sleep or food," said Adelric.

"Or nourishment, or warmth," added Cadman. "Or any of the other basic necessities required by every other army on the face of Esfah."

Adelric turned to face Cadman. "You sound so positive, Sergeant. Perhaps we should ride into their camp now and surrender, thereby avoiding a messy battle in the morning."

Cadman sighed, realizing the warlord was right. Negative talk—however true—had no place among the commanders. "My apologies, Warlord."

Adelric ignored the apology and addressed the patroller. "I want multiple sentries watching them all night long. You announce the call to battle as soon as there is movement."

"Yes, warlord," Assandro said, spinning on his heels and hurrying back to inform the sentries under his command.

As he watched Assandro leave, Cadman felt compelled to speak. "Warlord, I'm—"

Again, Warlord Adelric lifted his hand. "Never mind that. We have a strategy to prepare."

Cadman realized that his remark had already been forgotten and it would be best to move on rather than dwell upon it. "Yes, milord," he said.

Across the bay in Galatea, Dorian watched the waters of Delmara Bay roil and churn until well after sundown. After hours of observation, it became more and more obvious that there was a pattern to the waves. It seemed as if one set of waves came from the north while another moved west across the bay.

Now, the only question was what could be the source of these patterns? Some fell portent, perhaps? Regardless of whatever the source turned out to be, their points of origin were certainly less of a mystery.

The northern waves seemed to curl southward, suggesting they originated along the northern shore of the Dehnlee Peninsula. And the west-moving waves began just off the coast of Dehnlee, making it painfully obvious that some sort of geographic upheaval happened on the peninsula. If that was the case, then perhaps Adelric and the people of Dehnlee could be in danger.

The thought of it quickened Dorian's heart.

With darkness falling, he decided he would make the trip at first light.

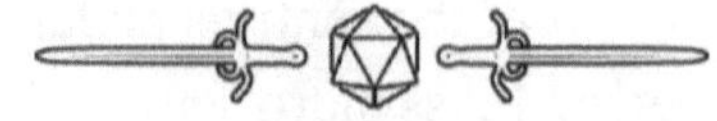

Although the sentries kept a close watch on the undead army, the dwarves kept their fires low in anticipation for swift action.

Small fires clotted around the vagha camp. Four or five soldiers huddled around each one, talking over the day's battle and preparing themselves for what was sure to be a fierce fight in the morning. Those who had not been involved in the day's fray listened to tales from those who had.

"I've never come across such an adversary," a soldier said as he sharpened the heads of his crossbow bolts. "Never in my life have I seen my quarrels strike a target to such little effect."

"Aye, it was an unsettling sight to be sure," said another.

"And then when my ammunition was spent, I stabbed an undead creature a dozen times or more—the same one that I'd shot with my crossbow—and instead of dying, it just looked at me with those vacant, white eyes and that rotten, yellow-toothed smile." The crossbowman shivered. "I doubt the sight of it will ever leave my memory."

"And it doesn't help to know we'll only have to meet more of them in them in the morning."

The crossbowman moaned. "Did you have to remind me?" he complained.

The second bowmen watched the other rearranging his ammo. "Why are you wasting your time with that? You saw for yourself that our crossbows might as well throw pub darts for all the good they did today."

The first bowmen stopped what he was doing and turned to look at his companion. "The usual ones had no effect on them," he said, holding a quarrel balanced between his fingers. "But this won't be no ordinary missile."

He chanted a couple of lines of rhythmic words and syllables and the stone broadhead suddenly burst into flame. It burned hot with flame that turned deeply blue.

"By the flame!"

"Exactly," said the first bowman. "While I doubt we'll be calling in another fire drake, it doesn't mean we can't fight the filthy cretins with fire. We are vagha, after all."

The second bowman watched the arrow burn for several more seconds before the fire finally died out.

"Can you teach me that spell?" he asked.

"Sure," he nodded. "So long as the magic of Esfah remains strong, all vagha, children of the goddess Firiel, can channel her power. It is the nature of magic…even if I heard some rumor from Ruskin's casters that something seemed to disrupt it out there, today. Some kind of festration, or a dweomernull. But that won't stop us from trying." And he winked.

Warlord Adelric, Sergeant Cadman, and the other commanders gathered around the largest fire that burned at the rear of the vagha camp.

It was a strange feeling for Adelric. Usually in these situations, his younger brother Evan sat at his right-hand side.

Like the other vagha gathered in groups, the assembled dwarves surrounding Adelric were trying to figure out a way to defeat the undead, or at least hold them off long enough to learn some new strategy that might prove effective.

"Darton was able to kill a few of them, milord," reported Sergeant Cadman. "And when he left them for dead, they remained that way."

"Really," said Warlord Adelric, intrigued. He looked around the fire until he located the scout. "Darton, how was it done?"

"Not easily, milord. I can tell you that," replied Darton. His response caused a ripple of laughter to circulate the group. "At times I thought I was fighting a practice dummy made of straw and timber. I struck blows at the creature's legs—both of them—and at the thing's trunk. But other than it oozing a foul black puss, it wasn't anywhere near out of commission."

"And yet, you destroyed it in the end. How did you manage it?"

"It's their heads, milord … I think you have to hit them in the head," Darton offered.

The words were followed by a low rumble of voices.

"I never thought to strike there since it's such a more difficult target for delivering a clean blow—after all, most of them are a full head taller than we are, mostly humans, trogs, and morehl—but since I'd struck every other part of the thing's body, it was all that was left to me." He paused, as if mentally revisiting the day's efforts. "When the blow of my ax hit a zombie in the neck, it seemed to slow its reactions somewhat."

"And then it went down?" asked Adelric.

"No." Darton shook his head. "It took four or five blows to put one down. Cleaving strikes are difficult in a battle, as you know. But I practically had to behead it before the thing toppled over for good."

"It makes sense in a way," said Cadman. "I mean, if its heart isn't beating, what else could be keeping going? It has to be the head."

"That sounds like a good theory, but even without their heads, some of the things still fought on. It's something at the base of the skull. When I destroyed that part, the body finally stilled."

Warlord Adelric nodded at Darton. "Thank you, that's a great help." He turned to one of the patrollers sitting around the fire. "Spread the word through the ranks. Their heads are most vulnerable."

"Yes, milord," answered the patroller before turning and scurrying away.

Before he left earshot, Adelric called out, "And see if longer ax handles can be fashioned before morning."

The reply was faint. "Yes, milord."

"Now then," said Warlord Adelric. "What else do you think kills these undead?"

"Well, there was the fire drake."

Adelric gave a slight chuckle. "I doubt we could get away with calling another of those unpredictable beasts. Especially so soon after the first, and so close to Dehnlee—a second red dragon might attract the first back to us, and then we'd never be rid of the pair. The enemy will be on our doorstep by the time we engage again, and I'll not authorize wyrmcraft so close to home."

Sergeant Cadman looked around, checking the faces of those gathered about him, no doubt to see if any were passing judgment on him for the earlier decision.

None did.

"That's not what I meant, milord," Cadman said. "The fire drake was successful in killing them off, but we don't need to call one up to start a fire."

The fire in the center of the group bathed the faces of the dwarves in shades of orange, red, and yellow.

"Continue," said Adelric, somewhat sorry he'd dismissed Cadman so easily before.

"We are vagha—dwarves attuned to the elements of fire and earth, Firiel and Eldurim. Surely we can combat these undead with fire magic. They are dead, decomposing. Fire harms them. Perhaps we don't need to engage them directly?"

A chorus of murmurs and nods circled the central pyre.

"...I think the sergeant's got something there..."

"...They burned right up, they did..."

"…I've heard of some folk purifying their dead with fire, it might work on these ones too…"

Warlord Adelric nodded thoughtfully. Then, he turned to Sergeant Cadman and smiled. "You might be right, Sergeant. If nothing else, you've given us a few ideas."

The circle drew closer around the fire and discussed strategy long into the night.

"They are vulnerable," Peregrine said. "Why not press the attack now? Either that, wait for just past midnight to lull them into a sense of safety?" He glowered at the heucuva, knowing that once she'd made up her mind to do something, she would not yield. It had always been that way—even before she'd died.

"No," Renata said huskily. She stared across the Wakefield Plain at the hundreds of distant, low flames which looked more like scattered embers. "They must believe they stand a chance at victory. If we press ahead in the dark, we will take them easily, but how many of the weak and unwary would escape us? We do not want just *this* army. *We want all of Dehnlee.*"

"But … You could send half the force to attack from the north and pinch the whole lot of them in…"

Renata snapped her head to fix Peregrine with those baleful, green eyes.

He quieted immediately, knowing that the former amazon queen may be dead, but she was as proud as ever. She did not appreciate Peregrine's input on her war.

## CHAPTER FOURTEEN

The vagha army stirred as the signal horns bellowed. Within seconds, every soldier stood to his or her feet and had weapons in hand. Sol's rays hadn't yet bathed the Wakefield Plain, but they verged on the eastern horizon.

Sergeant Cadman took the point position at the front of the army while Warlord Adelric rode in the middle of the pack, more than willing to follow Cadman's lead and offer support as the younger warrior needed.

The sergeant was the only one of the two who had faced this new terror, and that experience was enough to give him command of the army. The fact that Adelric wanted less and less to do with his role in the army made the decision to empower Cadman all that much easier.

The undead were about fifty paces away when Cadman stopped the army and let the flanks expand outward to allow the soldiers to cover a wider area. It formed a net to make sure the walking corpses could not slip around them and enter the city.

"Fire when ready!" he commanded.

Within seconds, flaming arrows began to whir overhead. With the dead still spaced out, many of the shots went wide, too far, or else hit their marks. The burning darts that hit the ground quickly hissed out; the ground had turned boggy and damp as some fell presence spread the bog's features to the plain.

Each time a zombie was hit, it burst into flames,, but not long after, it fell to the ground, where the damp land put it out. As a result, the fires didn't burn for long, and even when a zombie did sustain fire damage, the wounds were hardly enough to effect its ability to fight.

In the midst of the soldiers, Adelric could feel the morale level fall like a stone.

"Axes up!" cried Adelric, "This battle is yet to begin!"

Soldiers pulled themselves together at the sound of the warlord's booming voice. They adjusted their helms, raised their shields, and tightened the grips on their axes.

Although Adelric wasn't looking forward to a fight, he prepared himself for it just the same. This fight was about defending vaghan lives. He couldn't stand idly by and watch his fellows die.

Instinctively, he got down off his pony and charged forward, ready—if not entirely willing—to do battle.

Renata watched volley after volley of flaming arrows streak into the heart of her army. And as each one hit the ground and fizzled out in a wisp of smoke, she blew a little puff of air in their direction, as if blowing out candles.

She gave a low and predatory growl, like a feral cat.

Peregrine, knowing that defeating the vagha wouldn't be as easy as Renata would like to believe, rode out ahead of them to join the undead forces. He shook his head. Renata would win this war; it was the least he could do for someone he loved. It was enough to sustain him beyond his mortal life.

Adelric soon found that, as the others had said, the

undead were not exceptionally skilled fighters. They were adequate to make up a wall of bodies, but individually, they could easily be beaten…but it wasn't enough just to beat them if they could reform and continue the attack.

The warlord found himself face-to-face with what looked like a former morehl. Its decay-blackened skin had mostly sloughed off its face and body like a sheaf of pond scum skimmed off the top water. One side of its body had been hacked away, leaving most of its internal organs exposed, but indistinguishable, in their present state of decomposition.

Adelric let the zombie strike a few blows against his shield as he sized it up. The blows were solid enough, and all well on the mark, but they were nothing Adelric couldn't handle. Certainly nothing he couldn't hold off for an extended period. But while he managed the creature's attack, and did so for several minutes, he soon realized just what the others had been up against.

The zombie's blows were relentless. What's more--its twentieth strike was as strong and as accurate as its first had been. Adelric's shield arm soon grew sore, and he found it harder and harder to find an opportunity to retaliate.

Adelric decided he would use something other than raw strength. He attempted a minor spell to dazzle the enemy fiend.

Nothing happened. Instead of a flash of white-yellow flame, Adelric saw only the glint of the zombie's weapon as it arced toward his shield for yet another blow.

"What in the Sha'la'dinan is going on?" he cried.

And as he spoke, his right foot sunk into the ground. When he pulled it out, it came back out sopping, as if he'd stepped into a soupy bog.

But that was impossible. Boland Marsh covered the region to the north and extended only as far north and south as the Kendall and Trent Rivers. And even so, that spell would have worked in even a swamp.

Adelric's throat caught with rage. Something foul and magical was certainly at play.

Captain Ageeus looked out over the bow of the *Blackroc* at the rough waters of the bay. "It hasn't let up at all, has it?" he asked.

Dorian stood by his side. He'd been watching the water crest and churn since sunrise. The roughness of the water had not abated. In fact, it seemed to be getting rougher.

"No, it hasn't," Dorian said at last, glancing at Ageeus. He had personally requested the man to captain Galatea's finest ship. Luckily, its regular captain was away on leave, making that a possibility without serving as a direct insult.

"Not to worry," said the captain. "It's still nothing this ship can't handle." Ageeus rubbed the rail reverently. Sailing the *Blackroc* was every selumari sailor's dream.

"Perhaps," Dorian said under his breath. "But it's not this ship I'm worried about."

Warlord Adelric roared and pushed himself forward and into his adversary. It wasn't easy for him to gain any momentum with the muddy ground beneath his feet, but he was nevertheless able to knock the zombie over and onto its back.

Not surprisingly, the zombie kept hacking at Adelric with its blade, slashing and cutting into his shield. But while the zombie continued to fight, Adelric now held an advantage over the creature. He struck it first in the leg, knowing well that such a blow would not do significant damage, but he was unable to strike better hits on the flailing enemy.

Slowly, keeping the zombie pinned to the ground, Adelric struck blows, trying to create an opening. Eventually, he was able to get an angle on the zombie's head. He smashed it several times before it finally disconnected from the body. And just as Darton had reported, the body parts continued to fight.

They looked ridiculous, arms and legs flailing about in search of an enemy they could not see. It was a chilling reminder of how formidable these undead beings were. It crawled about, searching like a ravenous dog. The head dragged after it, trailed by a thin filament of black goo that remained tethered to the creature.

Just then, Sergeant Cadman came up to Adelric's side. "It appears the marsh may be expanding," said the sergeant, who looked at the grass. It wasn't just wet; it wilted as if poisoned and turned gray at its edges.

"Is this the first you've seen of it?"

"It was a little wet on the plain yesterday. The swamp moves with the enemy."

"It would seem that way," Adelric said, looking over at Cadman and taking his eye off the downed zombie. In a second, the arm clutching the morehl blade swung around and caught Adelric in the shin, cutting a small gash across the skin.

Adelric grabbed at his leg for a moment, then began hacking at the dismembered zombie. "I turned away for a second," he said incredulously.

"They are persistent," said Cadman, assisting Adelric in dispatching the zombie.

The old warlord dropped his ax into the thin, black filament, and severed it.

At last, the creature's parts lay still.

Adelric looked at the wound on his leg. It was painful in

the moment but would heal with time. He'd received worse over the years and never complained.

Cadman looked at his superior. "I think we need to formulate a different battle plan."

What they devised over last night's campfire was clearly not working; not under the shelter of whatever power devoured the land.

"I think you're right, Sergeant," said Adelric, who followed Cadman to the rear, his gait now marked by a slight limp.

The faces of the dwarven commanders gathered at the rear of the battlefield looked grave, and rightly so. They had devised several ways to defeat the undead, but now, it seemed that none of those methods would come easy. If anything, the undead were stronger than they had previously imagined—much stronger.

Adelric wanted this to be his last battle, but not in this particular way.

"Suggestions?" asked Adelric. He looked at the faces surrounding him, and none of them returned his gaze. He let out a sigh and challenged them. "So we're defeated already? Are we not vagha?"

The mapmaker Carswell Adar joined the group with a map tucked tightly under his arm. "You sent for me, Warlord?"

Adelric nodded. "Is that your best map of the plain?"

"Yes," Carswell Adar said.

"Let's see it."

He unrolled the map on the ground and weighted the corners with fist-sized rocks, adjusting the map so that Adelric had the best view of it.

Adelric studied the map for some time, noting the subtle changes in elevation and other landmarks. He looked to the regular extent of the Boland Marsh.

"What of this marsh?" asked Adelric.

"What of it?" replied Carswell Adar.

"It seems to be much bigger than what you have depicted here."

Although he'd been out scouting the terrain all morning, upon hearing Adelric's words, Carswell Adar turned his head and looked in the direction of the ongoing battle. "It would appear that way, milord."

"Then why isn't it reflected here on the map…"

Carswell Adar opened his mouth to speak, but Adelric cut him off.

"If we are to win this war, we need the most up-to-date information."

The mapmaker seethed. "Excuse me, *Warlord!*" He gave the title a sarcastic tone. "I am a mapmaker, not a fortune teller. I can't draw maps in anticipation of what the terrain *might become*. I have to wait until it changes, then record it." He paused a moment to compose himself.

"Obviously, the marsh must have been expanded in the last tenday since I would have recorded such an occurrence had I known about it?" His voice lowered, and he muttered under his breath. "I do possess a bit of professional pride, you know." He cleared his throat and spoke loudly once more. "My next map will show the marsh's true location, just as your war logs will eventually record the tactics best suited to fighting these abominations."

Adelric remained silent. He realized he'd been unfair with the mapmaker—that he'd been using the dwarf in order to vent his frustrations. The undead were difficult to figure out, and he did miss the presence of his brother, Evan. He wished that he was anywhere other than the battlefield, but none of that was reason to take it out on the mapmaker. "Forgive me, Carswell," he said at last. "I feel the battle wearing on my nerves."

"On *all* our nerves," added Sergeant Cadman quickly.

Carswell Adar nodded. "I understand."

Adelric took a deep breath. "Can you explain the shift in the marsh?"

"It would seem that whoever is commanding the undead, has also found a way to expand the marsh. I would say it's much like a piece of cloth placed over a wet spot on a table or floor. The water expands outward until all of it is absorbed by the cloth."

"And?" prodded Adelric, feeling as if Carswell Adar knew more than he was saying.

"Well, this is purely speculation on my part," he began.

"Of course," said Adelric, with a slight nod.

Carswell Adar continued, "The undead don't seem to be attuned to any specific elements in nature… only to Death, the bastard god. I don't think it's just a swamp. It's a deadlands—a festration."

Adelric considered Carswell Adar's assessment. It was sound reasoning, but it did little to help their current situation. He looked around the assembled dwarves and asked, "Now that we have an idea about what's happening, do any of you have any suggestions?"

The dwarves remained silent.

"I was afraid of that," sighed Adelric.

Peregrine returned to Renata's side from the battlefield

where the army pressed forward relentlessly. He had suffered a slash across the right thigh and another in the midsection, but otherwise, he was basically unscathed.

"How goes the battle?" asked Renata.

Peregrine looked up at her sitting upon her skeletal steed, as if she overseeing the play of some parlor game, and he felt a hint of contempt rise within him.

"The battle continues," said Peregrine, doing his best to keep his scratchy voice even keeled and emotionless. "But we are beginning to wear them down. Soon, they will begin to fall, one by one, and there will be nothing between us and the vaghan city they defend."

"Excellent!" she cried.

"You know," said Peregrine after a few moments of silence. "We could use you on the battlefield. Your magic powers could prove useful to the army's efforts."

Renata ignored Peregrine's plea, choosing instead to concentrate her gaze on what was happening on the battlefield. "Look at that!" she said. "They're retreating. They're running away … and soon, my minions will reach Dehnlee, where all its tasty morsels will be ours."

Peregrine turned to see what was happening and was astounded to see that what Renata said was true. The vagha forces were running from the battle. It seemed strange that the dwarves would suddenly turn and retreat as if they were about to be overrun—they were certainly holding their own, even if the overwhelming strength of the dead forced them back a step.

It just didn't make sense.

Renata, however, reveled in the apparent victory. "Run, you fools. You can run for your lives, but there will be nowhere to hide. My army will find you, embrace you, and kill you… and then you will join it."

Peregrine watched, still perplexed. Finally, he concluded that the vagha must have devised some new trick.

"After them," ordered Renata. "Chase them. Don't let them get away."

On command, the zombies began moving westward after the fleeing enemy. They moved more speedily than before; no longer the shambling monsters they were before.

"No," Peregrine countermanded. "No, come back; it's a trap."

"Silence!" Renata shouted. "We've got them on the run, don't let them get away."

Peregrine was about to counter her order once again, but Renata shot him an angry look, with her green eyes afire, and he dared not say another word.

Instead, he watched as a wall of flame rose up across the edge of the marsh. The rocky soil of the plain actually burned in a sheet of red, orange, and yellow fire.

*"No!"* screamed Renata at the sight of the flames. "Stop, get back!"

The zombies slowed, but not all of them stopped in time. Several of them continued on through the flames, burning as they passed through and appearing as balls of fire on the rocky side of the plain.

After the first wave of charging zombies pushed through the wall of fire, the rest slowed and retreated. Eventually, they pulled back and stood in place, as if wondering what to do next. They awaited Renata's new orders.

"Treacherous, stubby little dwarves," hissed the heucuva. The irony that she lost a sizeable chunk of her army on the same pursuit that had cost Renata her life did not go unnoticed. Once again, she blamed the vagha for it. "I'll make them pay for that."

Peregrine remained silent. He admired the vagha's ingenuity.

*Clever, but not quite clever enough.*

Renata continued spouting curses at the vagha.

Peregrine let her vent her anger, then said, "Relax, my queen. They've stopped, and this is only a temporary setback."

Renata looked at him. "Really?"

"Yes," he nodded confidently.

"Good," she said. "I could use the rest."

Peregrine looked at her and wondered what on Esfah she had done to tire herself.

Do you think it will be enough to hold them?" asked Sergeant Cadman.

Adelric watched the wall of fire burn across the perimeter of the marsh and wondered the very same thing.

There was no doubt in his mind that the wall of flame would hold back the advance of the undead, but would his magic-users be able to maintain the wall? Eventually something would give out. Either the wall of flame would burn itself out, or the arcanists' powers would falter to the point where they would no longer be able to sustain it.

Who could tell about these things?

It might even rain.

And when the fire went out, what then?

"It will hold them," Adelric said at last, doing his best to inject his voice with a bit of confidence.

Cadman turned to him. "And then what?"

"Now that—I wish I knew."

## CHAPTER FIFTEEN

"If we could cast a spell to send a stream of fire burning across the plain, it might wipe out their army where it stands," said Ruskin, the thaumaturgist who commanded the vagha's magic-users. "It would achieve the same result as summoning a fire drake, but without the unpredictability of the dragon's temperament."

Warlord Adelric and Sergeant Cadman considered the suggestion. It was one of many they had entertained through the day as they scoured the ranks for any suggestions about how to defeat the zombies.

Some of the suggestions had been unique and creative, while others had simply been bizarre. One of the younger dwarves had suggested they find a mammoth to simply stomp the opposing army into oblivion. It might work, but they could never acquire one in time.

There were many possibilities. But no guarantees.

Currently, Ruskin's suggestion held the most promise. Fire had been the one thing the dwarves had been able to use capably against the zombies thus far.

"That will require an incredible amount of magical energy," said Sergeant Cadman after giving Ruskin's suggestion some thought. "Tell me how you plan to harness that much? Fire bolts and dancing lights are one thing—even dragon and drakufreet summoning are not so bad—but *this?*"

Ruskin nodded, probably hoping someone in the group would have an idea about how to get around that problem.

"Well … I …" he paused for a moment. "I've heard that the gremmlobahnd produce items of incredible power, capable of vastly amplifying a caster's magic. It was their same craftsmanship that designed the dawn blade, the vorpal sword, and created the deadly flintlock forges in Karakto…"

A few grumbles circulated through the mental trust.

"…damned morehl and their gnomish lackeys…"

Adelric held up a hand to quiet them. The idea had merit—if it were based on anything more than urban legend. "Do you have such an item in your possession, Ruskin?"

The thaumaturgist floundered. "No… well … I heard from a peer in Vhandria that…"

"We have no time for that, then." Adelric pointed to where the front lines still fought, holding the enemy at bay as small knots of undead troops circumvented the wall of flame and harried the flanks.

"It seems to me," said Darton, clearing his throat, "that if we could draw them away from the deadlands, maybe it would enable us to defeat them in more conventional ways." He threw the ax handle into his left hand, which made a loud slapping sound to emphasize his point. "Maybe this supernatural toughness is all tied to it."

"Yes," said a sentry named Petrak, who had been invited into the command circle for the first time in his career. "We'll make them come to us, up into the highlands or even toward the coastline. I've no doubt we could hold the advantage on neutral terrain."

A low rumble of voices circulated among the group, as if in agreement.

"It's worth a try," said Cadman.

"Then let's do it," said Adelric. "Even if it doesn't work, at the very least, we might get the things off our doorstep."

While the fire edging the perimeter of the battlefield continued to blaze, Peregrine replenished his army's slightly reduced ranks. He slipped away from Renata's side for a time as they waited for the spell casters to burn themselves out. Their wall of flame could not hold forever.

"Pass me that arm over there," he said to one of the zombies under his direct control.

The zombie slowly picked up the arm and handed it to Peregrine, hand first.

Peregrine looked the arm over. It was a left arm, and he needed a right.

"Are there any more?

The zombie looked around, then shook its head. He noted that if he released more will to the creature, it became more like Peregrine: an animated creature of Death, but with its own mind and autonomy—much like the other members of Renata's court. Her undead were more than mere drones and cannon fodder that made up *this* army.

Peregrine shrugged and worked with the wrong arm. "All right then, this one will have to do."

He willed the black stuff within the dead to aid him. And the tiny tendrils of darkness reached through the skin and stitched parts of the corpse together, like the work of some invisible and poorly skilled seamstress.

Peregrine grinned and laughed as he completed his maniac work. His eyes caught that of his loyal minion, who smiled in return. And then Peregrine realized what power he had; he remembered drinking the black stuff in his earliest days beyond the grave… He had not just the power to create, but the power to control.

He stood for a moment and took a stutter-step backwards as realization flooded into him, like remembering a dream through a fog. Snippets of Peregrine's former life came back to him…just enough for him to remember more than his blind love and devotion to Renata—and how even then, he sometimes had to act in her best interests when she was set upon reckless courses of action.

Peregrine looked back to his loyal minion and asked, "What do you think of it?" He motioned to the creature with two lefts.

The zombie could not respond. There wasn't enough autonomy in its mind and so Peregrine focused his will. Peregrine concentrated on the dark forces within his mind and exerted the power he knew existed. Much like willing a clenched and cramped muscle to relax, Peregrine opened the zombie's free will.

"Ineffective," the zombie hissed when Peregrine was done. "Hindered by disability."

Peregrine nodded in agreement with his new adviser and then looked out over Renata's hordes. They were all disabled without the ability to act on their own. *We needed more than mere drones,* Peregrine thought. Or else he or Renata would have to spend all their energy directing every action. A battlefield was no place for micromanagement.

As the wrong-jointed mongrel zombie rose behind him, Peregrine meandered through the army. He reached out with his will and began his work: breaking the iron-clad bondage to Renata's authority and giving each one some semblance of self-governance. Not as much as he'd given his loyalists, but enough that they'd be more than walking heaps of flesh. They could react, at least, and that would make them better soldiers.

Deep down, a spark of pride lodged in Peregrine's gut. His love for the heucuva had not grown cold, but he knew what the army needed in spite of Renata. And he would make them succeed despite her… and *for her*.

The vaghan forces were in the middle of finalizing their battle plan when the perimeter fire flickered. All across the line, the flames diminished, until they winked out entirely in places. Leaving great holes in their line of defense.

"The time has come," cried Cadman. "It's now or never."

"Engage them!" shouted Adelric to his troops. "But don't exhaust yourself looking for a kill until we take the high ground."

Ruskin and a few of his charges had already moved north to prepare the cataclysmic spells they had planned to cast, knowing full well they would wreak havoc across the Wakefield Plain. Fire magic had proved a less than satisfactory answer, but the vagha were also children of Eldurim, the earth god, and could draw power from him as well.

The dwarves had repositioned so that they could funnel the enemy into their trap, but as the fighting got underway, it became apparent to Adelric that something was wrong. His army advanced much too slowly, as if they were hesitant to engage the enemy.

And then, a cry of terror rang out across the battlefield.

Adelric looked around him, expecting to see one of his soldiers struck with a fatal wound. Instead, his eyes caught a horrific sight.

The bloodless beast was a monstrosity. Its head was that of a goblin, but its body had once belonged to a massive lava elf, or perhaps a half-elf who had mated with an eldari lecher. The head had been stitched in place over the broad shoulders in a hurry, the eyes looking at an awkward angle. One of its arms, the right one, belonged in its socket, but the left arm had been replaced at the elbow by the lower half of a goblin's leg, which turned backward and moved wildly as the thing walked. The way it walked was another thing. It had two legs, both once part of the same elven body. But while the left leg had been attached correctly, the right had been put on backward, giving the creature an awkward lurching sort of step. While all the modifications had made the thing an ineffective fighter, its value as a weapon of terror was immeasurable.

When Adelric first saw the thing, he had to tense his gut to keep from vomiting. The soldier who'd first confronted it had fled, cowering from the creature as if it had some special power apart from being a poorly constructed abomination.

"Get back," yelled Adelric at the overwhelmed soldiers. "Move back onto the highlands!"

The footman turned and ran. Not exactly what Adelric had in mind.

One soldier paused, a low-ranked soldier who hadn't been privy to the commanders' plans. "H-highlands? But we're on the plains… The highest point is Dehnlee!"

In response, the ground rumbled as Ruskin and his troops cast their magic. Stones jutted up in massive, upheaving plinths. The ground rose north, creating a stone hill where there had earlier been nothing but flat land and tillable soil. Large furrows of jagged rock created a barrier to replace the flame wall, which funneled the undead directly to the vagha.

Adelric hefted his ax and rushed to hold off the monstrosity while Cadman sent out the word for vagha forces to pull back. He circled the beast in the opposite direction so it could not see him with its awkwardly tilted eyes. The warlord found an easy angle on it and hacked its head clean from its body.

The abomination fell limp and leaked a black ichor from its head stump. Adelric spat upon it, even more disgusted with this *thing* than with all the others. He vowed that none from Dehnlee would be forced into such an existence.

As expected, the undead forces pushed forward, mirroring the vagha's movements on the other, lower side of the jagged rows of stone.

The vagha hurried up the slopes to where Ruskin and the others waited, likely overtaxed from such a task; they'd be vulnerable for some time until they could marshal their strength again. Adelric felt joy at the feeling of solid rock beneath his feet. Finally, the undead began to ascend the slope… and then, they stopped.

The undead refused to leave the edge of their festration. They simply stood on the edge of the spongy, dying land and stared blankly at the dwarves, as if they were separated by a chasm.

It appeared that they had achieved another stalemate.

But appearances were sometimes deceiving.

"What are you doing?" cried Renata, climbing off her skeletal steed and running through the ranks. "We've got them running scared. After them!"

The zombies did not move.

"No," called Peregrine. He ran after her, grabbing her by the arm and bringing her to a stop. "The vagha have realized that they can't beat us while we're in these deadlands, so they've pulled back in hopes of drawing us onto more favorable terrain. Stripping us of our advantage."

"The disgusting swine," scowled Renata. "These dwarves do not fight fair."

"Oh, but they do," said Peregrine. "They continue to

fight us as if we are one of their usual enemies. But we are not the morehl, nor are we the trogs. They still fight a conventional battle against an unconventional opponent."

"I don't understand."

"I see their ploy and I laugh," Peregrine said.

"Then tell it to me. Explain it," Renata ordered.

Peregrine sighed. "We are an unconventional army. We have no supply lines. There is no army to feed unless we desire the taste of it—the black stuff sustains us by the power of the Death god, Malgrimm! Our soldiers don't even die when they're supposed to. If I were the vagha leader, I would surrender now or abandon my post."

"But our soldiers are just standing there. How can you be so confident the battle is ours when there is no fighting? You don't win a war unless the opposing army is slaughtered; the vagha must be killed."

Peregrine laughed. "That's if both sides play by the usual rules. But even if there's no fighting going on, we're winning this battle, Renata. We're winning *especially* when nobody is fighting."

"How do you figure that?"

Peregrine shook his head slightly. "Have you forgotten? The deadlands move with you. It grows around your presence and it never stops. The entropy will eventually overtake them, and then their city, and then…"

A smile crept across Renata's face.

Peregrine noted the look of dawning realization.

"The fools," she said, her voice suddenly dripping with contempt.

"Indeed," muttered Peregrine.

It was not a stalemate, Adelric realized. The undead and their commanders were content to remain at the edge of the slope, hemming the dwarves in, but refusing to take their bait.

From the higher vantage of Ruskin's hill, he could see the large swath of land where the undead army had moved. Everywhere they had gone, a gray blight of entropy seemed to sap the color from the land. Formerly verdant fields had blackened like ash and whither. The path snaked down from the Boland marsh, up to the Dehnlee graveyard, and then around to the eastern approach.

His gut churned with the revelation that the battle would be lost.

And eventually, they would lose a lot more than just the battle. Only a few hundred could escape by the sparse watercraft they possessed. All other lives in Dehnlee would be lost as well.

They needed a new, radical strategy. And quickly.

## CHAPTER SIXTEEN

The sun set on the day. With the dead's' progress halted, the dwarves made camp for the night. Sentries with long-looks and good eyesight posted watches outside the dwarven encampment and along the ridge Ruskin and his forces had raised to prevent access to Dehnlee. If the dead decided to try reclaiming the advantage in the black of night, the vagha wanted to know about it immediately.

Warlord Adelric held counsel again with his top soldiers. None of them had any new ideas about how this battle could turn to their favor. Adelric rubbed his face, wondering if his decades of strong leadership had stymied the growth of the soldiers under him—had he cast such a shadow that no others could stand in the light?

"We could dig a trench around Dehnlee," suggested a soldier. "The zombies would fall into it as they tried to near the city. Then it would be a simple matter of incinerating them with molten lava as they tried to climb up the other side."

The idea had its supporters, and Adelric conceded that fire had some merit. It had been one of the most successful weapons used against them.

"We have the time to dig the trench, " a soldier said, offering a word of support.

"It would have to be very deep, a chasm, in fact…"

The voices continued to call out support, but Adelric remained silent, listening patiently until the others were done. None realized the plan failed to address all this army's concerns.

"A trench would stop their approach," Adelric admitted, "and we could kill them off with lava, or Ruskin's fire bolts, but what of the encroaching blight? The land around them—around whatever controls the mindless dead—has turned the soil into a deadlands. A pit will not change that." He didn't bother to mention they would quickly run out of food and starve to death without access to the fertile soils of the Wakefield Plain. Adelric threw up a quick prayer to Tarvanehl that it had not all been turned to impotent silt and ash.

The assembled soldiers fell silent. "The Warlord's right," offered Sergeant Cadman. "We need to stop Death's encroachment on Dehnlee. It won't even matter if we destroy all the undead if we end up starving to death."

Adelric's eyes glimmered. He knew he'd made a right choice investing in Cadman.

The following silence drew long.

"Well, if a trench isn't such a good idea," said the dwarf who had made the suggestion, "what do you suggest we do, Warlord Adelric?"

Adelric was on the spot. He'd dismissed one suggestion and had to counter it with another, or else the army's morale would falter. He'd been in this position before, but previously, he'd always had the support of his brother, Evan.

He stroked the hair of his beard. They were in a losing the battle; one that became more difficult to win with each passing minute. If he didn't come up with an idea soon, there might well be an insurrection. Cadman, after all, had defeated the undead once by summoning a fire drake, and there were those who thought that summoning another drake—even two more—was their best course of action.

Adelric wasn't one of them. The undead might burn like wood under dragon fire, but so would the city…and all the vagha of Dehnlee, including the army that summoned such force.

This wasn't a battle that needed to be escalated. It needed thought, consideration, information... *intelligence.*

They had time to study the problem, and then act on what they learned. The rank and file wanted results; they wanted blood or whatever this black, sludgy equivalent was with these creatures. He had to come up with a plan that would gather information, and at the same time, satisfy the soldiers' desire to feel that they were winning the war.

"I suggest," Adelric began with a sigh, "that we infiltrate the enemy."

Blank faces greeted him. None knew what he meant, let alone how or why.

"Infiltration," Adelric repeated. "We must learn more about what drives this enemy. It cannot be mere hunger for flesh—we've seen some of our recently fallen fighting now on the other side. There is some mind driving these beasts."

The group seemed unimpressed. They desired blood and force, not stealth and knowledge.

Again, Adelric missed the presence of Evan. Usually in a situation like this, his brother was an ally quick to approve a risky idea that rallied the rest of the forces into one mind.

Instead, there were grumbles and dissent.

"Sounds like a crazy plan, if you ask me," muttered one.

"Might as well step into the Darkwell itself, " said another, calling on an old tale.

"I ain't no Davian Whisperwynd," commented a third, recalling the only hero to return from the lair of Death himself.

Sergeant Cadman cleared his throat. "I think it's a good idea, milord, and I volunteer to lead the mission."

The eyes of the assembled soldiers widened, perhaps eager to see if the plan gained support.

"Thank you, Sergeant Cadman, but no. You can't lead the mission because I will need you here in the camp to lead...I will undertake this mission."

A few gasps circulated the gathering.

Adelric knew that the only way to show his faith in the plan was to lead the mission himself, and Cadman was the future of Dehnlee's military—he was too valuable to send on this mission. Besides that, how could Adelric expect others to enter the undead camp if he himself wasn't willing to do the same? "Now, who's with me?" asked Adelric.

Thankfully, there was no shortage of volunteers.

Adelric took five others with him, including Darton, who had proved to be one of the best fighters of the campaign, and Ruskin. While all the soldiers were important to this mission, Adelric insisted on taking Ruskin before any other. Once they were across the battle line and into undead territory, it would be up to the spell crafter to make some sense of the magic being used against them. Hopefully, he would be able to discover something they could use to their advantage.

If not, dwarves would be going to a lot of trouble just to kill a few undead—something that would ultimately have little or no bearing on the eventual outcome of the war.

"Are you ready?" Adelric asked Ruskin, leaving the question unasked of the others; he barely had the time to recover whatever energies he had expended to create the high ground the vagha now occupied.

Ruskin nodded.

The crew headed north to avoid the cliffs the arcanists had summoned for Dehnlee's protection. Circling wide the perimeter of the arrayed enemy, Sergeant Cadman set the other part of the plan into motion. All up and down the battle lines and the ragged furrow that had once been a sheet of flame, soldiers lit alchemical fires that burned brightly for several minutes. After a few went out, new ones were lit further down the line.

The flames provided a diversion. They hoped the undead, with a justifiable caution for fire, would be entranced by the flames, watching them light up and burn out with single-minded fascination. That would give Adelric and his dwarves the chance to circle around to the north and allow them to cross over for a long look.

If all went well, they'd have time enough to explore. If it went badly, they'd likely be doing battle in the morning…

As members of the undead army.

"Look at the flames," said Renata. "The dwarves fear the dark."

Peregrine stared into the distance, unsure of her assessment.

"What do you think they're doing?" she asked for his input.

Peregrine scanned the darkness and focused on the distant fires. Great gouts of flame erupted up and down the battle line as vagha added flammable powders or oils to the signal fires.

He wasn't exactly sure what they were doing, but it didn't look as if it was being done to any great effect. "Well? " Renata prodded.

It wouldn't do for him to say, "I don't know." Renata expected an answer from him, and a knowledgeable one at that.

"They're trying to throw up another wall of flame to hold us back," he guessed, almost believing it himself. "But of course, it's not working."

Renata laughed. "The fools!"

She was pleased. Obviously, the answer had satisfied her. Peregrine, on the other hand, wasn't so sure. *The vagha are up to something*, he thought.

But what?

Adelric's band moved quickly through the deadlands. Their boots felt as if they grew noisier with each step and he heard his pulse between his ears. Adelric wasn't sure what he looked for, but he knew that the leaders of the undead would be easy to identify once found.

As they continued to make their way through the wilted terrain, he spotted a cluster of four undead shortly before midnight.

Adelric paused behind a large stone. Its bottom had rotted away under whatever entropic power moved with the enemy forces. It crumbled in the same way a piece of wood fixed in the ground for many years might rot. The stone's decay was rapid, and in another day or two it would be claimed by the deadlands--turned to dust by the Death magic that would eventually claim them all.

"Do you think we can take them?" asked Darton, as he sidled up beside Adelric.

"There are only four of them," whispered Adelric. "We are six. If we can't take them, we have no business being in the vaghan army."

Darton nodded.

"Take the others and circle this group. When I give the signal, move in."

Darton nodded once more before moving away. In moments, Adelric heard the others moving into position; their movements sounding like a wind sweeping across the plain.

Adelric waited a few more seconds, then rose up and peeked above the top of the rock. When he was sure all was ready, he gave the signal by clicking his tongue against the roof of his mouth.

The vagha suddenly appeared, as if out of nowhere. As the undead scrambled to engage, six vaghan axes cut them down, all striking deadly blows to the bases of their skulls. As the bodies toppled over, the ax blows continued in a whir of razor-sharp weapons, until all were left in pieces that could never be reclaimed.

It was over within seconds.

"Now get back," said Adelric, with a wave of his arm. "Out of sight."

The six vagha slipped back into the darkness, unseen. They kept on the move, darting from cover to cover.

Their slaughter of the undead boosted morale, if nothing else. In the long run, four undead wouldn't mean much, but those on the mission suddenly felt their fighting spirit reinvigorated. Hopefully, when they returned to camp, their enthusiasm would encourage the rest of the army.

They made their way deeper into the undead territory, moving quickly across open ground. Though they hid behind rocks and other cover when they came across numbers too large to handle.

At last, they came to a place that chilled their bones. Everything else had been the extant fringes of the festration… but the surrounding soil had turned black as grave soil.

Something in the air made the hairs on the dwarves' arms stand on end.

"Look at the ground," he whispered to Ruskin.

The thaumaturgist studied the growth and nodded. "It's unnatural. And only one known force defies Nature, Mother Ghaeial."

Adelric and the others had held out some hope that, instead of this plagued land, the swamps of the north had possibly flooded across the plain—that perhaps a dam had diverted water and choked the ground. The swamp had certainly festered and expanded, but the cause was more supernatural than a wetlands expansion could explain.

As Adelric took his eyes away from the foul ground, he scanned the shadowy darkness until his eyes stopped on something glittering against the black backdrop of night. Whatever it was shimmered like baubles or trinkets in the moonlight. It was quite out of place here in the midst of so much death and corruption.

Ruskin noticed it as well. "What do you think it could be?" he asked.

""I don't know," whispered Adelric. "But we came to find out."

"I'm right behind you."

The two vagha shuffled off, leaving the four others behind to protect their rear. They moved from rock to rock, moving ever closer to the source of the sparkling lights. When Adelric figured they were close enough for a good look, they crawled behind a good-sized rock and slowly raised their heads over the top to investigate.

Neither of them spoke.

As Adelric watched, he realized the source of all the glitter was the robe of one of the undead. It was decorated with sequins and shiny stones that sparkled in the light of the moon. Judging by the clothing alone, Adelric reasoned that she must be the leader of the undead.

She was tall and attractive, even if such a thing could be said. She had been human once—of that Adelric was certain.

He squinted and could just make her out beneath the pale light of the moon, Rhaudian. His heart soured the more he looked at her. *She resembles the amazon queen from the northeast... This would explain her disappearance and the Gwich'in's destruction early in the war against Garnock.* Adelric hadn't given the humans much thought since their requests for aid had gone unanswered during the first year of the Garnock war. He always assumed they had fled south to Xlinea. He had been too busy with the war to give it much thought.

To the woman's left stood another undead human. Adelric assumed the former queen in her robes was a magic-wielder and the source of the army's power, while the other commanded the military.

Adelric was tempted to rush across the open ground between them and hack them both to pieces, but they were not unguarded, and even if all six of the spies had been there, they wouldn't have been the gusto to defeat the undead guards and their two leaders. Besides, there was no guarantee that it would win them the war. It would certainly cost them their lives.

Adelric tapped Ruskin on the shoulder and jerked his head in the direction they'd come. Ruskin nodded. And together, they slinked back to rejoin the rest of their party.

"What did you make of that?" Adelric asked Ruskin when they were beyond detection.

"My guess is that she's a former human. I sensed magic all over her; a powerful connection to a god like I've never sensed before. "

"The human woman is not unknown to me—she was an ally at the start of the war against Garnock, though we lost track of her clan years ago, when the fighting began. And the other?"

"A soldier of some sort. I couldn't get a good enough

look at him to make a determination. But his proximity to *her* suggests a high position, I think."

"Can we defeat them?" Adelric wondered aloud.

"I think so."

Adelric was surprised and a bit relieved by Ruskin's answer. He was also perplexed. "How?"

"That I don't know," answered Ruskin matter-of-factly. "But consider the robe the leader wore."

"Gaudy."

"Exactly. It's something with no place on a battlefield. If she were alive and normal rules applied, I'd think her naïve or overly confident. Whichever it is, it means there's an excellent chance she'll make a mistake or overlook some small detail that will enable their downfall."

"Suggestions on what that might be?" Adelric realized he was repeating himself. But if there was a way to defeat these things, he desperately needed to know, and soon, so they could prevent more loss of life.

"As I said before," said Ruskin. "I don't know, but if you're patient, I'm confident an answer will present itself in time."

Adelric sighed. "Well, that's some consolation. I just hope it makes itself apparent before all of Dehnlee falls."

"So do I," said Ruskin. "So do I."

Adelric gathered the rest of the vagha together and headed north along the route they'd taken on their way into the camp. The mission, he decided, had been a success. Although he was nowhere nearer to discovering a way to defeat the undead, there was at least some reason for optimism. They now knew who guided this army.

And the fact that they had been able to infiltrate the undead camp suggested they were content to rely on the expanding deadlands to win the battle. And history had shown on many occasions that battles were won or lost due to multiple factors—not just because of a single overpowering weapon.

"Warlord Adelric, look!"

The urgency of the call snapped Adelric's meandering mind back to the present situation. They weren't home yet.

Before them stood five zombies, each with their weapons drawn and their malicious eyes that locked on the dwarven spies.

Adelric raised his ax and readied himself for the fight. They held a slight numerical advantage, but they were still well inside the undead camp. "Remember to target their heads," reminded Adelric. "And keep yours about you."

The two vagha at each end of the line rushed forward, letting out a battle cry as they charged ahead. Adelric was about to call for silence, but realized it was too late for that. This wasn't a battle they could win using stealth and cunning, but rather, through brute force and fierce fighting.

With that in mind, Adelric raised his ax above his head, let out a scream, and charged.

In seconds, there came the clang of metal on metal and the satisfying *shiff* of axes biting into long-dead flesh.

A straggler drew closer, another zombie arriving late to the fight.

Adelric pushed his opponent back, letting Ruskin take over. He prepared himself to engage with the newcomer. As the zombie approached, Adelric noticed it was about his same height, with short powerful arms and legs as thick as tree trunks. The thing had once been vagha and one of his former soldiers.

The blood drained from Adelric's face at the thought of hacking apart one of his own, but he steeled himself for the task at hand and readied for the oncoming zombie.

But as the creature neared, something about it seemed too familiar.

Although its skin had blackened somewhat since its death, and the fiery red hair had long since faded to a pale shade of brown, there was no mistaking the creature's face.

*"Evan!"* cried Adelric.

The zombie continued forward with an awkward, lumbering step.

"Evan," said Adelric again, choking back his tears. "It's me, Adelric."

The former Evan did not stop. It continued advancing, matching each step with a swing of its ax.

Adelric blocked each of the blows with his shield and retreated in a futile attempt not to engage his brother. "Don't do this, Evan," he said, backpedaling. "I'm your brother, *Adelric."*

The zombie kept advancing.

"It's me, Rickee!" he shouted, invoking the nickname Evan used to call him in their youth.

The Evan-zombie stopped in its tracks. It lowered its ax, tilted its head, and blinked at Adelric.

*"Yes,"* Adelric said in a voice that cracked. "You remember your pet name for your older brother, don't you?"

Evan stared at him.

As the seconds passed, Adelric slowly broke down, as if bits of his heart had chipped away and left in shattered pieces.

He was happy to see his brother again. But Adelric knew this wasn't Evan. This was an abomination: a mockery of everything he had so bravely stood for during his lifetime.

Evan was a free-spirited lover of life and Nature.

This... *thing* was a creature of Death and Corruption.

And yet, the ties between brothers were too strong for Adelric to deny. Despite death, they were kin, and it was Adelric's responsibility to care for his brother.

This time, all he could do was try.

"Evan," said Adelric. "Come back with me. Come back to Dehnlee."

The zombie let out a rough, grating whisper. "De-ehhhhn-leeee…"

"Yes, you used to live there."

"…ehhhn-leee…"

"When this is over, we can travel together. There are many powerful magic-users on the face of Esfah…like the sages. Maybe they can change you back. Make you a living dwarf again. "

"Vaa-ahhh-gaaa…"

"You remember now. You are…*were* a vagha. A brave and noble fighter. You belong among them, among those who love you."

"Killll Vva-ahhh—gaaa… " The zombie raised its ax and struck another blow against Adelric.

"No," cried Adelric, the tears beginning to stream down his face. "Don't do this, brother…There might still be a chance for you."

But the zombie continued forward, hacking and slashing with its ax.

Adelric took the blows with his shield, stepping backward to avoid the fight. But the Evan-zombie would not relent. It kept coming and would continue to do so until Adelric was dead.

Adelric let out a sigh, resigning himself to the fact that, while this might look like Evan, this thing was no longer his brother. Adelric had to kill this abomination. There was no other way.

If he didn't, it would kill him.

Brushing away the tears with a forearm, Adelric planted his feet in the ground and stopped his retreat. He raised his ax high above his head and matched the zombie blow-for-blow.

For each strike the zombie made against Adelric's shield, Adelric managed to connect a retaliatory blow with its body. In seconds, the thing began to falter.

When the zombie finally fell to the ground, Adelric continued the attack, hacking at the body until it was a mass of black and gray flesh on the ground.

Still, he continued to chop at it, making sure it would never rise again to mock the life of the noble vagha which Evan had lived and died trying to protect.

"Warlord!"

The voice belonged to Darton.

"Warlord! It's dead…"

Adelric didn't hear him as he kept hacking at the ground with continued force.

"We must hurry, Warlord," said Darton. "There are more undead on the way."

Adelric suddenly stopped and looked around. He recalled where he was, and all at once, the cold, hard reality of what had just happened came into context.

He looked over at Darton and said, "It was Evan. My younger brother, Evan."

All at once, the urgency went out of Darton's voice. "We better get moving, milord," he said softly.

"It was my brother," whispered Adelric.

Darton grabbed Adelric firmly by the arm and hurried him across the plains and toward the battle line, until they reached the safety of the highlands.

# CHAPTER SEVENTEEN

By the time Sol peeked above the eastern horizon, Adelric and his infiltrators found themselves safely back among the vagha soldiers. But while Warlord Adelric was safe and unharmed, he fell into a despondent mood.

No one could fault him for it. Having to put down one's own brother, regardless of the condition, would have brought the stoutest dwarf to his knees—yet Adelric still walked.

Upon returning to the camp, Adelric walked to the top of Ruskin's plinth. There he sat down, alone, and gazed upon the City of Dehnlee in the distance and refused to entertain any visitors. As the sun rose behind him and bathed the network of roads and stone buildings in the warm light of morning, he stared glassy-eyed and re-experienced every moment of anguish that Evan's death had brought him, like a healed wound torn back open.

In the end, Sergeant Cadman posted a sentry nearby and ordered him to prevent anyone from bothering the warlord until he came down of his own accord. Cadman knew pain and understood that if Adelric needed to be alone for a while, then he would help him remain in his solace.

The battle remained at a stalemate, so they could spare his ax. For now, at least.

And the undead weren't going anywhere, not anytime soon.

They were here?" hissed an incredulous Renata.

Peregrine looked over the ruined bodies of several corptic soldiers and shook his head in dismay. "It would appear so."

"If they were here, in our midst, then how far did they get?"

"Unless our soldiers suddenly turned against one another and hacked themselves to bits l would say, yes…vaghan spies penetrated our defenses. I don't know how far they got. But they all escaped alive."

Renata trembled with rage. "l feel so, so… " She paused to search for the word. *"Violated."*

"Indeed," agreed Peregrine.

"How did this happen?"

"We've been at a standstill since yesterday… " His voice trailed off. "Obviously, we weren't expecting them to act so boldly."

Renata turned toward him. Her eyes blazed a wild shade of green. "Are you telling me it's *your* fault we were unprepared?"

Peregrine had realized his mistake immediately, but the words were out of his mouth by then and the damage had been done. All he could hope for now was to control the damage.

"Not at all," he said, a malicious yellow grin creeping across his face. "It means that your brilliant strategy is working perfectly and that our enemy grows ever more desperate. They would have to be in order to take such unorthodox action."

Renata looked somewhat confused. "Are you saying we're winning?"

"Absolutely," said Peregrine. "We've practically got them on the run."

She clasped her dead hands together. "How wonderful!"

Peregrine let out a dusty sigh of relief, knowing deep down that if she granted her thralls a little more autonomy, the zombies might have formed patrols and spotted any incursion. But for now, Renata's plans still stood a good chance of success—and they didn't require him to risk his neck by correcting the mad heucuva.

The *Blackroc* pulled into the docks at Dehnlee to little fanfare. Since the elves' arrival was unscheduled and unannounced, only few people remained on the dock to welcome him, especially since most of the able-bodied vagha had been called up to join the military. But a cool welcome did not matter to Dorian. He was here on urgent business, not a diplomatic visit.

As he walked down the plank onto the docks, Dorian saw a curious dwarven boy looking at the sailing ship in awe. Although he couldn't tell how old the boy was, he certainly looked bright enough to know what—if anything—was going on in the city.

"Hello there, boy!" Dorian called.

The boy nodded. "You're the coral elf, aren't you? The enchanter?"

" Indeed I am. Listen, do you know where Warlord Adelric is right now?"

The boy nodded, but said nothing.

"Where is he, then?"

"On the plain. Big battle. Lots of dead."

Dorian let out a sigh as he considered the boy's words.

*Lots of dead*, he thought. Maybe the morehl had returned too late.

With a blank and unwavering gaze, Adelric watched the sun glint off the polished stone roofs of Dehnlee. He picked up a handful of stones and rattled them around in his fisted hands like dice. Then, he cast them upon the ground by his feet and wondered if his fate could be foretold by the simple patterns they made as they came to rest. Some spell crafters assured him of the art, but he remained a skeptic.

He studied the stones' placement, the shapes they made, and tried to put some meaning to them.. But he had soon wearied of the attempt and swept his hand across the ground, sending the stones flying in all different directions.

Trying to keep his thoughts away from his dead brother was a difficult thing to do. For a moment, he thought he'd seen Evan's face within the stones and the heartache flared anew.

He knew that he had done the right thing. That he had no other choice. Evan had died during the battle of Wakefield Plain. The thing that he met in the dark was not Evan. It was a monster, a facsimile of Evan, and an insult to his memory as one of the greatest warriors the City of Dehnlee had ever known. The creature had to be killed...No, *more than killed*. It had to be obliterated, decimated, annihilated, and utterly destroyed.

Adelric knew all this.

But the knowledge was contained within his head—his cold, rational, and practical head. A head that did not communicate well with his heart.

His heart ached, and no amount of reasoning could heal it.

Each time his mind replayed the horrifying image of

Evan's dead and rotting flesh locked into a rictus grin, another little piece of his heart withered. This time, he thought it might never be whole again.

The head and the heart.

Like two opposing elements.

Fire and water.

Life and death.

Perhaps over time, Adelric's head might grow strong enough to outweigh his wounded heart, or maybe time itself might do that job. For it was said that time had the power to heal all wounds. If that were true, then the only question was…

*How much time would he need?*

And did Dehnlee have that much?

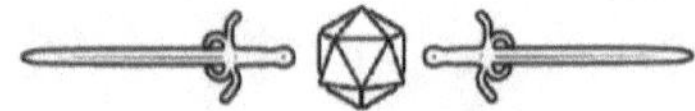

Where do you think you're going?" asked the sentry posted to guard Warlord Adelric's privacy.

"To see the warlord," answered Carswell Adar. He had a map tucked under one arm and there was a definite purpose to his stride. He did not slow as he passed the sentry. He only kept walking briskly up the hill toward the warlord who sat upon its crest.

"Sergeant Cadman has ordered that the warlord be left alone until he indicates his wishes to the contrary."

"Who?" asked Carswell Adar. "Sergeant Cadman or Warlord Adelric?"

"The warlord, of course."

"Oh," said Carswell Adar, not slowing his pace.

"I must instruct you to stop at once," barked the sentry.

"If you must, then do so," said the mapmaker.

The sentry jogged to catch up to him, then fell in line,

walking beside him.

The mapmaker realized he had put the sentry in a difficult situation. On the one hand, he was required to follow the orders of Sergeant Cadman. On the other, the military couldn't afford to detain any capable hands during a time of war. The sentry had quite a dilemma on his hands. "I'm going to report this to the sergeant," he said at last.

"Fine, bring him here. He might be interested in what I have to say, too."

The sentry peeled off and ran back toward camp, leaving the mapmaker alone with Warlord Adelric.

When Carswell Adar arrived at the crest of the hill, he found the warlord slumped over his crossed legs and holding his head in his hands. "Afternoon Warlord," he said.

The greeting went unanswered.

"I know you've made it clear that you wish to be alone, but I have some information that I feel is quite important and thought you might want to know about it."

Again, no answer.

There was a commotion at the bottom of the hill. Sergeant Cadman was on his way with several sentries in tow. Carswell Adar knew he'd only have one chance to talk to Warlord Adelric. He decided to step up the pace.

He dropped to his knees and spread out a fresh map of the battlefield. It was an elaborate rendering with several colored bands stretching out from what was once Boland Marsh. The widest band, a grayish-black one, extended all the way to Dehnlee.

"I've been studying the problem of the expanding wetlands and the ripples of decay that have come out from it over the past few days, and I've come to a rather unsettling conclusion about its rate of expansion."

Sergeant Cadman arrived on the scene then and spent a moment looking at the map at Carswell Adar's feet. Whether he was intrigued by the colors on the map or understood their meaning, Carswell Adar couldn't be sure, but it was obvious that he realized there was something significant there. He turned to the sentries behind him and sent them away.

Even though it appeared that Warlord Adelric still wasn't paying attention, Carswell Adar continued, "I've checked against my previous maps and have estimated that the area represented by the yellow band is the amount of expansion the wetland went through in the first few days after the undead's arrival. The outer edge of the band is where the wetland was when we first arrived on the plain…the blackish hash-marked areas are where the deadlands have taken firm root."

Sergeant Cadman knelt down for a closer look at the map.

"The red band shows where the wetland is at this very moment. As you can see, the deadlands' expansion is growing at a startlingly exponential rate."

"Meaning what?" asked Sergeant Cadman.

"Meaning," said Carswell Adar and looked directly at the Warlord. "It is growing faster and faster with each passing day. In another few days, it will have overtaken Dehnlee." He leaned forward to speak directly to the Warlord. "In a tenday, it will have have spread across the plain. Who knows? It might even infect Vhandria, taking Oxforge and Stonehome with it, along with all in Daurhedge." He paused, adding, "Small consolation--it'd take Garnock and the Red Rocks with it."

Sergeant Cadman inhaled a breath. He whispered, "Will the seas contain it or do you suppose it could cross the  Delmara to Xlinea? Or worse, to Galatea?"

Carswell Adar pressed his lips together and shrugged.

Warlord Adelric said nothing. He made no indication of even hearing Carswell Adar.

"The city will have to be evacuated. Those who are lucky might get away, but many, many others will die,"

Cadman mumbled, mostly to himself, wondering where they might be able to go to escape such a force.

Carswell Adar looked at Sergeant Cadman. The look on the sergeant's face suggested that he knew what Carswell Adar was up to. He nodded in approval.

Carswell Adar continued, "And when the vagha die, they will surely be revived by the undead, only to be pitted against their former friends and families...just like Evan."

Carswell Adar leaned closer and whispered, "If you don't do something, there will be more just like *him* ."

The warlord turned to face the mapmaker, then glanced down at the map.

A fire raged in his eyes and Carswell Adar jumped back, fearing the Warlord might harm him.

Finally, his lips parted, and he said, "No! Not while I still draw breath."

Dorian entered Warlord Adelric's home on the edge of Dehnlee. As expected, it was empty, but it surprised him to see how much ground in Adelric's prized garden had been upset by whatever turmoil affected the plain.

"He's not here," came a voice from somewhere behind him. Dorian recognized Hildegard's voice. He turned and saw the elderly, but hardy woman standing in the doorway.

"Hello, Hildegard."

"There's a war raging out on Wakefield Plain. And so soon after the last..."

"How bad is it?" asked Dorian. "A boy at the docks told me that there are a lot of dead."

Hildegard flashed him a wry smile. "Well, technically, I

suppose that's true."

Dorian cocked his head. "I don't understand."

"There are a lot of dead," she said. "An entire army of them, in fact."

"Double the sentries," Warlord Adelric told Assandro, the dwarf in charge of the defensive forces. They were mostly made of those citizens who received training, but were not full-time soldiers. "After our excursion last night, they might try to pay us back tonight."

"Yes, milord," said Assandro, who turned and hurried to carry out the order.

Adelric let out a sigh. He hadn't been away from battle for long and it felt natural to give orders again. And although his heart was still pained by the memory of his brother, at least now he was able to function as warlord. Carswell Adar had been right to inform him of the graveness of the problem facing them. The thought of more vagha dying only to be resurrected as undead was simply too horrible to bear. Adelric knew the heartbreak it caused, and he had vowed to never let such a thing happen to any of his kind. Not ever again.

But how was he to do it?

There was always that question.

*How?*

Ruskin had assured him that the answer would come soon, probably when he least expected it, but Adelric had dismissed that as the wishful thinking of a desperate magic-user. If the answer hadn't occurred to him by now, why would it ever?

Adelric made his way back to the rear of the camp,

where the army's mess had been set up. Cast-iron pots hung over open flames, while attendants stirred their contents. The cooks were mostly young dwarves, too old to be in school, but too young to have completed their training at Carlin Park. None of them resented the fact that their first battle experience came as mess attendants. They knew that before they could be added to the ranks of the vaghan army, they had to prove that they could follow orders. The mess was the perfect place to learn that discipline. Adelric took his place in the mess line when the sergeant, an elderly dwarf named Urbank who had been on as many campaigns as Adelric, maybe even more, spotted him.

"Warlord," he said. "Have a seat here. I'll send an attendant round to serve you."

Adelric didn't like to be treated any differently than any of the other soldiers, but he was still tired from the previous night's mission and hadn't slept a wink since. He didn't have the energy to argue and hoped that the rank-and-file soldiers wouldn't begrudge him the luxury this one time.

"All right," he said, pointing to a large rock. "I'll just be over there."

"Very good, milord."

Adelric walked over to the rock, climbed to its top, and sat down. The rock had been warmed by the sun's rays and felt good against his body. It was also high enough to give him a good view of the camp. He noticed the dark line crawling relentlessly westward as the jeweled undead arcanist commanded her blight. He saw the undead minions milling about beyond the slope.

He studied the terrain when the attendant arrived, carrying a stone slab. On top of it was Adelric's meal.

"Dinner, milord," said the attendant, placing the slab at Adelric's side. He was about to leave when Adelric grabbed hold of his arm. "Stay," he said. "Keep me company while I eat."

"Oh, y-yes, milord," answered the young dwarf. He seemed surprised by the invitation, and rightly so. It was an unusual request, but he made himself comfortable on the rock and sat patiently, waiting for the warlord to speak.

"What's your name?" asked Adelric, taking a sip from one of the metal cups on the tray.

"Mordecai," answered the attendant.

"A very fine name."

"It means warrior," Mordecai said proudly.

"I know that."

Mordecai's shoulders slumped forward as he realized that, of course, the warlord would know that. Adelric ignored the gesture, knowing there was no way to talk about the gaff without making it worse. Instead, he kept the conversation moving. "What type of soldier do you want to be?"

"I wanted to join the cavalry," Mordecai said with a hint of disappointment in his voice. "But the first time I climbed up onto a pony, it threw me ten feet into the air. I landed so hard I nearly broke my neck. When I got off the ground, I marched into Sergeant Cadman's office and asked to be transferred to missile training. He said he'd do his best, but I just know I'm going to end up as a footman."

"That's not so bad," said Adelric. "I started out as a footman. Just because you begin as a footman doesn't mean you'll always have to be one."

Mordecai smiled. "I suppose."

"Now, pass me that bowl before whatever's for supper gets cold," Adelric said.

Mordecai passed Adelric a gray bowl with veins of white running through its stone. "It's oatmeal.

"Oatmeal?" said Adelric. "For supper?"

"The mess sergeant hasn't been able to replenish his supplies. He has more oatmeal than anything else so he's serving it twice a day for the foreseeable future."

"Very well, then," Adelric sighed. He slid a spoonful into his mouth and nearly gagged. "Is there some milk on that slab?" he asked. "It's terribly dry."

Mordecai passed him the small container filled with warm milk.

Adelric took the container and poured the milk over his oatmeal, thinking about the last time he'd had oatmeal—it was during Dorian's visit. As he poured, his grip slipped, and he spilled too much milk into the bowl; the deluge of over-poured milk cut a furrow through the doughy substance.

He frowned. "Now it's too wet."

"You'll have to let it dry out again."

Adelric said nothing. Instead, he looked at the bowl with a strange fascination, gazing at it much like a caster might try to read the thrown stones—as Adelric had done earlier that day.

The attendant watched him curiously. He asked, "Is everything all right?"

Adelric picked up a spoon and began to stir his oatmeal.

It had turned thin and watery...

More milk than oats.

And suddenly, Adelric found the answer he'd been looking for.

"Yes, everything is all right." Adelric's smile turned into a laugh. "More than all right, in fact."

# PART THREE

Rotting corpses walked all around them, sniffing and sensing their presence, but unable to locate them. The two eldarim, Dhanriath and Nekarthis, meandered through the undead hordes, wary of drawing too close.

Finally, they reached the edge of Renata's army, where Dhanriath spoke of Peregrine. "He is restoring their freedom?"

Was he was not afraid the zombies would actually be a threat to them? His master had already expressed the importance of tipping their hand. Exposing themselves too soon would throw away one of the black shara's two weapons.

Nekarthis nodded. "In small doses, yes." Nekarthis motioned for his subordinate to follow.

"Where are we going?"

"To collect the coven, the other black shara."

Dhanriath looked over his shoulder, where the army of the dead waited for orders to crush their enemy. "But the battle…"

"Its outcome is inevitable," Nekarthis insisted, not stopping.

Dhanriath hurried to catch up to him. He didn't need to ask Nekarthis's thoughts. If he wished to share them, he would. And they weren't there to study the battle tactics of the dead, anyway. They were there to study the necralluvium, and Nekarthis had seen enough.

"The dead will win," the lead mage predicted.

Dhanriath cocked his head. "Truly?"

Nekarthis shrugged. "Yes, in the end. This fight doesn't matter. Not to us…Though I suspect it matters greatly to the residents of Dehnlee." A smile tugged at his lips.

"I have watched the dead since they first arose in great numbers on the slopes of the East Coast. I led their army against Farnoch until Empyreanoral revealed its soldiers," he continued. "I saw Leisterbane the Undying gift Sshkkryyahr the drider with the necralluvium. But observing the stuff's effect on the world at large is critical information.

"Before being dragged away to the sages' prison, Sshkkryyahr and her cult worked tirelessly to plant seeds of the Black Forest. Once they blossom, the weeds will spread. Malgrimm's power will set the races against each other, making them opposed rather than allied as the gods intended. Reports from Charnock already indicate as much across the Talvat and Far Seas."

Dhanriath nodded. "So long as the races remain divided, Death, the only element in true opposition to its siblings, will win."

Nekarthis tipped his brow with agreement. "They'll never figure that out. Not until it is too late."

## CHAPTER EIGHTEEN

Although he was near exhaustion, Adelric had finally formed a plan, and that fact had brightened his demeanor.

"You sent for me, milord?" asked an older dwarf named Budt. He was a little taller than most dwarves and somewhat thinner, but his wiry frame had a certain strength and agility about it. The age lines on his face spoke volumes about his experience on the field of battle. Because of his longer stride, Budt was also one of the fastest vagha in all of Dehnlee.

"Yes, Budt," said Adelric. "I have a job for you. There's a message I'd like you to deliver for me."

Because of Budt's speed, he was the army's top messenger.

Since the battle began, he had traveled back and forth to Dehnlee several times, but this time, he'd be going further. Much further.

"Wherever the message's destination, milord...I'll make sure it gets there."

Adelric nodded. His confidence was one of the things he admired about Budt. "I need you to go back to Dehnlee. Take a boat across Delmara Bay and get to Galatea."

Budt's face turned pale. The vagha had boats of their own, but they were mostly used for local travel and industry, not for navigating the waters of the bay. Nevertheless, Budt had given his word and forced his face to return to its default obedient smile. "Yes, milord!" he said.

"In Galatea, ask for Dorian—"

"The enchanter who was recently in Dehnlee?"

"Yes, that's him."

"What should I tell him?"

Adelric hesitated. After the silence became too long, Budt asked another question, "How many selumari soldiers should I tell him we need?"

"None," said Adelric.

Budt cocked his head in surprise, but he tried not to let it show on his face.

"Tell him that more soldiers won't help, and impress upon him that our problem requires his help—his special talents."

"Yes, milord."

"That's all."

Budt turned to leave.

Both knew that the time it would take for Budt to reach Galatea and return with the enchanter would amount to several days. Neither knew if Dehnlee would still be standing at that point.

"Good luck," said Adelric.

Budt turned back and smiled. "Thank you, milord. You too."

"They're sending another one back to the city," said Renata as she scanned the horizon with her dead, green eyes.

Peregrine busied himself making soldiers from fresh parts that scavengers had recovered from the battlefield. He was currently in need of a hand—left or right, it didn't matter—but all he had were feet. There were plenty of feet, as they weren't much of a target for the dwarves and usually came out of a skirmish unscathed.

"Do you think they're sending for reinforcements?" asked Renata.

"You ask that same question every time they send a messenger."

"Well? Do you think they are?" Renata pressed.,

"I don't think they have any more reinforcements."

Renata's laugh was almost a giggle. "You mean that's it. *That's* their army?"

"That's what I'm saying."

Renata *did* giggle.

Peregrine felt relieved he'd been able to tell her what she wanted to hear.

He couldn't be sure of anything about the vagha numbers. They could be stalling; a whole new army could be on the way. Vhandrian forces could be riding down from the Daurhedge for all he knew.

He could not know for sure, but they'd hear the approach of an army large enough to overwhelm them from the rear, and nobody had seen a messenger bird sent east for help.

All Peregrine could do was make sure his troops were as ready as they could be for when the fighting began anew.

With that in mind, he grabbed a foot and summoned the supernatural black stitching to connect it to the wrist of the zombie he pieced together. If nothing else, the creature would be able to kick with his arms.

After watching Budt head off toward Dehnlee, Adelric sought out Sergeant Cadman. He found the sergeant checking one of the sentry posts where the deadlands bled towards them like fingers from a hand.

"We couldn't stop it before, and we're just as unable to stop it now," Cadman told the sentry.

Adelric looked at the veins of blight bleeding through the rocky soil and simply shook his head. "Not to worry," he said. "If all goes well, it will be over in another few days."

Both the sentry and the sergeant looked at Adelric with confused expressions on their faces.

"What do you mean?" asked Cadman. "Have you found a way?"

Adelric smiled, realizing it might have been better to keep things quiet for the time being. "I have an idea, but that's about all I'll say." He turned to the sentry. "Just keep an eye on it. If it starts changing any faster, let me know."

"Yes, milord," said the sentry.

Adelric nodded, then asked that Sergeant Cadman take him to the magic-users. Naturally, Cadman was curious, but Adelric said nothing more about his plan.

The magic-users were stationed toward the rear of the camp. There, they used their powers primarily in a healing capacity. The arcanist corps were fairly well rested as a result and were eager to ply their craft to help end the stand-off and return to their homes in Dehnlee.

Ruskin noticed Adelric and Cadman approaching and came out to greet them. "What brings you back here, milord?" asked Ruskin.

"Your magic," said Adelric.

Ruskin laughed, then shook his head slightly. "I'm afraid I don't understand. We've tried ... we tried magic..." He gestured to the theurgists scattered about. "We couldn't fix whatever is plaguing the soil."

"Who said anything about changing the land?" asked Adelric.

"What are you talking about, then?" asked the

thaumaturgist.

Adelric simply said, "You'll see."

"Look!" cried one of the sentries.

"I see it," called another. "Magnificent."

Adelric turned to see what all the commotion was about and could hardly believe his eyes. He'd been told such a thing was possible, but he could never have imagined it to be such an incredible sight.

Approaching from the north, floating low over the horizon, flew a selumaric air ship—the *Blackroc*—made of coral polished shell. Adelric had seen ships on the water before, but the sight of one sailing through the air was awe-inspiring.

The craft had webbed fins like a fish for gliding through the air. An immense ship-sized air bladder sat within a central mast and kept the craft aloft. Adelric knew that an airship meant the likelihood of spell crafters who could help propel it.

The mouths of the nearby vagha hung agape as the ship swept down over the battlefield, trailing a thick plume of fog behind it as if the obscuring mist was the very thing pushing it through the air.

As the ship made its first pass, Adelric wondered how on Esfah Budt could have journeyed to Galatea in such a short time. Unless Budt knew the secret of teleportation, it was impossible. Even if Budt had utilized a path spell to send him to Galatea in a fraction of the time, there was no way that even a coral airship could have made the trip by now.

But as the ship came by for a second pass, Budt could clearly be seen standing on the bridge next to Dorian. If Adelric read Budt's face right, the dwarf appeared to be sick—sea-sick, air-sick, or perhaps a combination of the two.

After taking another few minutes to turn the ship around, Dorian and the captain brought the wondrous vehicle to hover not twenty paces from where Adelric stood.

"Hullo!" Dorian shouted, waving to the vagha who had gathered around the ship. It slowly descended just as the air bladder depleted.

A cheer erupted from the troops on the ground. The rank and file hadn't been informed of the plan, but obviously Dorian's arrival was enough to lift their spirits—any reinforcements were welcome against the enemy. The army only knew that something was happening and hopefully, it would change their fortunes.

When the ship came to a rest, a ladder dropped for boarding and unloading.

Adelric walked to the ship. He wore a smile for the first time in days.

Dorian set foot on the rocky soil and clapped Adelric in a heartfelt embrace.

Behind them, a greenish Budt stumbled his way down the gangplank and fell to the ground, groaning and holding his stomach as he tried to stand up.

Adelric looked at his messenger. "I trust you had a pleasant trip?"

"It was..." Budt began, but stopped himself before he threw up his breakfast. Budt made a motion as if to speak but stopped himself before managing to get a word out.

Dorian explained his arrival, "On my way back to Galatea, the waters of Delmara Bay proved rough. Certainly far choppier than any natural summer storm could have made them, and they acted strangely, as if some foul magic were at play."

Adelric listened intently.

"By the time I arrived back at my home, the waters had become more than rough. They churned abnormally, off-color and, well in a sickly fashion. I suspected that something was amiss near Dehnlee."

"But how did you know?"

Dorian shrugged his shoulders. "I can't explain it. Something drew me back to here and the closer I got to the city, the more certain I was of that feeling. I'd like to think it was the bond forged between us...Perhaps you were subconsciously calling me back."

Adelric commented, "I'll not deny that I wished for your arrival."

"Maybe it was from your wish, or perhaps it was the spirit of your brother looking out for you in his own way." Dorian's voice trailed off with a simple shrug of his shoulders.

Dorian's words shocked Adelric. Perhaps they held some truth. Evan had been a great warrior, a supportive brother, and close friend. Just because he died didn't mean he had forsaken Adelric. And just because his body had been resurrected and pitted against his former allies, it didn't mean that his spirit wasn't still looking out for Adelric any way he could.

Words never made it out of Adelric's mouth. He was just glad that Dorian was here now. He could wonder about the how and why of it later.

Behind Dorian, Budt groaned once more.

"You've done well, Budt," said Adelric. "You should be proud. But perhaps rest now."

Budt's body stiffened, just before he finally retched.

"We picked him up on the outskirts of Dehnlee," said Dorian. "You can't imagine how good it felt to hear him say that you had sent for me. Between you and me," Dorian's voice lowered to little more than a whisper, "I was beginning to think that I might have gone mad with my suspicions." He cleared his throat then and spoke much more loudly. "But when he said you didn't require soldiers, I understood and was grateful that I had thought to bring evokers and conjurers from my court. They are what keep the *Blackroc* in the sky. *Blackroc* is the only ship in Galatea's fleet finer than the *Atalante,* if you remember me saying."

"You've brought your magic-users?" asked Adelric.

"Of course."

Just then, the green-robed corps of spell crafters exited the ship, stepping gingerly onto the foreign soil.

"Excellent," said Adelric. "They're just what I need."

"Why?" asked Dorian. "What seems to be the problem?"

Adelric turned and began walking slowly westward.

Dorian took up a position to Adelric's right and walked with him.

After a few steps together, Adelric spoke. "It all began with an old dwarf named Standish."

"Oh, I believe I met him."

Adelric nodded slowly. "Standish is dead. And that is only the beginning of it…"

Renata and Peregrine were as impressed by the flying ship as the vagha had been. But soon after the ship touched down, Renata worried over the significance of the ship's arrival.

"They're winning, aren't they?" she asked, her green eyes flickering with an uncertain light.

"They're not winning anything," answered Peregrine, tiring of the heucuva's pendulous mood swings. "Nothing has happened yet. Nothing has changed."

"But they will win it now, won't they? They've got the help of the selumari and now they'll emerge victorious." She curled a lip, thinking on the fact that she had wanted to invade, but Peregrine had urged restraint.

"No, not necessarily," said Peregrine, realizing too late that he should have been emphatic with his denial. "Coral elves are like any other. Their arrows will prove as ineffective as the bolts fired by the vagha. If anything, they will prove lighter and more fragile. And there cannot be many warriors on the boat—certainly not enough to change the course of the battle."

"What about their magic-users?

"What about them?"

"How powerful are they?"

Peregrine hadn't given the magic-users much thought. He was a fighter, not a magician. Despite having instigated the whole resurrection of the dead, he had always preferred hacking and slashing over arcane craftsmanship.

Renata asked again, "I said, how powerful are they?"

Peregrine didn't have an answer for her. "I don't know," he said at last.

"You don't know?"

"I suspect their magic-users are as good as any," he said, losing ground to the heucuva. "But they're far from home…I suspect they'll have no particular advantage."

He nodded his head to further prove his point.

Renata, however, was not satisfied with his answer.

"I don't like it," she said. "I don't like it at all. They're planning something. Something big. They're figuring out a way to stop us."

"Should we turn back?" asked Peregrine. It was a logical question, as far as he was concerned. Perhaps they hadn't thought through their strategy as well as they could have. The expanding deadlands were their best weapon and it would not be a surprise to the enemy. The only different tactic left was to pull back, regroup, and invade at a later time. But as logical as the thought was to Peregrine, articulating it had been the worst thing he could have done in Renata's eyes.

When she turned on Peregrine, her eyes burned an

intense shade of green, and it seemed that the light shining from them was powerful enough to cut him in half. Although Peregrine's cold, dead body was incapable of it, he felt a shiver under the intensity of Renata's gaze.

"No, we will not turn back," she spat. "I want action. You will take a group of zombies. Cross into the vagha camp and kill the selumari as they sleep…just as I did to the northern firewalkers years ago."

Peregrine shook his head. "I don't think…"

The words died in the ghoul's throat as Renata's right hand clamped around his neck and began to squeeze. Harder. And harder.

"I'm sorry," Renata said, tightening her grip. "It sounded as if you were defying me?"

She released her grip slightly.

"I can't just walk in and…"

She closed her hand again and the dead cartilage that made up Peregrine's windpipe began to crack.

"I'm still having trouble hearing you," she said, bringing Peregrine's face within inches of her own. "It sounds as if you're having trouble agreeing with me…"

Peregrine had known the heucuva was strong, but this display of brute strength was unlike anything he'd witnessed before.

Either she augmented her usual strength by magic means—which would make it easy for her to crush his throat— or her anger amplified her power. Whatever the reason, Peregrine couldn't stand it much longer. Besides, if he disagreed with her again, he had no difficulty imagining that she might squeeze hard enough that his head popped right off his body.

He attempted a nod.

Renata must have felt the subtle movement. She eased up on the hold around his throat.

"I'll do it," Peregrine croaked.

Renata growled. "I knew you would see the error of your ways sooner than later. I'm glad. Later was not an option." She released her hold and tossed him to the ground in a single motion, as if he were little more than a dirty rag.

Peregrine landed with a heavy thud.

"Stop wasting time," said Renata as she looked out over the silent battlefield. "It'll be dark soon."

Peregrine tried to answer. Instead, he rubbed his damaged throat and moved out to collect a team of his loyal minions.

Under the vigilant watch of Renata, Peregrine gathered his loyal zombies and reluctantly moved west to cross into the vagha camp.

It occurred to him to head east instead. Just walk off the battlefield and continue home. But he knew he wouldn't get far traveling in that direction. Renata would surely stop him. His destruction at the hands of the vagha would be less painful and far quicker than anything Renata might inflict upon him.

And so, he chose the lesser of two evils. Peregrine led his soldiers across the plain, where waves of loyal minions milled about until he found what he was looking for: a gap in the vaghan sentry line. The rift of tectonic movement was not impossible to scale here, and with his team of zombies almost as free as Peregrine was, they rivaled nearly any living person for mobility.

Minutes later, they slipped over the ridge in the dark and into enemy territory.

"Do you smell something?" asked a sentry.

The next sentry down the patrol route sniffed the air. "It wasn't me," he joked.

"No, not that. Do you smell something bad?"

Again, the second sentry sniffed the air.

During the standoff, the pervading reek of dead and festering bodies had lessened thanks to a gentle and easterly blowing wind. But now the smell had returned, even though the wind still pushed slightly against their backs. It was the same winds the selumari had sailed in upon.

"I smell it," said the second sentry. "It's the dead all right, they're getting closer."

"That's what I thought. Keep an eye out and send word down the line."

Peregrine led his zombies only a few dozen paces into the vagha camp before they were found.

"Who's there?" cried one of the vagha.

Peregrine and his soldiers remained silent—dead silent.

"I know you're there," said the sentry. "I'd know that stink anywhere."

Peregrine knew he should remain silent, that keeping quiet might help him get away, but his contempt for the vagha was too strong and he couldn't resist.

"Yes," he hissed. "Whenever the vagha gather in groups, the stench can become quite palpable."

No one laughed.

Instead, a torch in one vagha's hands burst into flames and the undead were bathed in an orange-red glow. The vagha were caught by the same light.

There were only two vagha there, but with a signal torch lit, there would surely be more of them soon.

"Get them," Peregrine said, ordering the two zombies in front of him to engage.

The lead zombies raised their scythes and charged.

The vagha holding his torch dropped it to engage the oncoming enemies. Torch flames flickered as they hit the ground, and for several seconds, it nearly burned out.

Peregrine used those moments of uncertain light and confusion to make his escape. "This way," he instructed his four other companions to follow, leading them northward.

The light from the sentry's torch regained its brilliance, but it dimmed in the distance as Peregrine and his four remaining troops moved quickly over the rocky terrain of the vagha camp. Judging by the sounds, the two zombies he left with the dwarves put up a good fight. He expected they would overpower the sentries before seeking out other guards and setting upon them.

But there was still a camp full of vagha just beyond.

*Killing the selumari is impossible now*, he thought, shaking his head at the absurdity of the assigned mission.

Peregrine took a moment to consider his options. He could return to Renata's side of the battle lines. While that would be the easiest route to take, it also meant that he would have to report that the mission had failed.

His ruined neck throbbed at the mere thought of it. He dismissed it as the poorest alternative.

He could press on and try to execute the visiting selumari, but with the sentries alerted to their presence, Peregrine doubted they would make it any deeper into the vagha camp.

There seemed one other course of action left.

Escape.

Although nothing had happened to change the actual course of the battle, Peregrine sensed what bothered Renata: the hands of Fate had flipped. Whatever the vagha and selumari were planning, they would likely defeat the undead with it.

Renata was doomed.

It seemed so obvious now.

*And perhaps,* he thought as a sly grin stretched across his mottled gray lips, *it was for the best.*

With Renata out of the way, he'd be left to claim the castle ruins for himself.

He could try again, with a battle plan and strategy that was less ambitious. He could start slowly and expand. He could build an empire unplagued by Renata's particular failings—one free of the destructive emotional pendulums.

He stopped himself mid-thought.

He wasn't even out of his predicament, and he was thinking about conquering other cities, other races.

It would all come to him in time. Luckily, Peregrine was patient.

But for now, he was left with only one goal—escape. He would take his crew north and watch at a distance. If Renata emerged successful, he would claim they fought in the rear and rejoin her in the end. If she fell, he would assume her mantle.

He continued northward, under the cover of darkness, bidding his time.

## CHAPTER NINETEEN

"Very clever," said Dorian, after Adelric explained the events of the last several days. He also detailed his plans for how to deal with the dead.

"Thank you," responded Adelric, a wide smile on his face. "And do you think you can help with this scheme of mine?"

"I think so."

"Are there even spells for this kind of thing?"

Dorian considered the spell crafters he'd brought with him. He cracked a broad smile. "No, there aren't."

Before Adelric's optimism could fall, Dorian reassured him, "But that doesn't mean it can't be done."

"'What's taking him so long?" Renata wondered aloud. She gazed over the battlefield with her keen eyes, but she couldn't see anything except for a few dying fires.

Her question went unanswered, and that felt odd. She had become used to Peregrine answering her questions and belaying her fears. She now realized how much she needed him.

For a brief moment, she felt a tinge of remorse over the way she'd treated the ghoul. And then, as quickly as the feeling came, it dissipated—completely forgotten and unlikely to ever return.

"A coral elf ship isn't anything to worry about," she said aloud. Her voice boomed as if the more volume she gave her words, the more they would ring true. Renata realized that those words sounded very much in her head like Peregrine's.

She continued muttering to herself, keeping strings of words alive to avoid focusing on the fact that she was suddenly alone. And for the first time since she'd left the castle ruins, she felt unsure what do to next.

Renata paused a moment to scan the horizon once more.

"Well, bring them on. Bring on all the selumari you like. It won't make any difference how many soldiers you add to your army, *dwarf.* Every time we kill one of your soldiers, we shall gain one. Bring them on, as many as you can. Why, I'll even take them on myself…My magic is strong." She paused a moment and touched the hard lump on her breast where she remembered Death—Lord Malgrimm—placing his boon within her.

The upper arc of the sun crested over the horizon, and she raised her eye to the dwarven camp one more time, hoping to spot Peregrine returning across the battlefield, splattered with the green hues of selumari blood.

He was not there. Neither could she find any evidence of Peregrine's presence in the camp.

She lowered her eyes and folded her hands in her lap. "Where could he be?" she asked. Then, off-hand, "Oh, I hope he's all right…"

"You sent for me?" asked the master mapmaker,

Carswell Adar.

"Yes, I did," said Adelric.

The mapmaker stepped forward. As usual, there was a map tucked under his arm.

"I trust you've been keeping an eye on the shifting terrain?"

"Yes, Warlord."

"And?"

"And it's as I feared. The wetlands expand. The deadlands grow. Parts of the plain have become borderline desert. Dehnlee will become infected before the end of the tenday."

Adelric took a moment to ponder the news.

"Is that all, Warlord?"

"No, it is not."

At that moment, Dorian appeared from behind a stand of rocks where he had been working with one of his subordinates. He came up alongside Adelric.

"You remember my good friend, Dorian?"

"Yes, of course," said the mapmaker, nodding politely. "How are you?"

"I'm as well as can be expected under such circumstances," Dorian said, returning Carswell Adar's smile."

"I trust you found a good spot for the map I gave you," said Carswell Adar. "It's one of my better pieces of work."

Dorian seemed surprised by the mapmaker's words. While it was understandable that he liked to hear his work appreciated, this wasn't exactly the time or the place for it.

"It was actually Dorian that asked for you," interjected Adelric. "He wishes to see your latest map of the area. I assume you've updated it to show the current extent of the wetlands?"

"Absolutely, Warlord," said Carswell Adar, sounding slightly offended that Adelric felt he had to ask such a thing.

"Good, then let's have a look at it."

Carswell Adar nodded, knelt down, and unfurled his map.

Even before the mapmaker had finished putting the map into place, Adelric could see that changes had already been made since the previous day. Differently shaded bands represented the rate of progressive decay. It was worse than he remembered it. But despite his alarm at the sight of the map, Adelric and the others present waited in silence as Dorian studied it. He seemed unconcerned about the shaded areas and kept looking to the east at the source of the Boland Marsh's water.

"These rivers, here..." He pointed to the Trent and Kendall Rivers. "Are they very deep or wide?"

Carswell Adar took a moment before he answered. He looked at the map, then looked up to the sky. "Fairly deep. Maybe ten or fifteen paces wide."

Dorian nodded. "Is there a good water flow and a lot of water in them?"

"What do you consider being a lot?" asked Carswell Adar.

Each of the vagha looked at Dorian. It was an interesting question since the coral elves were attuned to air and water, while the dwarves were attuned to earth and fire. What was the common unit of measure between them?

Dorian struggled to find the words, which Adelric mused, was a very uncharacteristic moment for him. At long last, he opened his mouth to speak. "What if the river were a vein of granite or some such rock, and what if you had to dig out that vein for some reason, dig it out completely ... How much area would the granite cover?"

The mapmaker smiled and nodded his head. Obviously, he could answer the question more easily now, as could any of the vagha present.

"I would guess there would be enough stone to, uh

...cover the entire plain." Carswell Adair immediately looked around to see if the other dwarves were in agreement. They all nodded.

"Excellent," said Dorian, looking around to make sure the mapmaker's assessment appeared correct. "If that's the case, then it means it can be done."

Adelric simply smiled.

The sun had risen and with it came a sweltering heat. Renata scanned the battlefield again in search of Peregrine or any of the zombies he'd taken with him, but to no avail.

He wasn't anywhere to be found. Renata thought about his potential fates. There were only so many possibilities.

The first thing that came to her mind was that he had run away. The thought of it sent a ripple of rage through her body. *But* why *would he run away?* The thought seemed ridiculous. He had helped create this army--pulled it up from the ground. She gave him leadership to lead it in a triumphant march over these stupid little vagha and their city of stone. He owed it to her to return to the army.

*Peregrine was nothing without me.*

She held the power, the *real* power.

Together, they would conquer the four corners of Esfah.

*Maybe he was still carrying out the mission?*

Yes, that was possible. He could be waiting patiently for the perfect time to strike, and then, with one powerful swing of the scythe—no more selumari.

But what if he'd already accomplished his goal?

Perhaps that's why there was such little activity in the camp? Everyone was busy investigating the surprising overnight deaths of the selumari?

But then, if he had completed the mission, why hadn't he returned?

She inhaled a gasp at the thought.

What if he's stuck deep within the vagha camp with dozens of soldiers between him and the battle line and with no way out? He could be stuck there for days, waiting to return to her.

Days in which she would be left alone to lead the army.

She wasn't interested in the tedium of battle. Her army would have to fight in order to conquer Esfah, but Renata was only concerned with reaping the rewards that came with winning each of those fights.

She took a moment to calm her nerves, which threatened to come back to life. She also took a moment to think.

After a few moments, a tactical course of action seemed obvious to her. If Peregrine was stuck there in the vagha camp with no way out, she had to rescue him.

After all, it was the only way to save herself from the obligation to lead this army.

The sentry squinted against the glare of the morning sun as he scanned the undead camp for what seemed to be the hundredth time. A sentry's job usually entailed many hours of sitting around and waiting. The hardest part was staying awake during the longer periods of inactivity.

Except for the two undead soldiers that had walked into the midst of their camp by mistake the night before, there had been no activity since Ruskin and his arcanists created their current hill.

As if proof of that fact, the sentry at the next position slept through most of his morning shift. He considered going to wake him, but the thought of catching a few winks in the afternoon when the now-sleeping sentry was awake and owed him a favor was too tempting to ignore.

What was the harm, anyway?

It felt like they were all sitting around and waiting for the rug to be pulled out from under them. A rumor spread that the Warlord and his selumari contact had figured out a way to beat the undead, but if that were true, he didn't understand why they were taking so long to get it over with? Most likely they were stalling; maybe the plan required the zombies to attack first.

Fat chance.

The sentry scanned the horizon yet again. They hadn't moved in days, except for the previous exception.

He was just about to complete his visual sweep when something caught his eye.

A movement of some sort… A fluid motion like a trickle flowing down an embankment.

He concentrated his gaze on the spot, then took out his long-look in an attempt to discern whatever it was he'd spotted.

It was movement, all right. Troop movement.

The undead were gathering—amassing their forces. And if he wasn't mistaken, they were forming ranks and likely preparing for an attack.

The sentry collapsed the long-look and scrambled down the hillside as fast as his stubby legs could carry him. As he neared the back of the camp, nearly out of breath, he yelled, "Warlord! Warlord Adelric!"

The warlord was holding a conference with Sergeant Cadman and some of the selumari. As the sentry approached, they stopped and raised their heads expectantly.

"Warlord Adelric!" the sentry said one last time.

"What is it?"

"The undead," gasped the sentry, his chest heaving. He took several more breaths. "They are gathering together—I think they are preparing to mount an offensive attack."

The warlord nodded and smiled. "Thank you," he said.

He looked around at those surrounding him, still smiling. "Well—it looks as if we have our plan fleshed out and just in time." He turned to Sergeant Cadman. "Get everyone in place. The final battle is about to begin."

## CHAPTER TWENTY

As instructed, the vagha soldiers spread themselves as wide across the battle line as possible, hoping to thin out the enemy. Adelric and Dorian walked up and down the line, boosting morale—there was no guarantee the warlord's plan would work. The last thing they needed was for the vanguard to falter. One or two of the men losing courage could cause the whole army to backpedal.

Still, judging by the faces of the dwarves they passed, Adelric spotted eagerness rather than fear.

"How are you feeling, Darton?" asked Adelric, coming upon the rider where he sat in his pony's saddle. On the slope of risen stone, the cavalry hoped the sodden ground wouldn't render their mounts useless.

"Well, to tell the truth, Warlord," said Darton, "I'd rather see this battle come to an end. And as quickly as possible."

"As do we all," said Dorian.

Adelric nodded.

They continued back down the line. When they reached the end, they doubled back to check on the secondary line made up of magic-users. There, a young coral elf spell caster pulled tendrils of water vapor out of the air. The elf's hands moved in a series of dramatic swirls and arcs as tiny wisps of smoke-like mist trailed his fingers like pieces of thread.

The spell-casters would follow the soldiers into battle, but would not be involved in any of the fighting.

"He's warming up," said Dorian in a whisper.

Adelric nodded and watched the young evoker work his magic. He wondered how he could have ever imagined that such mildly entertaining magic could help to defeat an army of rapier, ax, and scythe-wielding zombies.

It seemed an unlikely scenario, yet for some reason, Adelric felt confident that the plan would work--that the combined magic of the vagha and selumari forces would be more than enough to end this wall of bodies once and for all.

The battle plan formed a two-stage strategy. The first part involved the soldiers. The second duty belonged to the magic-users. When the soldiers completed their task, they would hand the fight over to the magic-users.

It all rested with them. Hopefully, the magic-users could then end the battle.

It was an all-or-nothing strategy. If Dorian, Ruskin, and the others failed, then Adelric and the soldiers would perish. Dehnlee, and perhaps all of Esfah, would be doomed.

"Move!" cried Renata as she looked down at her army from atop her skeletal steed.

The zombies ambled forward, grasping the hafts of their weapons.

"Victory is ours for the taking," she hissed, but in the back of her mind she kept wondering where Peregrine was. He had started the battle, and she wished he was there to finish it.

The zombies slowed, uncertain about their next steps. One of them, which Peregrine had stitched together, refused to march up the slope.

"Where do you think you're going?" asked Renata.

The zombie didn't answer. It continued walking in the

wrong direction.

"I said, where do you think you're going?"

No answer. No growl. It did not even pause.

The rest of the zombies slowed their march, interested to see the outcome of the power play between Renata and one of their number.

"I'm giving you an order…"

Nothing.

Renata drew her blade and, in one swift motion, lopped off the creature's head. It flew in a gentle arch and landed in a moist patch of ground. The zombie took several more steps before the rest of its body crumpled. Renata hacked the fallen body to pieces. Finally, the body lay in a green-black heap of dead flesh.

Renata wiped the gore from her rapier, then looked around with baleful eyes. *How many of these were made by Peregrine rather than her?*

"Who's next?" she barked.

None of the surrounding zombies made a sound. Instead, they turned in the direction of the vaghan forces and resumed their slow march toward them.

Renata smiled with satisfaction. "Now that's more like it."

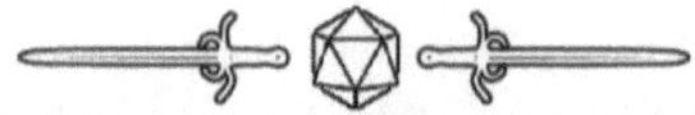

A horn blasted, signaling the army of the dead was on the move.

Through a long-look, Adelric could see the line of undead soldiers moving slowly west toward his troops.

Adelric was pleased to see the slow forward progress of the undead. Their reduced speed was part of their battle-plan.

As he pulled back the long-look, Adelric spotted his soldiers heading east toward the undead.

The armies would clash in a matter of moments.

"May Tarvanehl be with us," said Adelric.

Dorian stood beside him. He whispered a single word.

*"Indeed."*

## CHAPTER TWENTY-ONE

Darton saw the movement of the undead. The wall of rotting bodies had finally begun to move, like a dam breaking loose and flooding across the plain.

He sucked in a deep breath and tightened the grip on his ax handle. Knowing that some struggled not to flee, Darton fought the urge to rush out onto the battlefield and engage the enemy. His hatred burned hot.

Warlord Adelric and Dorian made it explicitly clear what was required of each soldier, and he certainly didn't want to be the one to doom the rest of them.

With his heart pounding in his stout chest, he remained where he was, waiting for the enemy to arrive.

The zombies poured up the battle line where they had previously stopped—at the edge of the rotting ground—and then crossed over onto the rocky terrain of the slopes. *Were they mad?* Darton wondered.

Again, Darton fought off the natural urge to rush forward and engage the enemy. While they might be able to defeat the enemy on the highlands, that still left them with the problem of the encroaching deadlands—the biggest problem they faced.

This was certainly an unexpected turn of events and Darton felt suddenly unsure of what to do… except wait on the warlord's order.

"They didn't stop at the battle line," said Dorian, an air of curiosity to his voice.

"They what?" Adelric said, somewhat surprised. He drew his long-look and spied the enemy's position. "They carried on across it," said Dorian. "They've crossed into your camp…Does this change anything for us?" asked Dorian.

Adelric studied the landscape for another moment, thinking that his soldiers were probably wondering the same thing. At last, he pulled the long-look away from his eye and said, "No. It just means our soldiers will have to show more restraint to make sure we have a chance to work our plan."

He turned to a messenger on his right and said, "Tell Sergeant Cadman that nothing has changed."

The messenger darted off without a word.

In seconds, the soldiers would be away, and the plan would be in action. Then, there would be no turning back.

Darton sat huddled behind his rock, waiting.

His heart pounded while he kept his breathing shallow and silent. His muscles grew taut and his legs strained as tightly as springs.

Suddenly, the vaghan soldier to his left jumped out and ran onto the battlefield. Then the one to that soldier's left burst out of his hiding place. Another second passed and the soldier to Darton's right rushed towards the dead.

The time had come.

Without another moment's hesitation, Darton leapt forward.

Once he was up, he kept running, eager to meet the dead.

"It's underway," said Adelric.

"Indeed it is," answered Dorian.

"I will go help out wherever I can on the battle line. It's in your hands now."

"Good luck," said Dorian.

"I was just about to wish you the same," said Adelric.

Dorian nodded.

After a moment of silence, Adelric turned to join the battle.

The sudden appearance of the vagha surprised Renata.

She silently cursed, wondering if Peregrine would have expected that, and then focused on the battle. One dwarf after another appeared out from behind the scattered rocks of the highlands.

There seemed to be more of them than Renata remembered. Hundreds of them rushed down the slopes, all approaching with a look of determination that would have scared any living creature.

She growled and directed her wall of bodies to engage the enemy, which they outnumbered by at least three to one.

Renata had come close to the vanguard, closer than she'd ever gone before—just as she'd seen Peregrine do.

Venting her frustrations, she launched a bolt of black eldritch energy from her fingers. A dwarf collapsed, struck dead. Her zombies pressed into the opening, and then one of the vaghan soldiers breached the line. He burst through with fire in his eyes and locked them on Renata, intent on taking out the undead leader. With his ax held high, he hacked the front legs off her skeletal steed and sent Renata flying through the air.

She landed on her right shoulder, tumbling into a roll that nearly yanked her fabulous, glimmering cloak from her body. Renata opened her eyes and found herself face-to-face with her attacker.

He stood over here, leering, as if challenging her to a fight.

Why hadn't he tried to destroy her while she lay incapacitated on the ground? She'd been exposed for a moment.

Renata rose to her feet and gathered the black rage within her. The green in her eyes snapped like shattering emeralds and her eyes roiled black as a storm. Still, the dwarf remained rooted in place, ax in one hand, shield in the other.

*What is he waiting for? Stupid little rock waddler! Why doesn't he attack?* She drew her blade, a ceremonial falchion she'd wielded in her previous life as a warrior queen.

Renata stepped forward, but he quickly stepped back, out of her range. She lunged forward, but the dwarf simply stepped back again.

Renata laughed. "You are retreating!"

Her face set as she tensed, like a coiling snake about to strike.

The dwarf anticipated her. He leapt out of the way and then began to run.

Renata laughed with a banshee screech. *"Coward!"* she shouted, pursuing him. "Craven little plaything, I will teach you the ways of the undying."

After running for a few seconds, the dwarf stopped, turned around, and resumed the fighting stance he'd taken before.

"Fool," she cried. "I won't fall for your tricks."

The dwarf remained where he was, his stance unchanging.

Renata laughed again, but then noticed something odd.

There were other vagha close by. They ran as well. Running, not from the powerful heucuva, but from her zombies. None had stood their ground—they'd broken the battle lines, circumvented them or pushed through—and entered the deadlands where they'd been so reluctant to fight before.

*What is going on here?* Renata wondered.

She looked around in the hopes that a broader view of her surroundings would give her a clue. Renata suddenly realized that it was a trick…some kind of trap.

The heucuva reached out with her mind, ordering the zombies to stop, but they would not. She felt her link to them crumble, much like the stones of the Wakefield Plain withered like petals in the heat. Something had freed her minions from her domination, given them just enough autonomy that they could act of their own accord in battle.

*Peregrine!*

He'd made them more useful in a fight, but they had enough psyche to overrule her order in pursuit of the prize. And now Renata could see something they could not—but she could not force them to stand down! They would keep on fighting, keep on searching out their enemy, without a care as to what direction they headed. They advanced upon the enemy, and that was all that mattered. To them, there was no bigger picture.

"Stop!" she screamed. "You're going the wrong way!"

But none of her soldiers heard her above the din of battle.

Darton found himself face-to-face with a former morehl. The fiend's blade was black and pitted. It reminded Darton that his job was not to destroy the undead creature—not unless that opportunity presented itself easily. Their task was to lead it back in the direction it had come from.

Now that he was merely trying to hold off the oncoming undead, Darton found his job significantly easier. It was tiring for the dwarves, but as long as they regularly changed shield arms, they could hold off an opponent indefinitely.

With each step Darton took backward, he brought the zombie closer, back to the source of their power: the wilted deadlands.

Again and again the zombie swung his blade at Darton, and each time, his shield took the blow.

Another blow and Darton realized that his shield had developed a crack. It showed signs of fatigue. Worst of all, the zombie still looked as fresh as when this battle began.

Darton backpedaled more quickly, drawing the zombie forward, trying to move quicker and absorb fewer blows.

Hopefully, his shield would hold out just a while longer.

Adelric joined the battle.

But while he was eager to join the fray, his presence didn't seem to be any great need. The vagha weren't trying to destroy the undead army; they only needed to keep baiting them forward, like a child playing keep away with a dog and bone.

As he walked the battlefield, he heard a raspy female voice screeching.

"Stop," she howled. "It's a trick, turn back around!"

Adelric couldn't see exactly who the voice belonged, but he suspected it was their leader—the one in the cloak. She must have realized what Adelric planned. If that were true, he had to silence her. If her orders were followed, the undead army would win the day, and not the dwarves.

He readied his ax and plunged into the mass of stinking corpses, searching out the source of the voice.

From his vantage, Dorian watched the battle progress.

As the vagha soldiers crossed into the deadlands, he signaled his selumari spell casters to move up the battle line.

They took up a position at the edge of the wetlands and prepared to engage their craft. Ruskin's corps of vaghan spell crafters followed Dorian's lead. Ruskin had taken two of his other theurgists and gone with Sergeant Cadman, sneaking deep into enemy territory.

Adelric found the cloaked, undead woman he'd seen on the previous raid, easily identifying her by her gaudy dress. He bullied his way into her path.

Her robes were unmistakable. But robes aside, Adelric could see her better in the light of day. She looked significantly different from the other zombies. Her skin wasn't as black and mottled as the rest of them, and she moved with a fluidity that the others did not seem to possess.

It had been many years, but the warlord recognized the warrior queen. He'd only met Renata once in passing at a diplomatic event, but Adelric remembered her from before the war against Garnock. Renata was a hard woman to forget.

Adelric pushed his way further through her forces and found another vagha had realized the same thing. He attempted to draw her along with the rest of the army. It was Budt.

"Greetings, Budt," said Adelric. "You're looking better than the last time I saw you."

"Feeling better too, milord," Budt said as he sidestepped an encroaching zombie.

"She doesn't seem to be taking the bait," Adelric said, pointing in the direction of the tall, lithe undead with his ax. He used the weapon to shove a shambling enemy aside and keep the path clear of deadly threats.

"I don't know why. The rest seem to be playing along," Budt said.

"Perhaps she doesn't like the odds," said Adelric. "Perhaps she'd prefers it more like four against one?"

Budt smiled.

"Hey, Queen of the Damned…You bloated, festering, maggot-fodder!" shouted Adelric.

The undead woman turned toward them. Her eyes, even at this distance, burned with a strange light.

"Do you think you made her mad?" asked Budt.

Adelric swallowed nervously. He realized that for her to take the bait on an insult, she must have possessed a deep intellect that the drones did not—but a smart enemy was a dangerous one. "Oh, I hope so."

Darton took another step backward and felt his feet reach the spongy ground turned to bog. He'd reached the deadlands.

He continued ever deeper and all the while, the zombie he fought followed. He followed the same pattern, hitting the creature, dodging the return strike, and stepping backwards. Darton drew the undead soldier ever eastward.

*It will be over soon,* thought Darton, satisfied he'd done his job. He only wished he could feel the same way about his shield. It was practically in ruins after so much damage.

He glanced around and saw that the other vagha recognized the same thing: they had nearly won. What came next was up to the magicians.

"Come and get me, you monster!" shouted Adelric.

The undead woman looked incensed. She moved quickly, shoring up the ground between herself, Adelric, and Budt.

"We better get moving, milord," said Budt. "This one isn't like the others."

"I think you're right."

Just before Renata could reach them, the two ran towards the river. But before they reached its bank, Renata cast a spell and a wave of sickness fell over them.

Both Adelric and Budt were caught by the wave of power and stumbled as they sprinted, falling to a tumbling roll.

Adelric wiped the spittle from his whiskers and found Budt vomiting.

The warlord hauled Budt to his feet. "Let's not wait to find out what else she's got in her bag of tricks. We've got to get moving."

Darton saw Warlord Adelric and Budt's approach. Throughout the enemy territory, vagha soldiers clustered together. The entire undead army swarmed around them, ready to crush against the dwarves and finish them once and for all.

"Welcome milord," said Darton. "Glad you could make it."

"I wouldn't have missed this one for anything," said Adelric.

Budt nodded his agreement.

"Thank you," said Adelric, with a nod. He looked north. Flooding from the Trent River had seeped out from the Boland Marsh and spilled down into the boggy sections of the deadlands, creating an ample supply of water, just as Carswell Adar had shown them.

"I believe it's time we got a move on," yelled the warlord.

"Lead the way, milord," said Darton.

"This way, then."

The compressed remnants of Dehnlee's army began moving, a step at a time, pinning themselves against the burgeoning waters of the Trent River's flooding.

The vagha were running…running *away*.

Renata watched them go. Their stubby legs scurried as quickly as they could, reminding the heucuva of waddling ducklings fleeing danger.

"What are they doing now?" she wondered aloud.

It looked like a retreat, but how could they be fleeing again? That's all they had been doing throughout this whole battle. Besides that, it was clearly the wrong direction for a retreat.

But Renata wasn't so sure anymore. Perhaps they were surrendering Dehnlee and fleeing to Vhandria, or any of the other vaghan cities in the Daurhedge? The dwarves made little sense.

As she took another look around, her zombies had, at least, slowed their single-minded pursuit. They remained where they stood, stupidly looking at the enemy, which crept further and further into the mire of the transmuted plains.

Renata stared at the warlord in his horned helm. He pressed a horn to his lips and blew a signal.

The heucuva saw the colors on the spectrum of magic, a kind of extra sense few possessed except those gifted with eldritch talents. Her eyes locked onto a yellow glow that surrounded the dwarven casters in their army. They summoned Eldurim's power and reshaped earth, creating another hill. As soon as they'd created it, the vagha disappeared behind and continued their retreat.

"It's a trap," Renata screamed. "Another dirty vagha trick!" She tried to make the zombies stop, to save themselves from whatever treachery the vagha had in store for them, but the zombies ignored her. She had yet to reestablish her control over them.

Again, she silently cursed Peregrine for interfering in the chain of control she'd instilled them.

After failing to move them again, Renata pulled her blade from within her cloak and hacked the creature's head off. She moved to her next target and lopped it free as well. After the third soldier toppled, those nearest her finally turned its attention to her and gave her heed.

"Who's next?" she growled.

The rest of the zombie horde had finally turned. "That's more like it," she said. "Now, back to Dehnlee. Kill and devour the civilians!"

The army slowly turned westward again—much too slowly for Renata's liking.

"Hurry up!" she screamed, fearing the dwarves and elves might spring whatever nasty trap they had devised.

But the zombies moved no faster.

Renata felt the first stirrings of magic coming from the west.

It wasn't a large or powerful spell, but rather like many small ones joining together to form a great effect. One that grew stronger with each second.

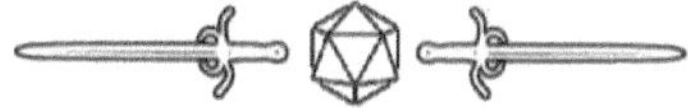

In the distance, Dorian could see the vagha running across the plains. They had looped back around to the south and hurried toward the battle line and the safety of the rocky terrain beyond it. From this vantage point, Dorian thought them painfully slow, but Dorian knew that, for the vagha, they likely believed they were running like the wind.

As they neared, Dorian continued scanning the horizon

for any undead quick enough to pursue them. It looked like there were none visible on the deadlands, and he could proceed according to plan.

But then, Dorian spotted something approaching. The object was little more than a blur streaking across the plain. It moved faster than anything he'd ever seen before.

And it appeared to be heading straight for him.

Adelric had almost reached the battle line when he heard a shrill scream cut through the air like an ax.

He turned to find the undead leader approaching. She moved quickly, her robes flapping behind her like flags in a hurricane. Judging by her speed, some kind of magic propelled her across the plain; nothing in Nature moved so quickly.

And given the direction she traveled, it appeared as if she were headed straight for Dorian. She must have sensed that the magical corps of casters were her greatest threat and deduced they were critical to the dwarves' countermeasures. She couldn't be allowed to reach them. If she did, she would most certainly kill Dorian, the most skilled of the spell crafters present, and prevent the magic-users from following through with their part of the plan. Winning the war would then become impossible.

Adelric couldn't let that happen.

There was no doubt in Dorian's mind that the figure

streaking across the plain was headed for him. There was also no doubt in his mind that the figure was an undead magic-user who intended to do him harm.

A great deal of harm.

His natural inclination was to defend himself, but that wasn't a viable option this time around. The spell was already in motion—he simply couldn't afford to stop the current spell—even to save his own life. If he did, the entire operation might fail and many, many vagha and those present selumari would die, and eventually rise as undead.

He took a deep breath and hoped for a miracle.

"Over my dead body," yelled Adelric as he ran northward to intercept the approaching heucuva.

When he was within striking distance of the streaking figure, he dove forward, throwing his body directly into the undead's path.

Renata hit him with bone-crunching force, sending him flying a dozen paces through the air. After hitting the ground with his shoulder and rolling several times, Adelric came to a stop in the dirt. He blinked to regain his focus and saw her lying on the ground some distance away. Her fancy robes splayed out like spilled blood, though she was a member of the bloodless: those beyond death.

A moment later, she rose to her feet. With a terrible, wet clicking noise, she flexed her muscles and forced dislocated joints back into their sockets.

"Where do you think you're going?" Adelric growled as loud as he could manage.

She looked over at him. An angry scowl pulled on her

face and her eyes burned with rage.

"If it's a fight you want," said Adelric. "I'm ready to hack you down like cord wood … *Renata!*" he spat her name. He had to do everything he could to keep her away from Dorian.

Renata did not take the bait. She turned towards the magic casters even as her undead hordes darkened the horizon, following their leader.

The warlord could not allow that. He grasped for words that might enrage her.

"I can't believe it's you again," Adelric barked. "I thought surely the trogs and morehl had killed you all off for good—erasing the Gwich'in and blotting out your mongrel species from the Plain. Humans—*bah!* Abominations of Tarvanehl with no true ties to Ghaeial. Will we never be rid of you?"

Adelric's lie struck a nerve in the heucuva. She whirled back to face him with one hand held out before her like a set of claws. She snarled, seeming more like a daemon, the physical form the spirits sometimes took, than a human.

But before she halved the distance between them, Adelric felt her magic crackling with the energy that preceded a storm. His throat closed up, and he found it difficult to breathe. Before he could cry out, he felt his heart beginning to fail; its beating became both irregular and labored.

Adelric watched her approach, saw her hand open and close, and knew that she used some kind of black magic on him. He'd heard of many such spells focused on Death magic; Kelda Whare spoke of them often when she taught soldiers at Carlin Park.

"Did you say something, dwarf?" she hissed as she approached. "I thought I heard you say something about a fight?"

She laughed before closing her hand into a tight fist. She

clenched as hard as she could.

Adelric felt his heart coming to a stop, just as his head felt fuzzy and gray.

She continued to laugh, grabbing him by the neck and physically squeezing his throat shut while dangling him like a child's plaything. "You're nothing compared to me. *Nothing.*"

Renata gave his throat one final squeeze and threw him to the ground as if he were a rag doll. She laughed at him one last time. Her contempt for the vagha, who she clearly begrudged for failing to aid the amazons, was painfully evident in her voice.

And then she turned away, leaving Adelric for dead.

Dorian watched helplessly as the heucuva toyed with Adelric, treating him like nothing more than a minor obstacle on her way toward him.

He desperately wanted to help his friend but knew he couldn't jeopardize the plan.

There was just too much at stake.

He closed his eyes so he wouldn't have to watch his friend die and concentrated on completing the spell.

As Renata turned away, Adelric suddenly caught a breath. He gasped, scattering dust where he laid face-down in the dirt.

He opened his eyes and saw that the magic-user turned

towards the dwarven battle line and Dorian.

"No!" he whispered with what little breath he had.

If she heard Adelric, Renata ignored him.

With considerable effort, Adelric dug his smaller hand ax out of his waist belt.

And then, with his last bit of energy, he threw the ax at her.

The weapon whirled through the air. Its wooden handle spun around the head like a crank.

Renata heard it buzzing through the air and turned, just in time to see the ax bite into her neck and slice it clean off her shoulders.

After a moment of stunned incredulity, Renata toppled forward. Her head separated from the neck in a wisp of black smoke, and her body fell to the ground in a pathetic heap.

"Warlord Adelric, are you alright?" Adelric recognized the voice as Darton's, but he could not move or otherwise gesture to acknowledge him. He could also hear Darton's striking blows nearby. No doubt his vagha were hacking the heucuva to tiny pieces to ensure that she never rose again.

Moments later, he felt dwarven hands lifting him off the ground and carrying him to safety.

## CHAPTER TWENTY-TWO

After taking far too little time to catch his breath and allow his heart to recover, Adelric insisted on being taken to the crest of a hill so he could watch the final stages of the battle.

Those attending him brought him to a ledge where he found Sergeant Cadman sitting comfortably on a large flat stone, watching the battle proceedings through his long-look.

Almost immediately upon Adelric's arrival, the sergeant got up and offered the warlord his seat.

Adelric grumbled unintelligibly as he eased into place upon the rock. Although he hadn't been physically injured by Renata, he was in a lot of pain. As he reached for his own long-look, his only thought was the same that he'd had repeatedly since the war against Garnock ended. He was definitely getting too old for this kind of life. When this battle ended, he would hand the title of Warlord to Cadman and spend the rest of his days tending his garden.

It was time.

After taking as deep a breath as he was able, Adelric peered through the long-look and watched Dorian's magic-users work in time with Ruskin.

Ridges as high as most dwarves rose from the ground and formed a fence. It hemmed the zombies in. Another ridge raised behind them, creating a channel with jagged peaks and sharp objects jutting out at odd angles.

"It's starting," said Adelric. "The beginning of the end of the undead."

The ground rumbled slightly as the trapped zombies scaled the jagged stone hedges. A small tsunami poured forth from the north as Dorian and his casters swelled the river to a flood and forced it to pour out from the Boland Marsh. Ruskin and his vagha guided it through walls with teeth like swords.

Adelric and Cadman watched as the floodwater poured through the channel like ocean breakers, catching every one of the undead who still pursued their enemy. Swept away, the roiling currents dashed the corpses through the jagged rapids and smashed them against the sharp turns and bottlenecks which the dwarven magicians had crafted through several leagues' worth of channels.

The enemy busted apart like spices broken with mortar and pestle. And then, there was silence. The waters quit churning, and everything came to rest.

Adelric breathed deeply, scanning the flat surface of the mud for any signs of life…or unlife.

There was none.

By the end of it, each of their bodies had been smacked hard enough to sever heads and break spines.

The plains drained, and scores of dead bodies—or what remained of them—lay encased within the sediment. Slowly, the vagha magic-users transmuted the mud left by the subsiding waters into rock, burying the remnants of Renata and her army forever.

Adelric watched them work until dark, at which time he felt well enough to walk down the hill to congratulate Dorian on a job well done.

Peregrine felt drawn to it—something that radiated

power. It beckoned to him like a hot pie calls to a hungry nose.

The morning light had not yet arrived, and the dwarves of Dehnlee had retired hours ago.

Presently, Peregrine and his small cadre of followers skulked about the battlefield, nibbling on whatever fallen soldiers they could find. They had watched the end of the battle unfold as the waves took Renata's army.

Peregrine and his troops had survived. The selumari and vagha hadn't gotten rid of *all* the undead.

He realized that he could return to the castle ruins and take the heucuva's place. The small remnant she left behind in her macabre court would follow him once they realized he had the skill and knowledge to create more of their kind—and that he had the power to both free and to enslave undead minions. He could amass another army, a stronger army that did not rely on the whims of the powerful and misguided heucuva for its power. His army would be a true army culled from the best soldiers he could find, trained in tactics and weapons—and it would not only consist of zombies to be used as fodder.

Peregrine arrived at the thing that drew him nearer. He looked to his feet, where a mound of flesh had been heaped upon a shredded, glimmering cloak. It smelled overwhelmingly delicious and looked like a mound of poorly chewed vomit. But Peregrine knew what he was looking at as he sank to his knees, overpowered by the urge to eat.

It was Renata's remains.

And though he had long loved her, he dug his hands into entrails and gore and feasted, urged to continue until his fingers grasped something hard as stone and cold as ice.

Peregrine pulled it from the heap and examined the violet hued crystal. The jewel seemed to whisper in his mind and Peregrine knew intrinsically that it had been the source of Renata's power.

He stood and spoke in a low voice that brimmed with

confidence. "I shall return," he said. "I shall return," he repeated it as a vow. But deep in his heart, without Renata, he wondered if it was true. The only thing he had left to him was his rage… his rage, *and it*. He opened the palm of his hand and stared at the gem. The gleaming crystal he'd pulled from his beloved's remains.

Staring at the prize in his grasp, he began walking north. His minions followed him, though he did not point himself at the collapsed castle. He walked without true destination or purpose; instead, he stared at the gem as he walked away from Dehnlee.

With one finger, Peregrine stroked the deep purple facets and mumbled, "How very … *exquisite.*"

# CHAPTER TWENTY-THREE

It was over. Sol had risen, bathing Dehnlee and her citizens in fresh light.

The vagha and selumari staggered back to their homes in the dark, where they'd promptly fallen asleep in much need for rest. Now that morning drew near, flasks of wine and harder spirits appeared and the liquids flowed freely.

"You did well, Dorian," said Adelric, giving the enchanter a well-deserved pat on the back.

"Thank you, friend, but you and I both know the plan was yours. It's you who deserve the credit, not only for ending the war, but for saving my life."

Adelric looked at Dorian and raised his mug of ale, winking as if they hadn't quite earned the right to drink booze for breakfast. He flashed him a grin. "I was only doing what any friend would have done."

"I only hope I would be able to do the same for you under similar circumstances."

The longer he looked at Dorian, the more Adelric became aware of the upturned corners of his mouth—a wry smile. Finally, the dam burst, and Dorian grinned from ear-to-ear.

Adelric found himself laughing as he described the final moments of the battle. "I saw it all. It was quite impressive," he said.

"No, *you* were impressive, my friend," said Dorian. "Taking on a powerful spell caster with nothing more than a hand ax. Fantastic!"

Adelric shook his head slightly, as if in disbelief. "I must have been mad...likely from the lack of oxygen when she'd nearly choked the life out of me."

Dorian laughed and raised his glass.

"It was a decisive victory," Adelric mused.

Dorian nodded. "Both our histories will look upon this victory as one that could never have been achieved without the help of the other. If my previous visit had opened inroads between our two races, this victory has paved the way to a long and fruitful partnership."

"Always the diplomat, eh Dorian?"

The elf smirked. "I'm sorry, but it's in my blood."

"I understand," said Adelric. "What's more, I enjoy listening to you speak."

"You're too kind, Adelric. Too kind."

Adelric simply smiled at him, drained his mug, and said, "I know."

## CHAPTER TWENTY- FOUR

The garden behind Adelric's home had returned to its former glory. The grass appeared a lush shade of green and covered the ground like a thick and inviting welcome mat. The trees grew healthily and stood upright to catch the warmth of the sun's rays. Their branches were covered with green leaves, new buds, and colorful blossoms.

Tranquility had returned to the place once again, signifying that all was right in the surrounding lands. The forces of Death and Corruption had been vanquished, and life could now continue in peace and harmony.

At least for now.

## EPILOGUE

Respen, a selumari ship captain, shuddered from a chill as the tall man boarded his boat at the Dehnlee port. The captain had just recently decided Dehnlee was safe, following the nasty business with the undead.

His guest wore a dark cloak and robe that hid his face, but he could tell by the figure's size and gait that he was probably an eldarim, one of the "old-folk" whose race, although rare, had been the inhabitants of Esfah since before any of the ancient monsters had lived there—and reportedly since before even the dragons—the most ancient of the creatures native to Esfah. At least, depending on what bard you listened to and believed in.

Biting his lip, Respen watched the man board from the corner of his eye. Something about this passenger creeped him out. Respen often made the trip from his home, Galatea, to Dehnlee. Their selumaric diplomats assured traders the place was free of danger—better in fact, the dwarves were giving trade incentives as thanks for the help offered by Dorian the Enchanter.

The coral elf captain watched as a number of men, similarly clad to the first, walked up the landing planks; they pulled a cart behind them. It clanked with the tinkling of glass, as if the wagon were laden with bottles. A bolt of fabric covered the contents to keep them secret. With the figures dressed in matching dark cloth, they looked more like members of a religious order than anything else, and Respen assumed the bottles' contents were not likely to be strong drink.

A second cart, slightly larger than the first, followed. It too was shrouded with a heavier fabric meant to keep light from leeching through, but the second cart did not clink or rattle. It towered taller and its base was built sturdier and made from metal.

Respen decided not to ask any questions. Whatever their intentions for the cargo in Galatea was none of his business, provided they paid for transport up front.

As if he'd read Respen's mind, the tall one approached and compensated him with gold coin enough that he could have easily purchased half his own boat. The captain nodded and signaled for his men to cast off. Shortly after, Dehnlee's coast and its vaghan traders shrank into the distance.

With the ship cresting waves and heading through the Delmara Bay and bound for Lemeliandor, and the coastal city of Galatea, the tall man approached the captain. He drew his hood back to reveal his white hair and pale skin. He wore tattoos that Respen did not recognize. Some kind of charm hung from the figure's neck by a filigree chain.

"You are going the wrong way, Captain," he stated, eliciting a guffaw from Respen.

"I do think I know where Galatea is…"

"But we do not wish to go there," the mysterious man said. "You must take us to Dereh'Liandor."

Respen laughed even harder, nearly choking. "I'm afraid you've gone cracked. Dereh'Liandor is clear on the other side of the world."

The eldarim stared at him with hollow, unflinching eyes, as if he knew exactly what he had requested.

The captain held his gaze, refusing to budge.

"Very well, then." The man withdrew the item at his neck, revealing it to be a fine ocarina made of some strange metal. He pressed it to his lips and blew a note. To Respen, it sounded like the most beautiful tune he'd ever heard in his life. Like light had enveloped him and filled his soul. Soon, Respen became one with that light.

All around Nekarthis, the selumari sailors aboard the ship dropped dead. Dhanriath pulled his hood back to match his master's, and he nodded to the subordinates behind him. They rolled back the heavy weave of fabric to expose the necralluvium samples. The stuff roiled and churned within their vials, and the cultists each took one.

Carefully, they poured one drop upon each of the murdered sailors. Moments later, the zombified elves stood to their feet and then resumed their sailing duties. The damned sailors changed riggings and rudder, turning their ship to its new destination.

"We have gathered enough information," Nekarthis said without even looking at Dhanriath, his protégé. "We have confirmed the power of the Necralluvium. And now, we will use it to break the world."

"Dehnlee was just a test?" Dhanriath asked.

Nekarthis nodded slowly. "A scout foray in the prelude to war. A war which will soon begin in earnest."

"Shall I alert the Black Forest?" Dhanriath asked.

"As soon as we next make landfall. But first," Nekarthis said, "we must stop and retrieve our corps of slaves. The artisans who will build the weapons with which we will use to break the world for the sake of our master."

Dhanriath knew of who he meant. "The gremmlobahnd?"

Nekarthis nodded. "The gnomes are the key to it all. Not

just their weapons, but also their ability to unlock the gates between dimensions. We will unshackle the beast, Dhanriath. With the gnomes' craftsmanship, we'll free Malgrimm to walk the face of Esfah. All creatures will be his playthings, and we shall reign as princes in the realm of Selurehl. Forever."

"If the gremmlobahnd learn your aims, they will activate the dracolem, their protectors."

Nekarthis smiled wickedly. "They will not come. Not so long as I hold the one thing that they fear...*the drekloch*." His eyes flitted momentarily to the second cart, the reinforced one shrouded with the heavy cloth.

Dhanriath turned his gaze to match his master's as they stared at the mysterious creature hidden beneath the dark cloak and caged within the bars beneath it.

Nekarthis turned and pointed his face into the wind, staring east towards the far-off Dereh'Liandor. The land that had been his home before the drider had enslaved him in his youth.

"Finally," he whispered. "After all this time...I am going home."

## THE END

# APPENDICES

# Glossary of Terms

Abyss – the home of the Void, a realm where silence reigns aside from pockets of terror and chaos where unknown gods reign. This is a similar concept to Greek myths of an underworld.

Ailuril – the second born of the Esfahan gods. She is represented by the color blue and has power over the air elements.

Agamid – a winged type Drakufreet

Aguarehl – the fourth born of the Esfahan gods. He is represented by the color green and has power over the water elements.

Amazon – the race of mankind said to have been deposited whole upon Esfah as one of the few races created by Tarvanehl himself. Amazons are the warrior caste of human race.

Areosa – commonly known as the frostwings, a frigid felinoid, winged race with magic resistance.

Bloodless – another common name for the undead.

Deadzone – synonym for the Abyss, except from the point of view of the trogs or morehl. Within their respective religions, versions of the afterlife differ wildly and as often as they align in geopolitical goals, neither could imagine spending an eternal afterlife in the company of the other.

Death – the half-brother god who is the child of Nature and Void.

Dragons – these beasts come in two forms: Drake and Wyrm. Drakes have wings, and wyrms do not. Though the dragonkin are a kind of subspecies, they are not the same thing, no matter how similar they are. They used to live hidden across Esfah, but were nearly eradicated in the Dragoncrusades. Dragons have eternal spirits and when they die, they return to the plane where they now dwell. Dragonmagic came in two forms and it summons them from this realm or from nearby (the older form of this magic which has now been forgotten since these mythic beasts have largely gone out from Esfah.)

Drakufreet – the dragonkin come from the same realm as dragons and appear as a type of draconic hybrid race. They come in multiple types and subspecies. Agamids are a flying type of the subspecies which include Saurons (a gator-like humanoid variant,) Mokole (a rideable dragonfolk that is something of a mix between Sauron and Suchia,) Suchia (a buffalo-sized drakufreet that can make an excellent mount). Of these, the Champion sized are the largest and most fearsome, ranging up to three quarters in size of a dragon's size.

Eldarim – a human-like race that emerged over eons from Esfah's primordial soup and predated the gods-made races. The eldarim are versatile and have proven the capacity to breed with many of Esfah's races. They are called eldarim, meaning "from the earth."

Eldurim – the firstborn of the Esfahan gods. He is represented by the color gold and has power over the earth elements.

Efflorah – the race of treefolk.

Esfah – the world and one of two planets revolving around Soll.

Empyrea – known commonly as the firewalkers, a war-loving mercenary race.

Faeli – commonly known as scalders or steam dancers. These creatures are fickle and capricious and were once captured and tormented by Death.

Festration – a kind of location so tainted by evil activity that the very land itself has become corrupt and avails itself to wickedness.

Firiel – the third born of the Esfahan gods. She is represented by the color red and has power over the fire elements.

First Age – everything from the beginning of creation to the year 863.

Frehlasuhl – also called the Forsaken or Mudbloods. They are the offspring of selumari and morehl unions. They cannot breed with each other to have children, only with one or the other race, but they are rejected wholesale by both.

Ghaeial – the mother goddess known more commonly as Nature.

Ghwereste – called the "feral folk." These are a hybrid of animal and man created at the dawn of the Second Age.

Kreethaln – there are three of these mystical artifacts made of an unknown metal. Little is known about them except that they each possess some kind of arcane power. Their names are Life-bringer, Wisdom-giver, and Spell-crafter.

Leguin – a sister planet to Esfah that also orbits Sol; it can often be seen in the night sky appearing above the horizon like a bright star.

Lich – a powerful undead spell caster. Lichs often possess necromantic capabilities, though their created undead are maintained by force of will, rather than by other means, such as the Necralluvium.

Mokole – see Drakufreet

Morehl – commonly called lava elves. They have red skin in addition to their elf-like features and their blood is said to smoke when exposed to air.

Necralluvium - a kind of magical potion with a seeming life of its own. This black filth can kill the living. The dead that are exposed to it become animated.

Rhaudian – the name of the moon. It circulates Esfah twice in a daily cycle.

Sarslayan – commonly known as swamp stalkers. These snake-men emerged in the Second Age as a result of Death using magic to twist the creations of his half-brother Aguarehl. They create more of their kind through magic conversion rather than by reproduction.

Sauron – see Drakufreet

Second Age – everything after year 863 of the First Age. This began when Ghaeial walked the face of Esfah and surveyed the damages of the myriad of wars. The 864th year is year 1 of the Second Age.

Selurehl – the name of the second god to emerge after Tarvanehl, usually known as Void.

Selumari – commonly called coral elves. They have blue skin in addition to their elf-like features.

Shara – what the eldarim people refer to themselves as when they communicate with each other. It means "little god-in-the-making."

Soll – the sun.

Suchia – see Drakufreet

Sukie – nickname for Suchia

Tarvanehl – the creator god who came first, according to all mythology and story; he is often known as Father Time, or simply The Father.

Teldrim – a race of extinct horse lords that bore many similarities to the Amazons. A creation of Tarvanehl, these were remarkable because the race could intermix with any other. They were eradicated by Melkior shortly after their emergence.

Trog – a synonym for goblin. trogs much prefer to live in boggy areas and tend to pollute the land.

Vagha – commonly known as dwarves.

Void – sometimes used interchangeably with the Abyss or, the power or person of Selurehl who is frequently referred to as Void just as his son Malgrimm is more widely regarded as Death. Context determines the meaning.

Warchief – a title of rank among the vagha. Below the king is a Warchief who leads Warlords and Warcommanders under them. It might commonly be understood as a sort of general.

# Timeline

Included is the general timeline of major world events in Esfah. Please note that, during the time before the Mother, Ghaeial, became a goddess and the First Age began, Prehistory spanned a scope of time measuring eons. In that time, verily, only *Time* existed. Despite the sage's attempts to capture much data and ancient knowledge, they did not begin tracking time and dates until the first passing of the Daybringer. The first three years of history might very well have been hundreds or even a thousand years as the gods (and the earliest race of eldarim) kept time differently.

*Prehistory N.D.*

Tarvanehl exists and creates within the realm of Void/Abyss and Esfah and Leguin are born; Ghaeial realizes she is a goddess and falls in love with Tarvanehl.

Turambar courts Leguin.

Selurehl, third of the brother gods grows angry.

Eldurim, the firstborn (earth) god-son of Ghaeial and Tarvanehl is born.

Ailuril, the second born (wind) god-daughter of Ghaeial and Tarvanehl is born.

Firiel, third born (fire) god-daughter of Ghaeial and Tarvanehl is born

Aguarehl, fourth born god-son (water) of Ghaeial and Tarvanehl is born

Malgrimm, the cursed bastard son (Death) is conceived and birthed after Selurehl's violence upon Ghaeial

Eldarim are birthed by Esfah and slowly emerge from the mire of her lands and water, evolving over long periods of time. They call themselves the Shara in their own tongue.

*The First Age*

03FA the Daybringer Comet passes Esfah for the First Time, the Sisters of Fate are birthed of Turambar and Leguin, Dragons and the Drakufreet are created during the schism of the god-children.

04FA Earliest creations of the gods: "monsters" are formed

15FA selumari are created

16FA vagha are created, trogs are created

17FA morehl are created

19FA The Dawn of War. morehl invaders overthrow the first selumari

22FA Humans arrive on Esfah via Tarvanehl's intervention

28FA Davian Whisperwynd leaves Maris-ta-Sehlim

32FA The proto-empyreans are birthed in the whirlwind

42FA Gundraokh Shatterfist finds the Bands of Turambar and renames the city of Orelod to Gundakhor

96FA Sshkkryyahr the Dread rises to power

103FA Malgrimm attempts to create a new powerful, destructive force within the Shadowlands, but the Areosan's magic resistance helps them maintain mild independence from the Death god and he abandons them to the frost plains.

143FA Undead created, Melkior is defeated upon the Raithlan Plains by the gods' chosen Champions

167FA Dilution of the eldarim race and the reduction of the Dragon population via the Dragoncrusades that eliminated nearly all the natural dragons of Esfah; the spells that compelled natural dragons that still remained in the realm became forgotten after this date in favor of those drawing eternal dragons through the interplanar rifts

341FA Existence of the empyreans is discovered when they aid the elder races in the first major Undead uprising.

447FA *Book of the Land, 1st Ed.* is published and immediately begins revisions

520FA morehl city of Karakto falls to the selumari

532FA morehl discover cursed bullets and retake Karakto

544FA Large load of Eldrymetallum discovered on the Karakto slopes

562FA Final version of *The Book of the Land* completed after 23 quintennial installments

836FA The Magestorm Wars erupt with the tectonic cataclysm that opens the Netherwold and nearly splits Dereh'Liandor in two; the Arcana Veil stiffens

842FA Disappearance of the gremmlobahnd and the genocide of the drakufreet

863FA Final battle of the Magestorm Wars ends the first age, the faeli are birthed in the Firequags and captured by the forces of Death and subjected to torments in the pits of the World Wound.


*The Second Age*

01SA Ghaeial walks the earth and surveys the damage of the elder races.

03SA Ghaeial creates the ghwereste

79SA The plagues of the World Wound and its evils continue and the first of the sarslayan emerge from the nearby Snekdenn Bayou

153SA The areosa race emerges from the Shadowlands. They are known mostly as rumors, but their existence is verified to the outside world.

209SA Whether the faeli escaped the torments of the World Wound or were released, none know, but they were so twisted by the centuries of abuse that they have become more children of Malgrimm than Ghaeial

233SA Under Ghaeial's wishes, the sylvan efflorah, existing as trees since even before the humans came to Esfah, picked up their roots and first emerged from forest and grove

602SA Lyandrica's Tournament of Champions begins. The fighting tournament happens during every cycle of the Daybringer Comet (27 years).

829SA Zephras "Thunderfist" dies in Cyrea defending Balgavarr Reaches from a dragon

967SA Geril sa'Ghuren "Dragonsbane" born

1021SA Geril sa'Ghuren rules in Balgavarr

1082SA Coryn Sa'Geril is born

1119SA Daybringer Comet makes its pass by Esfah

1122SA Kholkoro Wicebrow writes her commentary *Kholkoro's commentary on Book of the Land*

1127SA The famed "Adventurer King" Hy'Mandr sa'Meril is blinded

1139SA Melkior is revived

1142SA Daybringer Comet makes its circuit; 20th Tournament of Champions in Lyandrica.

0
200
400
Leagues
eliandor
Coral Cove
Galatea
Dehnlee
Delmara Bay
Boland Marsh
Hadden Bay
Reeve Island
Xlinea
Trellan
Lurneville Ruins
Ember
Kendall River
Trent River
Maris
Maris-tu
Vhandria
Stonehome
Oxforge
Daurbedge Range
Garnock Range
T

Coral Cove
Galatea
Boland Marsh
Trent River
Dehnlee
Delmara Bay
Kendall River
Hadden Bay
Garno
Trellan
Regsev Island
Xlinea
Lurneville
Ruins
Ender's Gulf
Undrakull
Niamarlee
People of
the Sun
Raithlan Plains
Irontooth Mts.
The Stonejaw Mountains
Charnock
Bralanthyr
Gods' V
Gnome Home
Jagra Flats

Stonehome
Oxforge
Daurhedge Range
ock Range
The Crechelands
Daur-Bor-Nin
the Darkness
Brooks...
Mezzoscarp Range
Southern Daurhedge
Lyandor's Pass
Narcea Marsh
Hagrond Mount
Em
The Birthlands
New Emmira
Talva
Lyandrica
Far Seas
Great Coastal Road
Co... Pass
Tenebrakth
ault
Barad's Spire
Tumult Straights
Kaerno
Diriath's Tower
The Broken Crown

# BOOKS
# IN THE DRAGON DICE UNIVERSE
# OF ESFAH

Rise and Fall of the Obsidian Grotto
Cast of Fate
Tome of Tarvanehl*
Heart of Stone and Flame*
Ashes of Ailushurai
Rise of the Champions
Drakuwar
Thunderfist and the Dragon**
Chill Wind
Eye of the Storm
Secrets of the Shadowlands
Army of the Dead

*These two short books were the first produced by TSR and are included inside the re-released (2020) version of Cast of Fate, which was originally produced in 1996.

**This short story is included inside the re-released (2020) version of Cast of Fate; large portions of it were released by SFR in the third edition rules book and it is a prequel to Chil Wind and the Cyrean Songs.

## About the authors:

Bram Stoker and Aurora Award-winner Edo van Belkom is the author of over 200 stories of horror, science fiction, fantasy, and mystery. His novels include horror titles SCREAM QUEEN, BLOOD ROAD, TEETH and MARTYRS, the fantasies BATTLE DRAGON, and LORD SOTH (Dragonlance™). His works for young adults include the WOLF PACK series and the anthologies BE AFRAID! and BE VERY AFRAID!. He has also produced the short story collections DEATH DRIVES A SEMI and SIX INCH SPIKES and the non-fiction how-to books WRITING HORROR and WRITING EROTICA.

He has also won a variety of awards including the Bram Stoker, Aurora, and Silver Birch Awards and a Truck Writers of North America award for fiction.

Born in Toronto, van Belkom graduated from York University, and then worked as a daily newspaper sports and police reporter before becoming a full-time writer. Edo van Belkom lives in Brampton, Ontario with his wife Roberta.

You can follow him at:
goodreads.com/author/show/169322.Edo_Van_Belkom
amazon.com/Edo-van-Belkom/e/B001HOPST6

His complete list of books are available here:
www.awfulagent.com/jabclients/edo-van-belkom

Christopher D. Schmitz is author of both Sci-Fi/Fantasy Fiction and Nonfiction books and has been published in both traditional and independent outlets. If you've investigated indie writers of the upper Midwest, you may have heard his name whispered in dark alleys with an equal mix of respect and disdain. He has been featured on television broadcasts, podcasts, and runs a blog for indie authors... but you've still probably never heard of him.

As an avid consumer of comic books, movies, cartoons, and books (especially sci-fi and fantasy) this child of the 80s basically lived out Stranger Things, but shadowy government agencies won't let him say more than that. He lives in rural Minnesota with his family where he drinks unsafe amounts of coffee; the caffeine shakes keep the cold from killing him. In his off-time he plays haunted bagpipes in places of low repute, but that's a story for another time.

He has a special offer for readers on the following page.

You can connect with him via the following links:
**http://www.authorchristopherdschmitz.com**

Follow me on Twitter:
https://twitter.com/cylonbagpiper
Follow me on Goodreads:
www.goodreads.com/author/show/129258.Christopher_Schmitz
Like/Follow me on Facebook:
https://www.facebook.com/authorchristopherdschmitz
Subscribe to my blog:
https://authorchristopherdschmitz.wordpress.com
Favorite me at Smashwords:
www.smashwords.com/profile/view/authorchristopherdschmitz
My Amazon Author Profile:
amazon.com/author/christopherdschmitz
Follow me at Bookbub:
www.bookbub.com/authors/christopher-d-schmitz

# Special Offer:

Get on the Esfah Sagas mailing list and author Christopher D. Schmitz's newsletter and get the first chronological book in the series.

www.subscribepage.com/getfreedragondicenovels

Enter your email address and then collect your book which will be sent to you within moments. It's that simple!

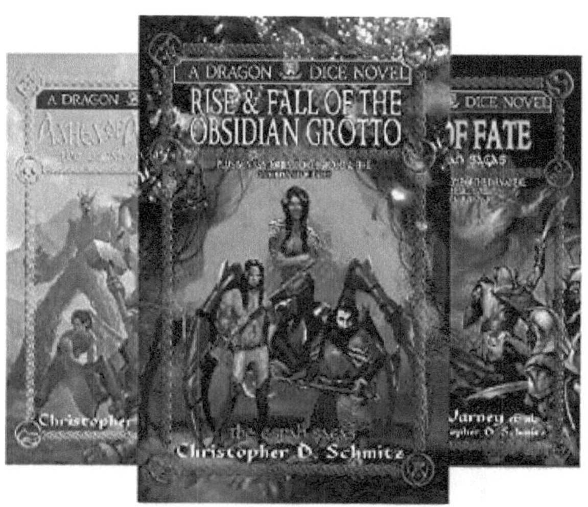

Edo Van Belkom &
Christopher D. Schmitz

# DRAGON DICE

Dragon Dice™ is SFR Inc.'s core product. We are constantly working to create a quality game that everyone can enjoy. Dragon Dice™ was originally created by Lester Smith and produced by TSR© in 1995. After several years, TSR, now owned by Wizards of the Coast, had put Dragon Dice™ on hold to work on other projects. In October of 2000, SFR Inc. purchased the rights to Dragon Dice™ and now will continue to support and create NEW! products for the game.

Dragon Dice™ is strategy game where players create mythical armies using dice to represent each troop. The game combines strategy and skill as well as a little luck. Each person tries to win the game by outmaneuvering the opponent and capture 2 terrains. Of course, eliminating your opponent completely is another acceptable way of winning.

Get online today and "Roll your way to victory!"

http://www.sfr-inc.com

www.ingramcontent.com/pod-product-compliance
Lightning Source LLC
Chambersburg PA
CBHW061310190726
48288CB00002B/433